THE WORST GIRLFRIEND IN THE WORLD

SARRA MANNING

atom

www.atombooks.net

ATOM

First published in Great Britain in 2014 by Atom

A CIP catalogue record for this book
is available from the British Library.

ISBN 978-1-907411-01-4

Printed and bound in Great Britain by
Clays Ltd, St Ives plc

Papers used by Atom are from well-managed forests
and other responsible sources.

MIX
Paper from
responsible sources
FSC
www.fsc.org FSC® C104740

Atom
An imprint of
Little, Brown Book Group
100 Victoria Embankment
London EC4Y 0DY

An Hachette UK Company
www.hachette.co.uk

www.atombooks.co.uk

Thanks to the crack team of Atom-isers: Kate Agar, Kate Doran, Karen Ball, the former Sam Smith of that parish and all the rest of the cake-loving gang. Also thanks to my amazing agent, Karolina Sutton, and Catherine Saunders, Norah Perkins and all at Curtis Brown.

Dedicated to the best and worst girlfriends who were my partners in crime during my own wild teen years: Karen, Caroline, Jacqui R and Jacqui J. "I'm telling you we had a time. Didn't we? Didn't we have a time?"

'She's my best friend and I hate her.'

HEATHERS

1

'Right, so after you've nicked a traffic cone, you need to climb on top of the bus shelter and leave it there, along with one personal item. First one to complete the mission gets an amazing prize.'

Alice stood there, her hands on her hips, blonde hair rippling in the breeze – though it seemed to ripple even when there wasn't a breeze, it was that kind of hair. It was obvious that *she* was the amazing prize.

It was a Saturday night and we were hanging out on the High Street, though Merrycliffe-on-Sea doesn't really have much of a High Street, just a forlorn parade of shops. It doesn't have much merry either, so we have to make our own fun. As we were both too broke to go to The Wow, watching Alice ensnare two lame boys and make them do her bidding was as good as it was going to get.

'I wonder how long they'll be,' I said to Alice, after the boys had trooped off on their quest to prove they were worthy of her. 'Want a chip?'

Alice sat down next to me on the low wall in front of the betting shop and shoved her hand in the grease-soaked bag of chips that one of the boys had bought for me because Alice had told him to.

Soon all that was left were the crispy bits floating in an acidic slick of vinegar. Alice looked up at the big, navy sky studded with pinpricks of starry light and ominous wisps of cloud. 'I think it's going to rain,' she said. 'If they're not back in five minutes, we might as well go home.'

'Next week, we have to go to The Wow.' This week, I'd lent my mum thirty quid because she hadn't got to the bank. It always took her ages to repay me too, not until I'd dropped brick-sized hints for at least a week about illegally benefiting off child labour.

'How long does it take to nick a traffic cone anyway?' Alice asked me. 'I hope they haven't got into trouble. Like the time Marc got caught trying to steal a wire basket from outside the pound shop, remember?'

'Don't be mean,' I said as Alice hooted, but I started laughing too because Marc from Year 12 trying to bomb it down the seafront with a wire basket and two security guards in hot pursuit had been one of the highlights of the summer before last.

In the end, to get rid of the evidence, he'd thrown the basket on top of the mini-golf ticket office where it remained to this day. 'Do you remember the security guards trying to find a ladder to get their stupid basket back? Then they decided that they couldn't climb it because of Health and Safety regulations.'

'And Marc didn't get arrested . . .'

'And he turned out to be quite a good snog so it was all OK.' Alice gave me one of her sideways smiles, her little snub nose twitching, eyebrow arched. It was the look that had all the boys bringing their milkshakes, fries and extra ketchup to Alice's yard.

Talking of which, limping down the road with only one of his trainers on was Chris, or was it Joey? He was holding a traffic cone aloft like it was an Olympic gold medal.

'I don't think this one is going to be a keeper,' Alice murmured, like that was anything new. 'But he'll do for the next ten minutes.'

She stood up, still tiny even in her five-inch heels. Alice was small and curvy. In ye olde days they'd have called her a pocket Venus. Boys wanted to protect her as much as they wanted to get with her. She had the previously mentioned ripply blonde hair and huge blue eyes that twinkled whenever she said something suggestive, which was all the time. It was like Alice came with an inbuilt nudge and wink as standard features.

Like she said, 'If we weren't best friends until the day we die, then you'd probably hate my guts, Franny.'

But I couldn't remember a time when Alice and I weren't best friends. We'd met at a Mother and Baby group; there's photographic evidence of us in nappies and a gummy, smiley embrace and barely a thing had happened to me, from losing my first tooth right through to almost getting my first kiss (let's not even go *there*), that Alice hadn't been witness to.

Right now, Alice was all Joey had eyes for, as he presented her with the traffic cone. 'Trainer on top of the bus shelter by the roundabout,' he announced. Losing a trainer lacked imagination and meant a tricky walk home but Joey was fit in a dull Merrycliffe way, which was about ten years behind the way really fit boys on style blogs looked, so Alice was eyeing him speculatively.

'OK then,' she said without much enthusiasm. 'To the victor, the spoils.' Off she went with Joey, swinging her hips in that artful sway she'd worked hard on ever since she got hips three years ago.

It was another five minutes before Chris came into sight minus a traffic cone but carrying one of those little lights that hang on the side of skips so people don't go crashing into them in the dark.

'Where's Alice?' he asked in dismay. 'I just left my second-best hoodie on top of the bus shelter.'

'Sorry to be the bearer of bad news, but Joey beat you to it.'

Chris looked at his little skip light and sighed. Then he came and sat next to me on the wall. My buttocks were pretty much all ache at this point.

'You got any chips left then, Franny?'

''Fraid not.' I was the poster girl for bad news. 'Got some chewy though.'

I gave him a stick of Wrigleys and he settled back with a sigh, arms folded. 'I mean, technically, she's not even *that* pretty. Vicky is prettier and Shayla's got bigger tits and you, well, your legs are insane, Franny.'

'Thanks for the validation.' I was only being a little sarcastic. The rest of me was quite glad that my love of an opaque black tight and a very short skirt wasn't just me trying to work a sixties mod silhouette when my legs weren't up to it. I knew I wasn't sexy. I wasn't that pretty. My hair was more mouse than blonde, my eyes were blue but not deep blue like Alice's. Just blue, and I usually had a couple of spots and I worried that maybe my lips were too thin but I had long, skinny legs and because I did work a sixties mod silhouette I had a rep for being cool. In Merrycliffe it didn't take a lot to get a rep for being cool. Anyway, that all added up to me being attractive on a good day. But not so attractive that boys wanted to get with me on a regular basis, or, like, ever.

'Alice is such a bitch,' Chris huffed. 'I don't know why I bothered.'

'But you did bother and you agreed to her rules so don't start hating on her just 'cause you lost. No one likes a hater.'

'I'm not being a hater.' He was, but I couldn't be arsed to argue about it. 'I'm just saying no wonder there's that graffiti in the bogs . . .'

'This isn't some new graffiti?' I asked sharply.

'No, it's the same old graffiti.'

I slumped in relief, because I was worried that some boy Alice had cruelly rejected might have got nasty and written something rude, possibly involving blow jobs, but it was just the old graffiti: Alice Jenkins is the worst girlfriend in the world.

We didn't know who'd written it, because Alice tended to snog most boys for no longer than a week. We'd narrowed it down to Rajesh, because they'd gone out for about three whole weeks, or George, who said he'd gone out with Alice when he hadn't. Though he had gone through a phase of leaving Alice bars of chocolate on her doorstep every morning until she'd told him to stop or she'd report him to the RSPCA because Pucci, her chihuahua, had eaten one and had explosive diarrhoea for three days.

Anyway, it wasn't like Alice had been offended. She'd persuaded someone to take a picture of the graffiti to use as the cover photo for her Facebook and Twitter profile and she was particularly fond of quoting it like she was doing the voiceover for a big Hollywood movie.

'Alice Jenkins is,' she'd say in a deep gravelly voice, 'the worst girlfriend in the world.'

No, Alice could never be accused of false advertising so there was no reason for Chris to look so mopey. There was also no reason for him to suddenly shift closer to me so that his leg was pressing against mine.

'Don't even think about it,' I told him sternly. 'I'm not the loving kind. I'm wedded to my career.'

'You're sixteen,' Chris pointed out, like that had anything to do with it.

'Also I'm a person in my own right. I'm not some consolation prize when you fail one of Alice's tasks.' It was my turn to fold my arms.

'Sorry,' he said. Then we sat there in silence and it wasn't

Chris's fault that he'd fallen for Alice's charms. It also wasn't his fault that he was rubbish at nicking road safety items.

'Let's head back to the bus shelter to get your hoodie and hang out there until Alice and Joey are done, all right?'

It was another fifteen minutes before Alice texted me. I was sitting in the bus shelter with Chris and watching old break-dance videos on YouTube on his phone. It was another fifteen minutes before she came to get me, by which time Chris had pinched the rest of my chewing gum and a blackcurrant Strepsil I'd found at the bottom of my bag. She was really pushing the limits of my good nature tonight.

Alice, inevitably, looked remarkably unsnogged. She'd reapplied her lippy, didn't have a hair out of place and was still managing to walk in her five-inch heels. Joey, following behind her, looked like he'd just seen God.

'Let's go, Franny B,' she demanded. 'We've things to do, places to be.'

Which meant she needed to change into her trainers but not when there were boys present.

'So, I'll see you. We'll make plans to hook up,' Joey said, then swallowed hard, amazed by his own daring.

'Yeah, great, BBM me or whatever.' At least two of us knew that she would never return any of Joey's messages, texts or invitations to chat, but at least Alice was letting him down gently.

'So, Franny, thanks for the chewy,' Chris said. 'See you Monday then, right?'

'Well, see ...'

7

'Wrong,' Alice interrupted in a flat voice. 'You're not going to see Franny on Monday. None of us are going to see Franny on Monday, because Franny doesn't go to our school any more.'

'I'm going to college to do a fashion BTEC. You know, after the school got all pissy about my GCSE results.' I shrugged. 'Like, whatever.'

'It doesn't matter about your GCSEs, Franny,' Alice said, like she'd been saying ever since my results had arrived. 'You're going to be a famous fashion designer so why do you need Maths anyway? Franny got on to the fashion course on the strength of her portfolio. Like, she actually has a portfolio,' she added proudly, not that Joey and Chris seemed to care.

As we walked away from the boys and I waited in the doorway of one of Merrycliffe's eleven charity shops for Alice to change into her trainers, I wondered if I'd ever get my BTEC, then get the hell out of Merrycliffe and go to London to find fashion fame and fortune. Or would my Saturday nights always be like this?

'Oh, cheer up, Franny!' Alice exclaimed, tucking her arm in mine. 'I wish I was going to college and not stuck at school. School is so immature.'

'Your mum still won't budge then?' Alice's dad owned five hair and beauty salons and Alice would much rather go into the family business than study for five A levels in subjects she didn't care about, but her mum wasn't having any of it. She let Alice work in the Merrycliffe salon on Thursdays after school and all day Saturdays, but she was convinced that Alice was going to be the next Alan Sugar – a younger, prettier, femaler

Alan Sugar. She was also convinced that Alice was going to go to Oxford or Cambridge to study Economics. It was kind of amazing how little she knew her only daughter.

'No, but Dad's on my side.' Alice's dad was always on her side. 'I just need to come up with a cunning plan.'

'You'll think of something,' I said, as we turned on to the seafront. 'You always do.'

'Oh God, I don't want to think about school. It can wait until Monday. Come on! Let's run!'

Alice and I grabbed on to each other's hand and ran, screaming into the wind, not caring that we might wake up the residents of the many old people's care homes that populated the seafront.

That was the way we rolled. We lived for kicks, even if the kicks were hard to come by.

It wasn't long before we got to my house. It was a huge Victorian beast of a house that had been a hotel back in the days before aeroplanes, when people had to holiday in Britain. I couldn't believe that anyone would come to Merrycliffe of their own free will. Like, on *holiday*, but that was the olden times for you. Now Merrycliffe was known only for being Europe's eleventh largest container port and our house was just a house, its sky-blue paint job corroded by the salt in the air, which had also rusted its metal balconies.

It wasn't much but I called it home. 'Let's do something tomorrow,' I said to Alice as I unlatched the gate. 'To celebrate our last day of freedom.'

'Something exciting,' Alice agreed.

We stood there for a while, a minute at least, trying to think of something exciting we could do.

'Oh, look, come round mine and I'll do your nails and then we can order some food and watch repeats of *Jersey Shore* and try really hard not to die of boredom,' Alice said finally. 'Sound like a plan?'

'Let's skip *Jersey Shore* for *Made in Chelsea* and that sounds like one wild Sunday afternoon right there,' I said. Then we air-kissed three times, 'cause I'd read that up in London, if you're in the media or generally fabulous, three kisses are industry standard. 'See you tomorrow if I don't get a better offer in the meantime.'

Alice snorted. 'Like, that's going to happen. *Here!*'

2

The house was in darkness and felt cold and stale as if it had been shut up for a long, long time, the rooms unaired, furniture swathed in dust sheets.

Except it hadn't, but my mother refused to open a window because she thought that the fresh air was full of toxic germs. Don't even get me started on the badness of putting on lights – apparently it had been proven that even energy-saving bulbs could give you cancer but what*ever*, I put them on anyway. Blazing a path from hall to kitchen, where I shoved two pieces of bread in the toaster, stuck the kettle on, put on even more lights as I climbed the stairs and knocked on my mum's door.

There was no reply. I pushed the door open and peered into the darkness.

'No ...' came the piteous whine from the lump of flesh

huddled under the duvet as I turned on the light. 'Turn it off.'

'Making toast. What do you want on it? Marmite? Jam? Is it too late for cheese?'

'No ...'

'Peanut butter? Tell you what, I'll let you have some of my Nutella.' I sat down on the edge of the bed and poked at what I thought might be her arm. 'As it's you.'

'Please, Franny.' Her voice was muffled until she pulled back the covers enough that I could see her face, all squinched up in case she might accidentally breathe in some fetid, airborne virus. 'I can't eat.'

'Well, tough, you're eating 'cause I'm not going to bed until you do. I'll just stay in here talking and talking and talking until you can't take it any more and go down to the kitchen of your own free will and end up eating the whole box of those weird Polish cocktail sausages with the use-by date of January 2019 just to get me to shut up. Your call.'

There was no response. It didn't surprise me.

When I came back fifteen minutes later with a laden tray, the bedside lamp had been switched on but she'd disappeared under the duvet again. I put the tray down on the bedside table. Right next to her pills, which I was sure she hadn't taken.

There was still no response as I sat back down on the bed, but I made sure that I was pretty much sitting on her leg so she had to shift over. With a deep sigh she sat up. I shoved a mug of tea at her so she had no choice but to take it, otherwise there would have been hot tea all over the duvet and spills drove her to the very edge of her nerves.

A huge number of things drove my mum to the very edge of her nerves.

'Been out then?' she asked, her voice rusty because she hadn't used it all day. She took three sips of tea and I let myself relax ever so slightly.

'Yeah, with Alice.'

Because she'd started to nibble at the toast now, she had the energy to pull a vinegary face. She didn't like Alice. Thought she was a bad influence, though she should have known, being my own mother and all, that I wasn't the type of girl who was easily influenced.

But tonight, I went along with it. I told her about Alice's re-enacting *The Hunger Games* with two dumb boys and it was the distraction she needed to drink the mug of tea and eat her two pieces of toast. She even looked at the tube of hand cream on her dressing table like she was thinking about putting some on.

'Alice . . . she's one of those girls who'll get pregnant before she's even finished school. She's probably pregnant already,' she said disapprovingly.

'She's not. She won't. She doesn't do *that* with them, she just likes to make them suffer,' I explained. 'There's not much else to do round here on a Saturday night, if we don't go to The Wow.'

'I suppose.' Mum smiled so fleetingly I almost missed it. But I didn't and for that microsecond she was who she used to be, then she was gone.

I stood up. 'I'm going to run you a bath. I put a wash on

before I went out. Should be dry by now. I'll get you a clean nightie to change into.'

'I don't really feel up to it.' She was already trying to retreat back under the covers.

'Oh, you'll feel much better once you've had a bath. And tell you what? I'll change the sheets while you're soaking.' I pulled back the covers and didn't quite haul her out of bed, but I came pretty close to it.

She didn't shout at me. Or swear. No threats or tears, just a little bit of grumbling as she swung her pasty white legs over the side of the bed and took hold of the hand I was offering to pull her up. This was a good day.

Once she was in the bath, which I'd generously doused with lavender bubble bath 'cause I'd read somewhere that it was meant to be all soothing and stuff, she let me wash her hair. 'You can do the rest,' I told her, as I handed her a sponge and the bar of lily-scented soap I'd bought her last birthday.

I went back into her room, opened the window to let in five minutes of fresh air and checked the pill bottle by her bed. There were twenty-three tablets in it. There'd been twenty-three tablets in it all week. There should have been only seven left and I should have been nagging her about going to the chemist to pick up her repeat prescription. I was too tired to think about that. Instead, I stripped her bed.

I could hear a faint splashing as I came back up the stairs with clean linen and fifteen minutes later she was back in bed. Her hair was damp and she wouldn't let me use the hairdryer because she said it would just blow dust around the room, but she was sitting up, she'd taken her pills with the glass of water I'd got her and was looking like she was present, rather than, like, absent.

'Tomorrow, I might do a supermarket shop,' she said. 'We'll make a list at breakfast. Maybe I'll drive, so we can go to the big Morrisons in Lytham. What do you think?'

'It sounds great,' I said with a lot more enthusiasm than I felt. I didn't want to spend my last precious Sunday free from the yoke of further education traipsing round the big Morrisons in Lytham. Besides, there were ten hours between now and breakfast tomorrow. A lot could happen in ten hours.

I bent down to kiss her cheek, wished her goodnight and said I'd see her in the morning.

When I got to my room, I had the sick, panicky feeling I always got when I thought about what she might be like in the morning. The only way to stop it was to stop thinking about her. To shove her far back into the furthest reaches of my head, as far back as I could, then the sick, panicky feeling would go.

Instead I looked at all my college stuff laid out, though college was still two sleeps away. I had new stationery: a really expensive set of fibre-tip pens for drawing, an A3 sketch pad and a lime-green notebook my sister Siobhan had bought me which had **DESIGNERS I MET AND LIKED** embossed on it in gold letters. I had my sewing kit in a little vintage attaché case: three different pairs of scissors, pinking shears and my chalks. Measuring tape, pins, thimble, reels of cotton and finishings. Really, it was a thing of beauty.

Draped over the back of a chair was the dress I planned to wear on Monday. It was a candy-pink and white sweater dress I'd found in a chazza. I'd put a corded trim on the unravelling hem, and fake-leather patches on the elbows like you get on old men's cardigans. I was going to wear it with black tights and a pair of amazing cork-wedged sandals because I love an open toe with a matt tight.

(It's very fashion to refer to things like jeans and tights in the singular. 'I was rocking a skinny jean with a five-inch heel,' you might say, though Alice said you'd only say that if you were a gigantic wanker.)

Apart from the pile of college stuff, my room is actually very minimalist in a space age, pop art way – probably because my sewing stuff is in the room next door, though I like to think of it more as my design studio. I'm on the third floor, just below what would have been the staffrooms in the attic. Mum never ventures up this far and Dad's always away so I can pretty much do what I want in here.

What I wanted to do was to paper my walls in silver foil. Yeah, Christmas turkey tin foil. It was very fiddly, but I was inspired by a place in New York called the Factory, where the artist Andy Warhol had lived and worked in the sixties. He was famous for making art that riffed off of all sorts of weird random stuff like Campbell's soup cans, Marilyn Monroe, even Brillo soap-pad boxes. He also directed black and white films full of sixties hipsters and he had a house band called the Velvet Underground sometimes fronted by a really cool German model called Nico and then Edie Sedgwick would dance on stage with them. Edie was this doomed, mad, utterly beautiful heiress, who's my absolute style icon and glamour hero and numero uno inspiration. I discovered Edie when I saw a picture of her on a style blog. She was wearing just a T-shirt and black tights and was posed in an arabesque while perched on a stuffed rhinoceros. No wonder I was intrigued. Once I started obsessing on Edie, it didn't take long to find out about Andy Warhol and his whole scene. I would have loved to be part of a scene like that, except for all the drugs and nudity, that is.

As well as clearing the Spar of all its tin foil so I could have shiny, silver walls, I also have a huge blown-up photograph of Edie, Andy Warhol and another guy called Gerard Malanga on the wall right opposite my bed. It was taken in New York, obvs, because New York is totes the centre of the universe, and they're on the street. Literally *on the street*, rising up out of a manhole, Edie leaning back against Gerard, her long, black-clad legs stretching up to infinity, Andy staring straight ahead at the camera with his own camera poised.

Whenever I was feeling unsure and down-hearted, like I was tonight, I would climb into bed and stare at Edie, Andy and Gerard and it always made me feel better.

That photo represents everything I want to be. The problem is that I'm just not sure how to get there.

3

On Monday morning, walking through the college grounds, after the trudge up the long hill from Merrycliffe town centre, felt like walking the green mile.

Obviously I wasn't the only new person starting college that day. But I felt like the only person hanging solo and I was getting some smirky looks because of my candy-striped dress, tights and open-toed sandals. Merrycliffe College wasn't ready for a tight and an open toe.

I styled it out by putting on my big dark glasses – they're a lot like the ones that Audrey Hepburn wears in *Breakfast at Tiffany's* – and assumed my best 'bitch, *please*' expression.

It got me through three hours of filling in forms and my first catch-up GCSE Maths class, then skulking around the canteen for the rest of the morning. It was weird not having a form room to hang out in but at least I could go home for lunch without fear of being accused of bunking off. At college you were treated as an adult, or else they didn't really care what you did – it was too soon to tell.

Mum was actually up when I got home. Not dressed, but she'd managed to make it down to the kitchen and was watching a repeat of *Location Location Location* on the little portable TV.

'Oh, there you are,' she said when I walked in. 'I know I never got round to it yesterday but let's make that list and go to Morrisons. It will only take me ten minutes to shower and change.'

She'd had the whole summer break, six weeks, to go to Morrisons with me instead of taking to her bed, but she chose today, this lunchtime, on my first day of college, an hour from my first official lesson in how to become a fashion designer. *Now* she decided she wanted to stock up on loo roll and fish fingers.

I also knew that if she really was serious, it would take her way more than ten minutes to shower and change. I could go back to college, then come home again and she might just about be ready to leave.

'Well, I have a few things I need to do first,' I said vaguely because I wasn't even sure that Mum knew that this was my first day at college. Dad had texted me that morning telling me to 'break a leg, kid'. Alice's mum and dad had given me a card yesterday and some salted caramel buttons from Hotel Chocolat. But as Mum spent most of her time in bed with the covers over her head, for her the days all bled into each other.

The only difference was good days and bad days and there hadn't been that many good days for a long, long time. 'I'm sure I'll be done by the time you're ready to go, but shall I make a cup of tea first?'

I made her tea and toast again. Started the shopping list. Had a slightly tense discussion about soap pads versus scourers and Fairy Liquid, then told her I had to pop out.

It was easier not to give her details but a brief, shadowy outline of what was happening in my world. That way no one got hurt.

'I won't be long,' I promised cheerily as I opened the front door. 'Call me on my mobile when you're ready to go.'

I was so late that I had to get the bus back to college, which meant a mad rush to the bus stop and I still had to chase down the bus until it stopped at the lights, then hammer on the door and pout and make sad puppy faces until the driver relented.

I didn't want to start my BTEC L3 Extended Diploma in Fashion and Clothing a red-faced, flustered mess, but we don't always get what we want.

I followed the signs to the art block, which was right at the back of the college grounds. Then I wandered around for a bit, getting more and more panic-stricken, until I found the right studio. I took a deep breath and pushed open the door.

I'm not entirely sure what I was expecting but it was something more exciting than seven other students sitting on stools in a semicircle in a workroom. Beyond them, I could see the workstations at the other end of the room; huge tables, each with a sewing machine built into it. I wanted to rush to the nearest one and get acquainted – but that could wait. First, I was curious and also more than a little scared to see who my sewing companions would be for the next two years.

Two of them obviously knew each other because they were jabbering away and also they were old, like in their forties at least. Probably retraining after being made redundant or something. By the look of them, they were hoping to open a boutique selling dresses covered in bits of frou-frou and diamanté. Not that I was judging. Me? Judge? Never.

There was a really pretty black girl with her own 'bitch, *please*' expression, and a girl who was totally orange 'cause she'd overdone it on the fake tan. She had fake everything else too: eyelashes, nails, hair extensions. I wondered if she'd got the wrong room and was meant to be doing a hair and beauty course. A lot of the girls who worked in Alice's dad's salons had the same look and they were perfectly nice but they weren't the kind of girls I wanted to hang out with on a daily basis.

Then there was a girl with pink hair who was working a Steampunk look – I was sure that's why she had clock faces sewn on to her billowing, gothy black dress. Last of all were two semi-cute boys. One wearing an old-fashioned three-piece suit, the other wearing jeans, a Fred Perry shirt, Adidas trackie top with Adidas Shell Toe trainers. It was a very old skool look.

21

Obviously the two boys were gay. My gaydar was infallible. I took a seat nearest to the one in the suit and there wasn't even time to make eye contact with anyone or open my *Designers I Have Met And Liked* notebook, before the tutor came bustling through the door.

I'd been expecting a Lancastrian version of Anna Wintour, the uber-chic editor of US *Vogue*, not a middle-aged woman who looked like she'd yell at you if you presented her with a crooked seam. She wasn't wearing anything amazing either but an olive-green jumper and boring black trousers. I couldn't imagine how she was going to teach me anything I wanted to know about fashion design.

Up until now, I was completely self-taught. I'd learned how to make clothes through trial and error; watching how-to videos on the internet and buying clothes from the 50p bin in the chazzas so I could take them apart to see how they were made.

'I'm going to assume that you know nothing about fashion design and start with the basics,' Barbara, the tutor, said. 'Though I do expect all of you to be able to thread a needle at the very least.'

We all laughed nervously and I waited for Barbara to tell us about all the exciting things we'd be doing, from learning how to make trousers to corsetry. While I waited, I mentally sketched out a perfect pair of cigarette pants and was just frowning over the zipper when I realised that Barbara had stopped talking ages ago and we were meant to be taking it in turns to introduce ourselves.

I'd already missed the two older women's intros. Barbara had moved on to the black girl, whose name was Sage (I wondered if she'd made that up), who was keen to pursue a career in costume design for film and TV.

Orange girl, as I'd suspected, admitted that the hair and beauty courses had been over-subscribed so she was here under duress, waiting for a wannabe hairdresser or aesthetician to drop out. Her name was Krystal with a K. Girls like that always have names like Krystal with a K.

Then Barbara moved on to Three-piece Suit who was called Matthew and was interested in menswear and tailoring. He even name-checked Fred Astaire and Miuccia Prada. He'd make a perfect fashion friend, I thought, and tried to smile at him welcomingly but I don't think he noticed.

The Steampunk girl was known to her parents as Dora and launched into an impressive but quite scary ten-minute rant about mainstream fashion and how she was only interested in avant-garde design and she'd 'like, rather die than have to ever design anything as mundane and boring as a raincoat or a pair of slacks. Honestly, I would totally die.' I could tell she and Krystal with a K were not going to be bosom buddies, but I thought Dora might be interesting to hang out with. Sitting next to her was Mr Old Skool, AKA Paul, who hoped one day to have his own sportswear empire even though he'd never so much as sewed on a button before.

Then it was my turn. I wasted precious time dithering over my name, which wasn't the best start. Officially I was called Francesca Barker, but that had always been shortened to

Frances. Anyway, everyone called me Franny B, had done ever since nursery school, though I couldn't demand that of new acquaintances – they kind of had to make that decision for themselves.

'I'm Frances. Franny, really,' I said after several long, long moments. Then I didn't know what else to say. I couldn't share my five-year plan, which saw me to my final days at Central St Martin's where my entire degree show was snapped up by Net-A-Porter and everyone marvelled at how a dump like Merrycliffe-on-Sea could have produced me *and* Martin Sanderson, who had his own huge fashion empire as well as being Creative Director at the French couture house Corres, and was an even bigger inspiration to me than Edie Sedgwick. Then Martin Sanderson would give me a job, preferably in Paris, and that was my five-year plan.

I couldn't say any of that because it sounded like I was really up myself, so I just said, 'Well, I love fashion and making my own clothes and I'd really like to have my own design house one day.'

Barbara looked down at her wad of papers, then looked back at me. It wasn't a good look.

'So, you're the girl who failed her GCSEs,' she said.

That was completely untrue. 'I didn't fail *all* of them,' I pointed out. I also wanted to tell her that it was blates unfair to share my academic shame with my new classmates. Wasn't there such a thing as lecturer–student confidentiality? Like when doctors aren't allowed to blab all your embarrassing medical stuff to people. 'I'm retaking Maths and English.'

Barbara stared at me like she was amazed that I could even form sentences. Everyone else was staring too and not because they were in awe of my fashion-forward first day look, but because they probably thought I was intellectually backward.

'We expect people on this course to have a minimum of four GCSEs including English at grade C or—'

'I *have* got four GCSEs. In fact, I've got seven,' I snapped in a way that had Barbara's eyebrows shooting up. 'As and Bs mostly and the other lady who interviewed me, the dean of art studies or whatever, said that as long as I attended catch-up lessons and retook Maths and English, she was happy to have me. I showed her my portfolio. I wrote a five-page essay on why I wanted to take this course.' *So why are you giving me such a hard time?* I thought, but I didn't dare say it out loud.

Barbara settled back down with a little huffing sound. She had a tape measure around her neck in case of any measuring emergencies. I wanted to strangle her with it. I also wanted to cry.

'I want to see your portfolio tomorrow.' She shuffled her papers unhappily. 'I don't have your interview transcript and I don't see a copy of your essay in your file either.'

'I'll print you out a copy.'

'See that you do.'

Even if I managed to stay on the course and pass my retakes, I had a feeling that Barbara was going to personally guarantee that my next two years would be abject misery. She probably wouldn't even let me operate a sewing machine without adult supervision.

I settled back down in my chair, hugging my notebook to me,

and kept my eyes fixed on a spot on the greying white lino. I wouldn't cry if I focused on just the one spot.

Barbara, who was now at the top of my shit list, number one with a bullet, wittered on about techniques and processes for ten minutes, then told us we could go. It was weird not having the day measured out by the sound of a bell ringing every fifty minutes but I couldn't wait to get gone.

I stumbled to my feet, shoved my *Designers I've Met And Liked* notebook in the Marc by Marc Jacobs canvas tote that Siobhan's mate had got me from London, hung my bag from my shoulder and tried to get to the door as quickly as humanly possible without any need for eye contact.

'You're Franny B, right?' demanded a voice.

I turned round to answer Krystal with a K's question. 'Yeah,' I said. I didn't sound that friendly but I don't think I sounded that *unfriendly* either. It was hard to strike a balance.

'Right, so you're mates with *her*.' Krystal with a K pretty much spat the last word. 'Alice Jenkins. You're her best friend.'

I nodded. 'We go way back. Why?'

I knew exactly why and I knew exactly what the next words out of Krystal with a K's over-glossed pink lips were going to be. And right on cue . . . 'She stole my boyfriend! She stole all of my friends' boyfriends and she's a sl—'

'Well, I'm sorry about that,' I said quickly because I really didn't want to hear *that* word. 'Anyway, they couldn't have been very good boyfriends if they were that easy to steal. So, you know . . .'

'Alice Jenkins? I only moved to Merrycliffe two months ago

and I've already heard all about her. It sounds like she needs to come with a public health warning.' Now Steampunk Dora was getting up in my grille. 'You willingly hang out with her?'

'She's my best friend.' I didn't approve of Alice's boy-baiting, but when strangers were giving her a hard time I'd defend her to the death. That was the deal with best friends. 'She's really funny. She does great impersonations. She absolutely doesn't need a public health warning.'

'Yeah, she does. She's a total whore. She's, like, riddled with STIs obvs.'

I couldn't believe that Krystal with a K would say that about Alice, about anyone. 'You know nothing about her. Just 'cause guys want to get with her doesn't mean she ever does anything more than snog them and why should it be her responsibility to check their relationship status?' I drew myself up to my full height, five foot seven inches, and my wedge heels took me all the way up to five, ten. 'Also, Krystal, it's really reductive to call other girls whores and condemn them for owning their sexuality.'

The last bit I'd totally nicked from my older sister Siobhan. Since she'd started university, she'd become a feminist and was all about reclaiming words like slut and sending me links to articles about expressing my individuality and not following the crowd. Whatever. Like I didn't already know that. I was the only girl in Merrycliffe brave enough to do double leopard print.

Dora stared at me like I was some kind of enigma. Matthew and Paul exchanged raised-eyebrow looks. Like it was impossible for a friend of Alice Jenkins to have any depth.

Which just went to show how little they knew.

4

'I can't believe how judgey they all were. It's not like any of them know you. They didn't go to St Anne's. We've never seen them down The Wow,' I said the next day to the girl herself as she sat on the counter of Sparkle Drycleaners and rummaged in a bag of pick 'n' mix. 'Krystal with a K, who's everything you hate about trainee hairdressers ...'

Alice looked up. 'How orange is she on a scale of one to ten?'

'She's at least a seventeen. She's ... thermonuclear orange.' I shook my head. 'She wears pink frosted lipgloss too. It does her absolutely no favours.'

'She sounds horrific.' Alice sat up straighter. 'Poor Franny! Having to put up with all those losers. You'd think fashion students would be more open-minded, but if there's one thing worse than being talked about, it's not being talked about.'

'Though *maybe* you could rethink the whole using-boys-as-blood-sport thing or at least confine it to a three-mile radius. Krystal with a K, and even Sage, live nearer to Lytham and they knew all about you. Oh! Don't look so happy about it!'

Alice tried to be serious but her serious face lasted five seconds and then she went back to looking very pleased with herself. 'But all I do is snog them for a little bit, then toss them back. I don't dole out blow jobs, I never shag them, I hardly ever let one of them even feel me up. You know it and I know it and we're the only two people whose opinions I value.'

It was like arguing with a slab of concrete. I shook my head, but I was smiling as I turned my attention to the jeans I was meant to be hemming. 'Just as long as you do value my opinion.'

'I do. Without you I'd never have mastered doing the flicky thing with liquid eyeliner,' Alice insisted, swinging her legs restlessly. It was four o'clock – the afternoon lull. It would get really busy twenty minutes before closing as people rushed to pick up their dry-cleaning or brought in dirty clothes that they wanted ready for collection first thing the next morning. 'Don't you mind being stuck in the window like that?'

I worked part-time doing alterations on Tuesday and Thursday after college and all day Saturday. I took up hems, let down hems. Sewed on stray buttons. Mended rips and tears and occasionally took apart a whole garment and put it together again with some extra material added in for Mrs Ayers, a yo-yo dieter who couldn't bear to abandon a perfectly good dress just because she'd put on a stone.

It was a great way to learn how clothes were put together. And it was a great job for a fledgling fashion designer, but it wasn't the most glamorous part-time job in the world. Sometimes the clothes that we had in for mending were quite whiffy and Mum was convinced that the dry-cleaning fumes I was huffing were carcinogenic. And no, I really didn't like sitting behind the huge sewing machine in the window so people could gawp at me like I wasn't even a real person, but at least I could watch the world go by. Not that there was a lot of world to go by.

'It's all right. At least I don't have to work in Burger King.'

'Or what about Katie? She stinks of fried fish.'

We took a moment to ponder Katie's sad lot in life, forced to serve behind the counter of her parents' fish and chip shop. That took a good thirty seconds and then we were back to matters in hand.

'So, basically you're saying that everyone on your course doesn't like you because they don't like me?' Alice clarified.

'Well, apart from Sandra and Karen but they're in their forties so, whatever.' I sighed. 'Anyway, I'm not there to make friends.'

'You sound like a reality TV contestant.' Alice held her finger up. 'The show's called Merrycliffe's Next Best Fashion Designer, not Merrycliffe's Next Best Friend. Look, I'm sorry if I'm cramping your style . . .'

'You're not. I don't want to be friends with them if they're going to hate on people they don't even know,' I said, because it was true.

'Yeah! You have to hate the haters. Is it wrong that I'm kind of glad?' Alice suddenly asked, swivelling herself round so she could sit cross-legged on the counter. 'I've been worried that you'd meet loads of cool people at college who'd get all your obscure fashion references, and then I wouldn't see you quite so often and when I did, you'd want them to tag along and you'd all have these little in-jokes and we'd drift apart and eventually we'd stop hanging out together. That would be awful. It would be even worse than if we had a big row. I mean, you can say sorry after a big row, give each other make-up presents, but if you just grew tired of me, well, there wouldn't be much I could do about that.'

This was the thoughtful side that no one else saw of Alice. They also never saw the really funny side of her. Once Alice had made me laugh so hard with her impersonation of Nicki Minaj at the self-scanning checkout in the supermarket (you kind of had to be there) that I wet myself a little bit. But it was OK because I knew I could trust Alice to take the secret that she made me wet myself just a little bit to her grave.

'You don't have to do anything about it because it's never going to happen,' I said, reaching across the sewing machine to give her a friendly punch on the arm. 'We're going to be little old ladies together, remember? Raising merry hell at the bingo.'

'Racing each other along the seafront on our mobility scooters.'

'Our pimped-out mobility scooters,' I added, because I planned to add hot rod flame decals to mine and do something

31

with the horn so it played Lady Gaga's 'Born This Way' at anyone who dared to cross my path. 'And we'll tear up the dance floor at the— Oh!'

'What? What dance floor?'

I was only dimly aware of Alice squawking in the background. All I could see was a smirky grin and a mop of dirty blond hair with bleached ends all tousled and rumpled like he'd only just got up. Then he was gone in a blur of a battered black-leather jacket and a hand maybe raised in greeting, maybe just scratching his nose.

Oh, Louis, Louis, I've got a crush on you.

I must have murmured it out loud because when I came back down to earth, Alice was giving me a knowing look. 'When you see him, I swear your ears prick up in exactly the same way that Pucci's do when she hears the postie coming up the path.'

Pucci, Alice's chihuahua, also yapped furiously and ran around in mad circles whenever anyone dared to approach their house.

'My ears are covered by my hair,' I pointed out, but it was less pointing out and more sighing rapturously. 'I just know that the world can't be *such* a terrible place when Louis Allen exists.'

Suddenly, none of it mattered. Not hostile lecturers and even more hostile new classmates. Mum and her inability to function on any kind or level. Dad never being around. Siobhan being in Manchester and hardly ever coming home.

It wasn't important because there were still reasons to cheer and the biggest reason was that Thee Desperadoes, Louis's band, were playing The Wow Club on Saturday.

'Oh great, I was looking for a new way to make my ears bleed,' Alice said sourly when I reminded her.

'They're not that bad.' I waved her disdain away. 'Anyway, who cares what they sound like . . .'

'They sound like what I imagine bowel surgery sounds like when they haven't given the patient any anaesthetic . . .'

I waved *that* away too. 'I don't care. All I know is that for half an hour they'll be playing and for half an hour I have gawping rights at Louis without anyone thinking that I'm a sad stalker.'

Alice smiled at me kindly. 'But you are a sad stalker, Franny. You're the girl who followed Louis all the way round all the amusement arcades in Blackpool.'

I regretted nothing. 'It was an afternoon well spent.' I grinned. 'I think he just waved, Ally! To get my attention! *My* attention. Like, he noticed me and he thinks I'm on his level. This is huge. It's a total game-changer.'

'I hope you're not going to spend all of Saturday night mooning around Louis with a line of drool hanging down from your chin,' Alice said. 'Note to self: remember to pop a pack of tissues in my bag.'

'Except you'll be far too busy putting the moves on some poor, dumb lad to worry about my drool issues,' I assured her and she brightened.

'You're probably right.' She looked pensive for all of five seconds. 'I need to think about who I'm going to snog on Saturday.

Indie disco. Pickings are going to be slim unless some university students wander in by accident. I mean, there must be some who live in Merrycliffe to take advantage of the cheap rents and excellent transport links.'

If they were we'd yet to meet them. I was saved from having to think up some names of boys that Alice hadn't tormented yet by the bell over the door tinkling, and talking of which . . .

'Yo! Yo! Yo! Looking superfine, Franny B!' The Chatterjees' son, Rajesh, swaggered his way through the door. 'When you gonna get with me?'

'Um, some time like never,' I said as I always said every Tuesday and Thursday at four-thirty, when Raj turned up and asked me the same question. 'But thanks for asking.'

Raj was pretty superfine himself, apart from the fact that he tried to talk like he was from South Central LA, which didn't really work with a Lancashire accent. Also, there was the fact that he was the apple of the Chatterjees' eyes and no girl was good enough for him – Mrs Chatterjee was quite adamant about that – and I intended to keep this job until I (hopefully) buggered off to do my fashion degree and then there was . . .

'Alice,' Rajesh said thinly, dropping his fresh and fly routine. 'You've got some front.'

She looked down at her breasts and smirked because she knew that it would really wind Raj up, the boy she'd dallied with for actual weeks, weeks in the plural, longer than she'd ever dallied with another boy, which made him her most long-term boyfriend. That had been over a year ago, and when she realised that there was a conflict of interest because dating my employers' son made things totes awk for me with the Chatter-jees, Alice had dumped him.

'No way am I letting a boy come between us,' she'd said when I'd told her that Mrs Chatterjee kept telling me that Raj was out till all hours with Alice and it was interfering with his studies. Then there'd been the whole incident with the lovebites. Mrs Chatterjee had come close to tears over that. Though I had told Alice that she could keep seeing Raj if she was *really* into him. 'Oh, but I'm not *that* into him. His snog-ging skills aren't up to my own high standards. Also, that whole gangsta thing is tragic, especially when the closest he's come to a ghetto is ... well, Raj has never, ever been close to a ghetto in his life. He's heir to a dry-cleaning dynasty.'

So, Alice had dumped Raj and now they were sworn ene-mies, which still made my life awkward because I was friends with both of them.

'Anyway, you were just telling me about all the hot guys at college,' Alice reminded me, though I'd been telling her no such thing.

'Yeah, the hot gay guys,' I said and I still had buttons to replace on three shirts, a pair of cords to take up and the hem on a skirt to let down before closing time. 'Both of you are dis-tracting me, so you'll have to leave now. Either separately or together. Your choice.'

'I is flying solo these days on account of all the pretty ladies who want a piece of me,' Raj said with a leer in my direction, which I pointedly ignored by hiding my face in a pink-striped shirt.

'Yeah? Name three of these co-called pretty ladies,' Alice said sweetly and Raj stopped leering and stared down at his trainers. 'Anyway I've got to go.' Alice lowered herself down from the counter. Raj's eyes were now fixed firmly on her boobs as Alice did a little shimmy like she was ironing out all her kinks. 'I'm meant to be Face-timing fit Declan from the Academy and Skyping my gran at the same time. I hate being double booked. I'll see you tomorrow, Franny B.'

Then she was gone.

Sometimes, I wondered if making boys fall at your feet was worth all Alice's time and effort. I'd much rather stay in and watch *The Great British Bake Off* instead of juggling boys like they were flaming torches.

Raj reached up to pop the collar of his hoodie, then remembered that his hoodie didn't have a collar to pop. 'Whatever. She's such a bitch,' he muttered and he looked to me for confirmation but I shook my head and pressed down on the foot pedal of my sewing machine so whatever else he wanted to say was drowned out.

5

I'd never been so pleased to get to a Friday. College was turning out to be way more stressful than school.

That morning, Barbara had made me stand in front of her desk while she read my entrance essay. It was about the end of clothes rationing (it had blown my mind when I discovered that clothes had been, like, *rationed* during the Second World War) and how Christian Dior's New Look of 1947 with its big foofy skirts had been all bye, bye austerity and hello opulence.

I'd also shown her the two prom dresses I'd made. My prom dress was a slinky, silvery, cap-sleeved shift dress with epaulettes fashioned from gunmetal-coloured paillettes. I'd painstakingly sewn two hundred of the bastards on each sleeve. I'd also made Alice a dress, though my Alice dress had been inspired by Alexander McQueen's 2008 collection and was my first attempt at boning a bodice and working with feathers. It hadn't been entirely successful – in the end Alice's parents had bought her a draped black dress from All Saints for £200.

I wouldn't have blamed Barbara for dissing my really tortured seam-work where I'd tried to insert the boning, but she just asked me where I'd found the pattern. When I said that I'd tried to make my own pattern, she pursed her lips, then said that she was happy to have me on the course, but woe betide me if I screwed up my GCSEs second time round.

She actually said 'woe betide' like she was from the days of Queen Victoria, but it was all right. I wasn't going to screw up my GCSEs. Barbara was stuck with me but I did wonder when I was going to *learn* something. We'd spent an afternoon sitting in front of the sewing machines and going through the annotated worksheets that told us what each bit did, though I already knew how to thread the bobbin and what happened if you accidentally pressed down on the foot pedal while threading said bobbin – a world of pain, that's what.

Sage was now hanging out with Steampunk Dora and Matthew and Paul, and Krystal with a K hung out with her orange-hued hairdresser mates and shot me evils and the two middle-aged ladies tucked themselves away and I hung out by myself. It was almost a relief to go home at lunchtime and check on Mum, who'd finally registered that the summer holidays were over and I was at college.

'I didn't realise that you'd started college already,' she said in a perplexed fashion when she found a whole load of course bumpf on the kitchen table. This was after she'd made it downstairs on Thursday lunchtime and I was nuking a spaghetti bolognese ready meal in the microwave for us.

'Started on Monday,' I told her for what had to be the fiftieth time.

'Oh, so you didn't want to go back to school?'

I furiously polished a handful of cutlery so it would come up to Mum's high standards. 'They wouldn't even let me start doing A levels until I retook my GCSEs and I wanted to do a fashion degree after A levels anyway so doing a BTEC in fashion is giving me a head start.'

'Can you even do a degree with just a BTEC? Will they let you?'

'Well, I hope so. As long as I don't screw up my retakes.' By then, I'd moved on to furiously polishing a glass.

Mum smiled wanly. 'So, it all worked out in the end, then. That's good.'

I managed not to shout but chewed on the insides of my cheeks instead because she'd been a little better this week. She was out of bed when I came home, if not at lunchtime, then later in the afternoon. On Tuesday she'd even had her friend Linda round who she'd met when she was still going to her support group. Mum was always in a better mood after one of her visits, even though all they did was sit around and moan at each other for a couple of hours.

On Friday afternoon when I got in from college, my oldest sister, Anna, was just parking in the drive. She was the last person I wanted to deal with. Anna always makes out like she's really busy looking after my nephews, Aiden and Jayden (I know, I *know*), and that she's practically a lone parent because my brother-in-law, Steve, works on the lorries like Dad, but she can't be that busy because every time I log into Facebook she's playing YoVille or Candy Crush or Bejewelled Blitz or whatever.

On Friday, when I was exhausted after a full week at college and two afternoons doing alterations, she greeted me with a cheery 'I hoped you'd be here to give me a break. Why don't you look after the boys while I have a chat with Mum? Oh, and I'll have a coffee if you're making it.'

Anna stayed for two hours, and told me off for plonking Aiden and Jayden in front of the television because they kept putting their sticky hands all over my stuff. Then she had a go at me for planning to heat up some pizza for tea, not that she was offering to cook us a meal from locally sourced fresh produce. Didn't even wash up her coffee mug, borrowed twenty quid from Mum (which was actually twenty quid from me, because Mum didn't have any cash on her), then had the nerve to leave a huge pile of mending for me to do. And breathe, Franny, breathe ...

The one good thing about Anna coming round is that Mum and I always bond over how badly behaved Aiden and Jayden are and how lazy Anna is and how she never had any ambition to be anything other than married. Once Anna had left with half the pile, because I refused to do anything more complicated than stitch up a hole or sew on a button unless she paid me, Mum and I ate our pizza and bitched about her.

'She's got a new tattoo of a rose with Steve's initials on the petals right on her left boob,' I told Mum, who sniffed.

'How common. I thought I'd raised her better than that.'

Ah, it was just like the old days.

What passed for a good mood carried Mum all the way through Saturday. When I got home from the Chatterjees' I was amazed to find her halfway through an internet supermarket shop though she was a little stressed about which anti-perspirant to get as some of them were more carcinogenic than others.

Mum getting her groove back meant I could go out with a clear conscience, especially as Linda had promised to come round with a couple of the other ladies from the support group. There was even talk of cake.

'First time I've seen your mum downstairs in weeks,' Alice remarked as we got ready to go out.

'I'm cautiously optimistic,' I said, as I carefully sewed the last piece of my dress together. I'd found some vintage cross-word material on Etsy – and I was making a very fitted dress. My dresses were getting more fitted as I got better at sewing. It was perfect for the indie disco. If we got bored, we could fill in some of the blank squares by writing cool words on it with my fabric pen. 'Maybe, just maybe, she might be turning the corner.'

'Well, about time,' Alice muttered, as she painted her nails with top coat. 'It's not right how she—'

'Oh, let's not,' I begged. 'It's Saturday night and we haven't seen each other properly all week.'

'Yeah! Sing it, Franny! Have you any idea how boring English is when you're not sitting next to me?'

'I wish you were at college with me. Is your mum still being really fascist about letting you train to be a hairdresser with all the orange girls at college?'

'Totes fascist.' When I was a fashion designer with my own line, diffusion line and a creative directorship at a French couture house, Alice would be a ground-breaking and innovative hair stylist who'd do all the looks for my runway shows. For now though she was stuck doing five A levels and working at her dad's salon to pick up what she could. It was a travesty. 'But at least she's a fascist who buys me alcohol,' she added brightly. 'I've got a bottle of vodka in my bag and some diet Red Bull but let's wait until I've finished my nails. I don't like operating nail polish while under the influence of alcohol.'

By the time we clattered down the stairs, we weren't pissed but on the way to pissed.

'I'll just say goodbye to Mum,' I told Alice as she slipped into her jacket.

'Be quick,' she said. 'Don't get into anything with her.'

Mum was in the kitchen putting nuts and crisps into little bowls. She looked up and smiled at me. 'Are you cryptic or general knowledge?'

'Am I what?' I looked down at my crossword dress. 'Oh! Cryptic, always.'

'Back here no later than midnight,' she said sternly. I couldn't believe it. Not the curfew bit but Mum being Mumly. 'How are you getting home?'

'Alice's dad is going to give us a lift when Alice rings him,' I said.

She fussed over two bowls of nuts, making sure the contents were absolutely level. 'Well, make sure you thank him.'

'Of course I will,' I assured her. 'So, you're all right then?'

'Getting there,' she said and she was cryptic too. Must be where I got it from. 'It will be nice to have the girls over this evening. Been ages since I last saw them.'

'Well, I'll be going then, Mum.'

She suddenly tutted and tipped some of the nuts from one bowl into the other and I stood there for a second, holding my breath, in case the nuts sent her nuts, but she was still smiling. 'Have a nice time. I probably won't wait up for you so I'll see you tomorrow morning.'

'I'll text you just to make sure everything's OK. And to remind you that if Linda brings her salted caramel cake, you have to save a piece for me ... '

'You don't have to text. I'm sure I can remember to keep a piece of cake for you,' she said a little waspishly as if she knew that I just wanted an excuse to check up on her.

'I'll still text you,' I insisted. 'It gives me something to do when Alice is being chatted up and I'm standing around like a spare part.'

'I heard that!' Alice popped her head round the door. 'You're looking sick, Franny. Maybe I'll be the spare part tonight. I'm dragging her off now, Mrs B. Nice to see you. Promise we won't drink too much.'

Mum snorted at that and I let Alice drag me off as Mum went back to checking the level of nuts in her snack bowls.

6

The Wow Club, underneath the crumbling arches of Merrycliffe's seafront promenade, was the place to go on a Saturday night.

Correction. It was the *only* place to go on a Saturday night, unless you fancied the nightclub in Whytecliffe, Kudos, which had four bouncers on the door and had gone down in legend after the time two lads had a fight and part of someone's *ear* got bitten off and spat out on the dance floor.

Saturday night at The Wow was indie night and they always had a band playing. The band was usually Thee Desperadoes because they were the only band in town (apart from a poodle-haired covers band that replicated the tunes of Def Leppard and Bon Jovi).

Alice and I didn't even like indie music that much. It was all whiny and guitary and the singers all sounded really up themselves. Mostly Alice and I listened to Nicki Minaj and

Azealia Banks and when it was just the two of us we tried to spit out rhymes, though we weren't very good at spitting out rhymes.

What we were good at was sneaking alcohol into The Wow Club. I had a water bottle filled with vodka and diet Red Bull tucked into my tights and held my bag very carefully over the bulge as it was searched by Scary Bob, the doorman. The Wow were meant to check ID and not let under-18s through its scuzzy portals but they were far more worried about under-18s bringing in their own booze. Alice had her bottle hidden down the arm of her jacket and as soon as we'd paid our entrance fee and had our hands stamped, we raced up the stairs and into the club itself, grabbed the first two empty pint glasses we could find, then hid in a shadowy alcove at the back of the room to decant the contents of our water bottles. We were old hands at this. Never spilled a drop.

'Cheers.' We clinked pint glasses and only then could we relax and take off our jackets and go to our usual table.

The Wow was a long low room split into two. The larger part of the room had the bar at one end and the DJ booth and the stage at the other, the dance floor in between. There were two archways at each end, which led to a tall skinny strip of space where there were tables and chairs.

Alice and I always sat at the table by the archway nearest to the stage because it was also next to a little unmarked door that led to backstage, though backstage was just a tiny room the size of a closet. Our table was in a prime spot because it guaranteed many Louis sightings, without it being obvious I was pining for him. Or I hoped it wasn't obvious.

One of the best and worst things about Merrycliffe was that everyone knew everyone else's business. So, when Alice and I had drunk enough that we felt uninhibited and able to dance, no one took our table, because it was *our* table. Except when we got back to our table after the DJ had played fifteen minutes of actual dance music, it was to find Steampunk Dora hovering uncertainly with Paul and Matthew in tow.

It was weird how you could not know someone and then all of a sudden there they were, in your face, all the time. She gestured at the chairs we weren't using.

'Can we?' she asked.

'Yeah, help yourself,' I said, thinking she'd take them somewhere else but the three of them plonked themselves down, even though Alice and I had barely seen each other all week and had lots to discuss.

'So, how are you finding college?' Matthew wanted to know. He was wearing only a two-piece suit tonight. I guess it was really too stuffy to wear a waistcoat as well as a jacket. 'Bit different from school, isn't it?'

He was talking to me *now*? He'd had all week to talk to me.

'It was OK,' I said with a slightly put-upon air. 'I thought we'd do some sewing instead of only being allowed to look at the sewing machines.'

'I was scared to even touch the sewing machine because that technician guy kept glaring at me extra hard every time my hand got too close to it.' Matthew gave a shudder and he seemed nice enough. Like he could be a new friend. Just a college friend though, because Alice, who was staring at him with arms folded, had the copyright on being my non-college friend forever.

'This is Alice,' I said, gesturing at her with a little flourish. 'Alice, Matthew. He's on my course.'

They looked each other up and down.

'And I'm Dora and this is Paul,' Dora butted in. 'So, you're at Saint Anne's, right?'

'Oh God, it's Saturday night, the last thing I want to talk about is *school*!' Alice glanced over at me as if to say, who are these freaks, then turned her attention back to Dora. 'I hope you've been nice to my girl, Franny, otherwise we're going to be having words.'

'Alice ...' I hissed, because she was coming on really strong, like she was confronting a playground bully. Which, not even, but it was good to know that Alice would always have my back. 'Sorry, we're a bit pissed. We've already had way too much vodka and diet Red Bull.'

'I could never drink anything that sweet,' Dora said loftily, like she only drank decades-old malt whisky or red wine with a cheeky bouquet, when actually she was clutching a pint of cider and black, so she was no better than us. 'Do you come here every Saturday?'

'Not every Saturday,' Alice replied truthfully, because some Saturdays we were broke and during winter we sometimes stayed in to watch *X-Factor* instead. 'We often go into Blackpool.'

We had gone into Blackpool on a Saturday night twice. Once was to see Little Mix but that was two years ago and so in no way could impact on how cool we were now. The other time was for Alice's cousin's birthday and we'd gone to a really tacky nightclub that was like Kudos on steroids, and Alice had pulled a seventeen-year-old who turned out to be married and I'd fallen over on the dance floor and split my skirt.

'Yeah? Well, I go to Manchester a lot,' Dora said defensively, like we were handing out cool points. 'Like all the time. We only moved to Merrycliffe because my dad's in logistics.'

I didn't know what logistics were but they didn't seem like a good enough reason to move to Merrycliffe, but that wasn't important. Not when there was a commotion to my left and I saw Louis walking towards me.

Well, I suppose he was really walking towards the backstage but he had to walk past me to get there so technically he was walking towards me. I was probably the only person who would describe Louis walking as a commotion but his long-limbed stride played havoc with my soul.

It wasn't just me. Everyone turned to look at Louis as he walked past. It was as if he came with built-in back-lighting and a wind machine. He also had an entourage, which consisted of Thee Desperadettes; three girls who thought they were it even though one was wearing shiny, metallic black leggings with a white shirt, which didn't even work as a look, and the three other guys who were in Thee Desperadoes. I never really paid much attention to Louis's backing band but now I noticed that—'

'Isn't that the studio technician who glared at us all the way through our thrilling sewing machine tutorial?' Paul asked me. I squinted at the guy's back.

'I think it is.' I worked my brain really hard. 'Hang on ... maybe he was in Thee Desperadoes last year and then he wasn't. He might have played the guitar or the bass guitar. Anyway, they had this other guy with glasses for a while but this one has been back for the last few shows. Hey! Do you think he's so moody because he has to wear those blue overalls with *Merrycliffe Technical College* stamped on the back?'

'I'd be in a bad mood if I had to wear them,' Matthew decided, then Dora said that it would be really easy to customise them and make them look a lot less like a prison uniform and I said that you really had to be a girl to work a boiler suit and maybe do some retro Rosie the Riveter thing with it. By then Louis had finished his progress through the club, which took a long time because he knew everybody and had to stop and chat to people, and had gone backstage and I hadn't had a chance to smile at him and hope he'd notice me.

Sometimes my crush on Louis felt almost debilitating. Like, going out and having a good time didn't count unless I'd had some acknowledgement from Louis that he was aware of my existence. Still, the night was young.

'... yeah, well, I wouldn't be seen dead in a crappy boiler suit,' Alice was saying forcefully. 'What would be the point unless you were painting a house or something? Like, if you're a girl and that's what you want to wear then it's because you can't handle having girl parts.' Alice looked at Dora, who was wearing some complicated Victorian-style get-up that was verging on goth, then down at herself and her girl parts, which were shown to their best advantage in clinging black Lycra. 'I'm sure you get where I'm coming from.'

'Yeah, everyone knows where you're coming from,' Dora sneered and Alice turned to me with a look that said clearly, 'I hate this Steampunk saddo. If you ever become mates with her, we are so over.'

Alice never had to worry that anyone, especially not *Dora*, could come between us.

'So, yeah, Alice, how about that thing that happened yesterday?' I asked.

Alice didn't miss a beat. 'Yeah,' she breathed, eyes wide. 'That thing. I doubt the stains will ever come out in the wash. I mean, how could they?'

I nodded my head. 'Right. Yeah. I know.'

Dora took the hint and turned to talk to Matthew and Paul, probably about how much she hated not just Alice but me too. That she hated me by association. I was, like, hate adjacent.

But I couldn't worry about that now. I'd worry about it on Monday when I was having a pity party about my lack of college friends. Right now, there was a flurry of activity, people coming and going out of the backstage door. I craned my neck to get another glimpse of dirty blond hair . . .

'Way to make it obvious, Franny,' Alice snapped. 'Be cool.'

I tried to be cool and I tried to listen as Alice told me about the Facetime chat she'd had with some guy who worked in the garage up the road but every time the door opened, my heart did this weird dive-y thing. I was practically vibrating.

It took a little while before I realised that I wasn't practically vibrating and that it was my phone. I'd had five text messages from Mum's mopey friend Linda, who was meant to be working her way through Mum's perfectly balanced snack bowls at that very moment.

Franny. Had 2 cancel @ last min. Car battery flat. Mum v. upset. Not answering phone. Pls check on her.

I sighed long and deep. The four other texts all said the same thing but with increasing panic.

I sighed even longer and deeper. Then I texted Mum. R U OK? Heard Linda bailed. Text me. F x

Now my attention was torn between the door that led through to the tiny dressing room, which was opening and closing every few seconds, and my phone, which wasn't doing anything. Meanwhile, Alice was still talking to me about the guy from the garage.

Mum. Pls text me! F x

I left it two minutes, in case Mum was in the loo, and then I stood up.

'I need to call my mum,' I told Alice, who sighed almost as long and deep as I had. 'I'm going to the foyer. It's quieter.'

'Oh, Franny, no! She was fine when we left. I'm sure she's all right.' Her words lacked conviction and when I shook my head she gnawed on her lip anxiously.

As I clambered over Paul's legs, the door opened again and one by one the four Desperadoes walked out, Louis last, his

51

pace a lazy saunter like heading towards the stage was no big deal. My body strained in his direction, but my legs went in another.

'Shall I come with you, Franny?' Alice asked.

'No. I'll be back in five,' I told her. 'Make sure you get our usual spot.'

Our usual spot was almost down the front but to the right, so we didn't look like totally tragic Desperadoes fans and also because Louis usually favoured the right side of the stage when he was strutting about.

'You're not going to miss anything,' Alice said at the same moment that the music was replaced with an expectant hum from the PA system. 'It's not like they suddenly got good since we last saw them three weeks ago.'

'Yeah. They're awful aren't they?' Dora exclaimed. 'I saw them at this all-dayer in Leeds and they pretty much got booed off stage.'

Alice clapped her hands together in delight. 'How hilaire! I bet the boos just slid off Louis's ego.'

I was desperate to call Mum, but I still had time to glare at both of them. I could handle them not liking each other but I could not handle them bonding over how crap Thee Desperadoes were.

OK, they were terrible; everyone knew that. There was no need to go on about it.

'Hello, Merrycliffe! Do you feel all right?' The double doors swung shut on Louis's enthusiastic greeting. It was really rather endearing the way he acted like playing The Wow at ten o'clock on a Saturday night was like playing Manchester Arena, I thought as I crouched down in the little gap between the cloakroom and the manager's office and called Mum's mobile. She didn't pick up, so I called the landline.

I got stuck on an awful loop of mobile and landline, then worrying that she was trying to get through while I was blocking the line. I must have called both numbers ten times but she still didn't pick up.

Then again, Mum wasn't me. She wasn't surgically attached to her mobile so sometimes she left it downstairs when she went to bed. And she often unplugged the phone in her room so it wouldn't wake her up. Also, it wasn't unprecedented for her to be in bed this early. In fact, it was entirely precedented but, but, but, but ... she'd been so much better today.

I could hear Thee Desperadoes churning their way through their 'ironic' cover of Justin Bieber's 'Boyfriend' and the easiest thing to do was to go back into the club, find Alice and nudge each other and delight in how awful the band were. The harder thing to do was to admit to myself that maybe Mum hadn't been better today, I'd just wanted her to be, so I could go out.

All that OCD crap with her snack bowls ... oh God, *not again*.

Have 2 go home, I texted Alice. Sorry. Luv U.

It took me seven minutes to run home. Seven more attempts to call Mum, who still wasn't picking up. As I unlatched the gate and hurried up the path, I saw that the house was shrouded in darkness, which wasn't that unusual but now, with

Mum maintaining phone silence for no good reason, the darkness and even the long shadows I made as I fished for my keys filled me with an ominous dread.

Though really, was there any other kind of dread?

'Mum!' I called out as soon as I was through the door. There was no reply.

I raced up the stairs. Mum's bedroom door was shut. I tapped on it gently. 'It's me! Can I come in?'

Still no reply. She could be asleep and if she was I didn't want to wake her, but there was no way I could move until I knew she was all right.

'Mum!' This time my knocking was a little more enthusiastic, not that it did any good.

The softly, softly approach wasn't working. I opened the door and switched on the main light.

There was a lump underneath the duvet and there was her phone on the nightstand. 'Mum! Jesus! You could have answered your phone! I mean, even if you had it on silent, it must have been vibrating like crazy with all my calls that you didn't take.'

I could cope with the misery. I could keep with the manic moods, but when she went silent it scared the breath right out of me.

'Please tell me you're all right.'

I approached the bed tentatively. My skin felt cold and clammy like it could creep right off my bones. I circled the bed, stretched out my hand, then snatched it back, unsure of where to touch her, what I might find.

And then I reached out and before I could retreat I was prodding a bit of her, a hipbone, I think. 'Mum? Mum?'

It was absolutely terrifying but also a huge relief when she suddenly flung back the duvet. 'What? What do you want?' She sounded flat and empty, like every word was a superhuman effort.

'Linda texted me and told me she'd cancelled and you hadn't taken it very well. And then when I tried to contact you, you'd disappeared. We talked about this! I said ... I *told* you that it wasn't cool, that it made me feel like ...'

Mum held up a hand as if she couldn't take any more, though she didn't say a word in her defence. Like, that was any surprise, but then she stirred herself into a sitting position so I could see that she'd gone to bed in the clothes she'd been wearing earlier. She looked at me but didn't look at me, as if focusing her eyes would have taken too much out of her, then she sank back down with a bone-weary sigh.

'Oh, just fuck off, Franny,' she said in a tiny voice that cut like the sharpest razor.

7

I wasn't surprised that Alice was in a mood with me about me bailing on Saturday night.

Not a huge mood, but on Sunday morning when we were having our usual post-Wow debrief, she said, 'I'm really sorry that your mum is back to being menty but you have to promise never to leave me alone with that Cora girl ever again. She's got a hell of a lot to say for someone who's just a sad old goth.'

'Her name's Dora and she's not a goth, she's Steampunk. Whole different vibe, apparently,' I pointed out, which was the wrong thing to say.

'Oh my God, do *not* stick up for her,' Alice had said in her really scary, really quiet voice and I'd changed the subject to something way less controversial, like if Alice had found anyone fresh and new to snog after I'd left.

'Not anyone. I think I've pretty much snogged every snog-gable boy in Merrycliffe,' she said sadly. 'But enough about that, how was your mum when you got home?'

I'd have much preferred to listen to Alice's snog woes. As it was, I couldn't bring myself to tell even Alice what my mum had said to me. 'She's having a blue period' was what I did say.

'Oh, no! Not *another* one of those! That sucks!'

I hadn't been able to crowbar Mum out of her bedroom since Saturday night. I sometimes heard her come out to go to the loo, and when I went into the kitchen in the morning I'd often find a mug and plate in the draining rack, which meant she was getting some form of sustenance.

The bottom line was she didn't want to talk to me and I didn't have the magic combination of words that would unlock the right bit of her brain and make everything OK. She was still better than how she'd been early last summer so I left her to get on with it.

While she was getting on with it, I went to college. I did all the reading and made lots of notes every time Barbara said something note-worthy and I went to my GCSE catch-up classes, but all the time I felt as if my head was in another place. All my go-to-get-happy fixes like fantasising about getting trapped in a small, confined place with Louis or meeting Martin Sanderson and him offering me a job on the spot weren't working.

It felt like life would never stop sucking.

On Friday as I walked home from college, I felt a bit like taking to my bed too. And then Alice rang. 'So, I just saw Matt from The Wow and he says that the band they'd got for tomorrow night pulled out and Thee Desperadoes are playing *again*. Do you want to get ready round mine or yours?'

There was a God and he/she was sending me an unscheduled Louis gawping session to make up for also sending me a really crappy week. 'Do you mind coming round mine again? I'll make sure I get some posh pesto pizzas from Sainos. They're much nicer than Dominos.'

'Posh pesto pizza every time. I'll bring the booze.' Alice paused. 'So, um, is your mum still having a nervo?'

'Well, if she is, it's a quiet nervo and I got a text from my dad and he should be back home on Sunday.'

'God, it's about time! You shouldn't have to deal with her having any kind of nervo. Anyway, what are you going to wear tomorrow night?' Alice asked – she knew all about my good stuff and my bad stuff and when I was absolutely sick to death of talking about the bad stuff. 'I just bought a pair of wedge trainers. They're surprisingly hard to walk in. I'm going to wear them with that blue drapey dress you made me.'

'The black and white ones in the window of Charlie Girl?' Charlie Girl was the only place in Merrycliffe that sold anything even remotely fashionable and I use the word fashionable in the loosest possible sense so it stops having any real meaning. I hadn't been in there since I was thirteen but as Alice said, I was a style fascist, when I reminded her of this.

The next evening Alice came round mine to get ready. I left Mum in bed with a bottle of water, a cheese and pickle sandwich and an apple hermetically sealed in a Tupperware container, so she wouldn't starve for fear of germs. I said a cheery goodbye and got the tiniest of grunts in return and then I was free. I'd discharged all my maternal responsibilities and as Alice said as we hid round the corner from The Wow Club so we could decant our vodka and diet Coke into water bottles, 'At least when she's like this, you know she hasn't got the energy to do anything stupid.'

'Yeah, she couldn't even summon up enough oomph to reach for the remote on her bedside table and turn on the TV.' It had only been through a system of blinks and sighs that I'd established that she didn't mind watching back-to-back repeats of *A Place in the Sun*. 'You know what? I'm not going to let her ruin another Saturday night. Anyway, Dad will be back tomorrow and then she'll snap out of it, like that!'

I clicked my fingers so fiercely that I nearly had Alice's heavily mascaraed eye out. She wore her new wedge sneakers and the drapey blue dress I'd made her. It had come up a little small but Alice didn't mind because she said it did awesome things to her boobs, even if she did have to wear Spanx under it, which she'd rolled down so she could manage half a pesto pizza.

I was wearing cropped trousers with my black lace-up brogues, a skinny-fit white T-shirt and a black jacket that looked like an iconic Chanel jacket if the lighting was dim and you squinted really hard. We didn't really have anywhere on our bodies to hide our alcoholic contraband.

'We have to organise ourselves better,' Alice said crossly, after I'd tried to force the bottles down my tight trouser legs. It looked like I had some kind of gross disease like elephantiasis. 'We can't both do body-hugging.'

'Would it kill you to wear an A-line dress just once in your life?'

Alice nodded frantically. 'Yes, yes it would.'

I surveyed our assorted limbs. 'We'll just have to neck it before we go in.'

'You know I can't ingest a large volume of liquid in a short amount of time.' Alice was close to tears. 'I'm not physically capable of drinking that fast.'

It was true. Alice had once taken four hours to get through an iced coffee when we went to Leeds for the day. 'I could always drink both bottles.' I smiled brightly. 'If it would help.'

'No, it wouldn't help.' Alice stamped one wedge-sneakered foot. 'Why did you have to wear a jacket with sleeves that don't reach your wrists?'

'I like it. It looks a bit Chanel. Kind of.' We looked round to see Dora standing there. Actually, she looked more as if she were floating than standing because she was wearing a huge, voluminous black dress. And I mean huge. Crinoline huge. 'You going to The Wow?'

She was talking to me, not Alice, which wasn't a surprise given how totally they'd not got on last Saturday. 'We are, except we're having, um, issues.'

Dora took a step closer. She had old-fashioned aviator goggles perched artfully on top of her huge pink beehive. I had to admire her for going all out in pursuit of her look. 'What kind of issues?'

I came to a decision then. I was going to be on the same course as Dora for two years and I'd rather spend those two years on friendly terms. So, she and me and Alice were going to have to find some common ground, which admittedly might be difficult, but now was as good a time as any.

'Alcohol issues,' I told Dora, even though Alice clicked her teeth and shoved me in the ribs. 'We have nowhere on our persons where we can hide two half-litre bottles of vodka and diet Coke.'

'That is a problem,' Dora said. 'Have you come up with a solution?'

'Does it look like we have?' Alice asked with a snarl and another stamp of her foot. 'I am not paying for drinks in The Wow. No way.'

'I would never pay for drinks in a club either,' Dora said. 'I'm always broke. It costs a lot of money being a full-time Steam-punk.'

I could feel Alice thrumming next to me like she was work-ing on some devastating comeback to that little insight into Dora's lifestyle choices. I gave her a warning prod. 'It's not that. It's a matter of principle. They water down all the drinks and they won't serve you unless you pretty much rest your boobs on the bar to get the staff's attention.'

'And Franny has no boobs to rest anywhere,' Alice said tartly.

Dora didn't say anything. Then she slowly lifted her skirt and I saw that I'd been right. She'd made a crinoline cage out of what looked like old coat hangers. I was quite curious to see how she'd done it, but that wasn't the most interesting thing under her skirts. No, that would be the carrier bag from the off-licence that was dangling from one of the hangers. 'A bottle of red wine and one of my rings doubles up as a corkscrew,' she said proudly.

'Oh my God.' Even Alice was impressed. 'You're my hero.'

We gave Dora our bottles and followed behind her as she glided into The Wow. Well, until her crinoline got stuck in the doorway and we had to give her a good shove, to the amusement of Scary Bob, the doorman, who was too busy laughing to even check if we were smuggling in alcoholic beverages. We sat at our usual table, which I guessed was going to be Dora's usual table too because she was on her own (apparently Matthew and Paul had gone to a sci-fi convention in Oldham, which must be secret gay code for something far more exciting) and she'd helped us in our hour of need. It would have been rude to make her sit somewhere else.

It turned out all right because Alice and Dora could talk to each other about make-up and how hard Dora found it to maintain the right kind of pinkiness to her hair, while I kept my gaze riveted on the door that led to the backstage. But, like, subtly riveted.

The door opened. I held my breath, but it was only the sneering studio tech from college. He glanced over at us as he walked past and then Dora actually said, 'Hi', to him, like it was no big deal.

'Hi,' he said and even his voice sounded like a sneer, as if he couldn't believe that she would dare to address him when he was in Thee Desperadoes and could talk to Louis any time he wanted and also when he was a studio tech and she was an annoying first-year fashion student who thought it was OK to touch college equipment with her grubby fingers. That was what he managed to evoke with his 'Hi'.

'Rude, much?' Dora said loud enough for him to hear, even over the sounds of some really bad moperock, and then she turned back to talk to Alice about the merits of Manic Panic over Crazy Colour Hair Dye and though I didn't want to miss anything, I was dying for a wee and it was better to go now than when Thee Desperadoes were on stage.

I could also feel one of my false eyelashes making a bid for freedom and was just trying to do a repair job in front of the mirror, when someone dug me in the ribs.

'Franny B!'

'Jesus Christ!' I almost jabbed my finger right through cornea, retina and all the other bits that make up an eye. I didn't, but it was pretty close. I looked behind me in the mirror to see two uncertain faces waiting to find out if they'd blinded me. 'Oh, hey! Hi! How are you?'

It was Ashleigh and Vicky from school. If Alice was the hottest girl at St Anne's, then Vicky was the prettiest. She always looked dewy like she'd just stepped from the pages of a magazine where she was advertising a flowery fragrance, but she wasn't at all stuck-up about the way she looked. Ashleigh was her best mate and she was scary-smart. She'd done half her GCSEs a year early and it was a little embarrassing to see her again knowing that she must know that I'd ballsed some of mine right up.

Maybe that was why she gave me such an enthusiastic hug. 'I said to Vicks that you'd probably be here tonight,' she said, eyeing my cropped trousers and inspired-by-Chanel jacket. 'God, you look so cool.'

'Yeah, like you should be on one of those street-style blogs,' Vicky added, looking anxiously down at her own outfit.

Vicky and Ash were wearing vests, unbuttoned plaid shirts, cut-off jean shorts, black tights and Uggs. It was what the Merrycliffe indie girls wore.

'You both look great too,' I said, because there was something, though not much, to be said for comfy instead of chic. 'I envy your Uggs. I can't wear tights with cropped trousers but my brogues are really pinching and my ankles are going to freeze on the walk home.'

'So, like, how's college? What have you made? Are there any fit boys? Parminder said that there are loads of hot, older art students.'

We talked about college for a bit and then Ash, who was scary organised as well as scary smart, wanted to know if I'd thought about my costume for The Wow's Halloween party (last year Alice and I had come as eighties Madonna and nineties Madonna, but it had been wasted on the masses) and if I was going to make T-shirts with sequinned slogans on them for Christmas again.

It was ages since I'd had a really good chat with Ash and Vicky. Probably long before I'd left school because they'd never talk to me when I was hanging out with Alice. Not many girls would. Which reminded me ...

'We should totally hang out one evening,' I said, as I put away my make-up bag, because we'd been yammering for ages and I didn't want to miss Thee Desperadoes. 'Maybe at half-term or something.'

They agreed that it would be amazing and then I nudged Vicky on the arm because she was a softer touch than Ash. 'I hate to think that Alice has to fly solo at school now,' I said softly. 'Don't suppose you could ask her to eat lunch with you—'

'You mean when she's not getting lunch with some boy that she stole from another girl?' Ash interrupted, eyes blazing, because there was history there. There was always history when it came to Alice and other girls. 'If Alice hasn't got anyone to go around with at school then it's her own fault.'

'Please.' I gave Ash my most imploring look, which involved knitting my brows so hard that it hurt. 'I'm not asking you to become best mates, but try to include her. Honestly, she is such a laugh when she's not—'

'Slutting around like a total slut.'

I actually hadn't missed the way Ash continually interrupted whatever anyone was saying.

'That's a really denigrating thing to say about another girl,' I said, which was what Siobhan said to me when I was commenting on other girls' extreme sluttishness. 'I thought you were a feminist.'

'I am! I totally am! Oh my God, I can't believe you think I'm a bad feminist when all I do is try to make things better for other girls. Alice has no respect for any girl.'

My good deed had gone bad. I held up my hands in surrender. 'It wouldn't kill you or put the feminist cause back to say hello to Alice each morning.'

'Excuse me!' said a furious voice from the doorway where Alice was suddenly standing. 'I don't need you to scrounge up friends for me, Franny, and actually, Ash, I'd have loads of respect for other girls if they didn't try and slut shame me just because I'm hot and they're not.'

I was mortified, though I hadn't done anything wrong. Not really. I was trying to do a nice thing but it had all backfired. Ash and even Vicky were glaring at Alice and she was glaring back at them and I was caught in the painful epicentre where their glares all collided. 'But if you take the boy thing out of the equation, then you guys would really get on,' I bleated.

'I don't think so,' Ash said, her eyes resting on Alice, who had her hands on her hips and looked like a tiny, furious Valkyrie. 'We have nothing in common. Not one thing.'

Because I was looking out for it, I saw the hurt flash up on Alice's face for a mere nanosecond before she sneered it away. 'You can say that again. I wouldn't be seen dead in a flannel shirt. And Franny, I came to tell you to hurry up otherwise you're going to miss the band, so move it!'

I moved it. 'I'm sorry,' I said as I followed Alice's stiff back as she stalked through the club. 'I'm pretty lonely at college and I know you're lonely too so I just figured that I'd try and find a way to make you, like, less lonely.'

Alice whipped round. 'Like I'd want to hang with that bunch of losers and haters.'

66

Out of the corner of my eye, I saw Louis surging through the crowd, the rest of Thee Desperadoes trailing after him. But Louis wasn't important right now. I turned to Alice, who was standing there, determined to chat this out even though we were right in the middle of the dance floor. 'Look, we've been through this a hundred times. They wouldn't be haters if you just maybe took a solemn vow that you wouldn't have anything to do with a boy who you knew was in a relationship.'

'It's very hard to keep track of these things, Franny,' Alice said. She held up her iPhone. 'Am I meant to make a note every time someone from school snogs someone? Or should I just stick to avoiding the male half of couples that have been together longer than a week? Or a fortnight? Or does sending a picture of your tits to a boy mean that you're in a relationship, because Josie seems to think it does?'

I wish I'd never started this. 'I don't even know why you'd want to get involved with any boy from our school. Even the Year 13s are immature.'

'You got that right,' Alice muttered. 'Look, with you not there, the boys are the only ones who will talk to me. And anyway, you're not lonely. You've got Dora, your new best friend.'

I shook my head. 'No, she's not. She's barely even a friend. She hardly talks to me at all when we're at college.'

'You're just saying that.' Alice didn't look quite so furious any more.

'I'm not. Why do I even need a new best friend what I have

an old best friend who totally rocks ... when she's not being a pain in the arse.'

'Ha! You're a pain in the arse too!' Alice scoffed as she tucked her arm into mine. 'Just as well we're friends 'cause nobody else would put up with us, right?'

'Their loss,' I said and I grinned at Alice as we carried on walking. My heart was no longer sinking, but lifting higher and higher. Then suddenly my heart was as free as the birds when two hands shot out to stop me from cannoning right into him and Louis, *Louis*, looked at me, really looked at me and he smiled and he said, 'Careful'.

Our eyes met, even though it was very muted lighting. I could feel the connection between us and his fingers burned where they touched. Yes, I was wearing my Chanel-esque jacket, but it was like we were skin to skin.

'Oh ...'

Then he was gone. He brushed past me and took his heat and his touch away and it was like everything had gone cold and dark.

My knees were so weak that Alice had to help me across to our table. I sat down so heavily that it jarred my spine and I smiled weakly at Dora, who looked like a very young, very cross Queen Victoria in her big black dress. I was just about to apologise for leaving her on her own for so long when Alice gave me a slow handclap. 'Wow! You almost managed to speak to Louis this time.'

'"Oh." I said, "Oh." Next time I'm planning on a whole sentence with a noun and a verb. Maybe even an adjective if I don't lose my nerve.'

Alice shook her head. 'How can you be the most edgy girl in Merrycliffe ... '

'Not *the* edgiest,' I protested. 'I mean, there's that girl who runs the milk bar on the seafront in summer. She's a vintage queen ... '

'Just 'cause she wears a lot of second-hand tat doesn't make her edgy,' Alice insisted. 'You are really edgy apart from when Louis Allen is within fifty metres of you, then you turn into a complete sap. I'm telling you this because I'm your best friend.'

Alice was right. It was lame the way Louis reduced me to a wobbly pudding of hormones and girl gloop. I needed to be told so I could at least pretend I wasn't rendered mute by him the next time our paths crossed.

Then the strobe light started flashing as it always did, five minutes before the band came on stage.

'We got back just in time!' I yanked Alice to her feet. Even though she was wearing a HUGE crinoline, I kept forgetting that Dora was still there and looking pretty pissed off that we kept ignoring her. 'You too.' I yanked her up as well. 'Come on, we're going down the front, but to the right.'

'To the right?' Dora asked, as I pulled her in that direction.

'Yeah, we don't want to go right down the front because we'd be the only ones down there and it would look really sad and Louis would know that I have a crush on him,' I explained as I wedged the three of us into a gap by one of the speakers. Dora groused but I didn't care because Thee Desperadoes were trooping on stage, shoulders hunched like they were walking in front of a firing squad.

Sneering Studio Tech crouched down in front of us to mess about with his guitar pedals. He looked up and caught my eye and I wished he hadn't but then Louis suddenly leapt on to the stage like he'd been jet-propelled.

SHOWTIME!

8

'Hello, Merrycliffe! Are you ready to rock?' Louis shouted into his mic.

He was met with a deathly silence.

As usual, there were a clump of older indie girls at the front that Alice and I called Thee Desperadettes because they were sad and desperate and followed Louis everywhere – they weren't even subtle about it. There was also Mark the mad dancer, ready to spring into action in the middle of the dance floor, and the two middle-aged men who went to The Wow every Saturday to leer at girls young enough to be their daughters, but everyone else in the club had now gathered at the bar.

That didn't stop Louis. 'Well, *we're* ready to rock! Come on, people!'

His exuberance was endearing and generally Louis was the bomb. Tonight he was wearing skinny black jeans held up by a big leather belt and a black Motörhead T-shirt. He looked like a lovely, sexy, black-clad angel, I thought as I rummaged in my pocket for a small plastic box.

Alice already had her earplugs in. I handed my spare, unopened pack to Dora. 'You'll need these,' I said, as I slipped my manky ones in.

'It's all right,' she shouted, as Thee Desperadoes launched into their first song with a squeal of ear-splitting feedback. 'I saw them last week. I've brought my own.'

Even with earplugs in, we could still hear Thee Desperadoes. Each of their songs lasted no more than two minutes, which would have been a good thing, if they didn't have so many songs to get through. The guitar sounded like it had been filtered through mud, the drummer couldn't keep time, I don't even know what a bass player is meant to do but the bassist wasn't doing it very well, and Louis was squawking and screeching about a 'blackhearted woman with legs as long as sin who done gone and left me'. His singing always reminded me of the time when Siobhan stepped on her plugged-in hair straighteners with bare feet and the unearthly screams she produced.

But, oh, *oh*, Louis was so very good at strutting and throwing shapes. Excellent at jumping up on the speakers and holding a pose. And he aced thrusting his hips every time.

I knew all his moves and exactly when he'd pull them out, but I was never prepared for the moment when Louis tugged off his T-shirt during every gig.

'Oh my,' I murmured as he ran a hand down his bare, *naked* chest.

'I've seen more muscles on my gran,' Dora shouted in my ear, like it was perfectly all right to diss the father of my future children.

'Shut up!' Who wanted a chiselled six pack bashing into you every time you kissed? Louis's chest was thin, hairless and totally rock 'n' roll.

Thee Desperadettes obviously thought so because they were all screaming and waving their arms. I would never behave like that. Instead I stood there trying to sway in time to the music, even though there wasn't much of a rhythm to work with, and memorised Louis's performance so I could play it back in my head over and over.

Half an hour later, they left the stage. I could tell that Louis was thinking about stagediving but it was doubtful whether Thee Desperadettes would catch his fall so he just bounced off with a casual wave of his hand, and didn't even catch my eye though I was willing him to with all my might.

'I didn't think it was possible, but they were actually worse than last week,' Dora said, as the three of us removed our earplugs.

'Yeah, they're weird like that. Every time you think that, yes, that was their crappiest gig yet, they still have it in them to be even crappier the next time.' Alice grinned slyly at me. 'Right, Franny?'

'I'm not saying anything. It would be disloyal.' I caught the eye of the sneering studio tech, who was unplugging something on stage. He gave me a stern look like he knew Dora and Alice had been slagging off his band, or maybe he thought I fancied *him*, what with all the catching of eyes, and he wasn't having it.

I wasn't having it either. There was only one Desperado I was interested in. I turned away. 'Let's go back to our table.'

The mood at The Wow always took a little while to recover after Thee Desperadoes had done their thing. By the time Alice and I had had another glass of vodka and diet Coke and Dora some red wine, the DJ had binned the moperock and was playing some shouty, boppy music that we could dance to.

Dora did really gothy things with her arms when she danced and Alice always does hoochie mama gyrations like the girls in r 'n' b videos. I just dance like a normal person with a few sixties flourishes I've incorporated after watching clips from really old music shows on YouTube. My favourite move is holding my nose and shimmying right down to the floor like I'm going underwater but I only pull that one out when I'm drunk.

I certainly wasn't drunk enough yet and there was no way I wanted to make a show of myself, especially when Louis took to the dance floor. He was with Thee Desperadettes, who had much more of a sexy vibe than the younger indie girls that went to The Wow. They were all at college too, but the year above me, and hung about on the patch of grass by the art block, smoking and poncing about with their iPads. It was quite hard to tell them apart. They all merged into a pretty, shiny-haired, 'Oh. My. God'-ing mass. Tonight, they were all wearing flouncy little skater dresses with Converse and Louis, my Louis, had his arm round two of them as they danced around to a Grimes track and all of a sudden I felt ridiculous and out of place in my silly cropped trousers and boy shoes and my jacket that didn't look *anything* like a Chanel jacket.

'You are worth more than the whole lot of them,' Alice said, because she could see where my gaze had come to rest. Her gaze was resting there too, but she had a superior smile on her face. 'I mean, did they get a group discount on the same skater dress from ASOS?'

I knew that Alice had the exact same skater dress from ASOS in black 'for my bloat days', but it was so like her to make me feel better.

'Girls like that are so boring and safe,' Dora said without pausing from waving her arms ethereally to the music. 'We are what we wear, so they must have really dull personalities if they all wear the same things.'

I looked at the three of us – Alice in her slinky blue dress, Dora looking like Helena Bonham Carter's little sister and me trying to do elegant, understated Chanel chic – and wondered what it said about our personalities, but then the music changed to an infectious thugstep and Alice took my hands so we could spin round and nothing else mattered for the three minutes that the music took us somewhere else.

After The Wow closed at midnight, it was time for another Merrycliffe Saturday night tradition. One of the few advantages of living in a town that was Europe's eleventh largest container port was the Market Diner.

For starters, it was open twenty-four hours to cater for the port workers, drivers and haulage contractors who rolled in and out of Merrycliffe at all hours. And secondly, it did the best bacon sandwiches in the world. Thirdly, its chips weren't too shabby either and lastly, everyone went there after The Wow because there was nowhere else to go.

When we arrived, Thee Desperadoes were already at a table. We joined a long queue because there was always a ten-minute wait for chips.

'At least they'll be fresh,' I said brightly, because Alice was getting that look like her feet and her Spanx were killing her and she'd already asked me quietly on the walk over, when Dora went on ahead, if we were going to be stuck with her all night.

I didn't mind getting stuck with Dora that much, not that I'd admit that to Alice. She was all right, and when Alice had gone to the loo before we left The Wow, Dora had said to me, 'You do know that Thee Desperadoes are terrible, don't you? There isn't a tiny bit of you that secretly likes their music, is there? Because if there is I'll have to rethink everything I'm thinking about you.'

I was curious about what Dora *was* thinking about me. 'Oh no, they *are* awful. It's almost like they're my penance for getting to spend half an hour doing nothing but stare at Louis without fear of reprisal.'

Dora had shrugged. 'He's not my type but he doesn't offend my eyes.'

'Louis looks like a young Terence Stamp,' I'd sighed longingly. 'I wish I looked like a young Jean Shrimpton.'

'Wasn't she gorgeous?' Dora had agreed. 'Something so timeless and elegant about her.'

So Dora knew something about sixties fashion icons and she

and Alice had bonded over hair dye and how rubbish Thee Desperadoes were, so it wouldn't be a bad thing if *occasionally* me and Alice became me, Alice and Dora.

'How long do you think Krystal is going to last?' Dora asked me as we waited for chips and I discreetly stared at Louis, who was demolishing a bacon butty. 'Matt says she won't get through another week.'

'Don't you mean Krystal with a K?' I asked innocently. 'The lost Kardashian.'

Dora snorted. 'In her dreams. How long must it take her to get ready in the morning? I thought I was high maintenance, but I can get from bed to bus stop in an hour.'

'She must have to set her alarm for about five o'clock.' I stopped to think about it. 'Unless she goes to bed in her make-up and just puts a light coating of new make-up over the top.'

Dora and I both shuddered. 'Dirty birdie,' she said in a creepy voice and we giggled.

Alice nudged me. 'Sorry,' I said. 'Krystal is that orange girl I was telling you about who ...'

'You know, you're right,' she interrupted.

'I am? Really? What am I right about?'

Alice tossed her hair back, which was silkier and shinier than any of the Thee Desperadettes' hair (they were further down the queue from us). 'About the boys at school being totally immature.'

'Oh, *that*! Well, yeah ... ' I looked at Alice, unsure if she was about to renounce her boy-stealing ways once and for all. Had I finally managed to get through to her?

'I deserve much better than that. Much, much better,' she said, almost under her breath. 'I've decided that older boys are where it's at. They have, like, wages and their own cars and it will give me a social standing that I don't have at the moment. Yeah, I'm definitely going to go older.'

'Glad to hear it.' I really was and I was also glad to hear that the chips were ready and piping hot and crispy. 'Even the styrofoam boxes they put them in can't ruin how yummy they are,' I explained to Dora as we shuffled down the queue to the condiment station.

I was a vinegar girl. Dora was one of those weird people who eschewed all garnishes and Alice suddenly wasn't there any more, but moving purposefully to where Thee Desperadoes were sitting, right in the centre of the Market Diner. They usually sat there if no long-distance lorry drivers had got the table first, and it was very convenient because it meant that a person (by which I mean me) could look at Louis without everyone knowing they were looking at Louis.

No one in the place was looking at Louis right at that moment though. They were all looking at Alice walking over to their table. If Thee Desperadoes had had any discernible musical talent, they could have written a song about Alice's walk, it was that good a walk, and it would have topped the charts in forty countries.

It was a measured, sexy, utterly nonchalant walk. I'm not even sure what nonchalant means but it felt like the right word to describe the unhurried sway of Alice's hips.

I had enough time to scurry over, intercept her, but how

could I? God knows I didn't want to get stuck playing the part of the needy best friend who couldn't function on her own so I took five steps forward then stayed exactly where I was – just out of shot but near enough that when Alice reached their table I could hear her say in a challenging voice, 'So, what's a girl got to do to get some tomato ketchup in this godforsaken place?'

There was plenty of tomato ketchup at the counter. Loads of it. In red plastic tomatoes so there could be no mistaking it for brown sauce or mayonnaise. They even had sachets of the stuff. It was the lamest reason ever for going over to Louis.

He picked up the red plastic tomato on his table and looked at Alice from under his extraordinarily long lashes. 'How much do you want?' he asked in a throaty way.

'Oh, I want a lot,' Alice said.

It was like they weren't even talking about the ketchup.

Louis started drizzling ketchup on Alice's chips and all the while his eyes were running over her curves in the blue dress I'd made for her and she licked her lips. It was the hottest, heaviest flirting I'd ever seen. This was Alice, my best friend, my soul sister, and Louis, the guy I'd been crushing on and dreaming about for the last four years. He was out of bounds, and a best friend and a soul sister should know that.

Each squeeze that Louis gave that bloody tomato was a stab right through my heart and instead of just letting this happen I was all set to storm over and drag Alice away from *my* Louis, and then I heard it. A snort. A small, snuffly snort. It came from Sneering Studio Tech, who then said, 'Don't you think there's enough ketchup on those chips now?'

At that moment I loved Sneering Studio Tech. Louis put down the red plastic tomato and Alice straightened up and walked back to where Dora and I were standing at the condiment station.

Alice flirted. It was what she did. Half the time she didn't even know that she was doing it, but this was different. When I saw Louis blatantly checking out her arse, it made me so furious that Dora put a warning hand on my arm even though I hadn't said a word.

'Not worth it,' she advised me, and then Alice was back with her chips lovingly ketchupped by Louis and a blank expression on her pretty face.

'What was that about?' I demanded as we grabbed a table. I had to demand it very quietly because I didn't want to cause a scene.

Alice selected a chip and munched it thoughtfully. 'Well, I love you, Franny, you know I do, and I've always got your back but in the four years that you've had a crush on Louis—'

I had to stop her right there. 'It's *not* a crush, it's much, much, much deeper than that. It's practically on a spiritual level.'

'What*ever*.' She actually rolled her eyes as if I wasn't me but one of the other girls who must have had similar conversations with Alice.

'Don't whatever me. In fact, just don't,' I said softly. 'Not to me. Please don't.'

'Don't what?' Alice was all wide eyes and innocence. 'What are you talking about?'

'You know what I'm talking about,' I said. Alice reached across the table to nudge my hand, even as Dora reached under the table to give my other hand a comforting little squeeze.

Alice gave me an exasperated look. 'Oh, come on, lighten up.' She made a fist and placed it against her heart. 'Chicks before dicks. That's my motto.'

'Yeah, but boys are my toys is another one of your mottos,' I reminded her and Alice pouted like she couldn't believe I was using her own words against her.

We argued all the time, it was what best friends did, but this particular argument felt different. Like Alice had crossed over a line and she didn't even care that she'd crossed it. I had to make her understand that.

'I can't believe that you even went *there*.'

'I hardly went *there*. Way to overreact, Franny,' Alice said, and she held out her hands, palm side up like she had nothing to hide. Like maybe I had been overreacting. Then her gaze shifted to Dora, who was sitting at an odd sideways angle to accommodate her crinoline. 'Anyway, it's not like I abandoned you. Not when you and Dora were so busy talking about all the stuff you get up to at college. I'm surprised you even noticed that I wasn't hanging around like a spare part.'

Not this again! 'I'm sorry that maybe I didn't give you my undivided attention for, like, one whole minute while I talked to Dora but you need—'

'I thought your curfew was midnight,' said a voice in my ear and I forgot that Alice and I were having a big, scary fight that felt different to all the other times we'd argued. I even forgot that every cool person in Merrycliffe was in the Market Diner, as I got up and threw my arms around my dad.

'You're back!' I exclaimed. He hugged me back and he smelt a bit ripe because he probably hadn't stopped for a shower in order to get back ahead of schedule but I didn't care. 'I wasn't expecting you until teatime tomorrow.'

'Thought I'd surprise you,' my dad said and for one moment his thin, craggy face lit up with a grin that not many people got to see. Even I didn't get to see it often. 'So, about this curfew of yours . . . '

'Oh, *that* curfew. Expecting me back at midnight on a Saturday is an infringement of my basic human rights.'

Dad smiled again and it was like since he'd been gone I'd been clenching all my muscles and holding my breath and not realising it. But now, he was back and standing in front of me in jeans and the navy shirt with his name embroidered on the breast pocket by my own fair hand and a jean jacket, though I'd told him a million times not to do double denim. But it was more than that, he was smiling at me again and holding my hand even though, at sixteen, I was far too old to have my hand held by my dad.

Six weeks ago, when he got into his lorry to deliver fridges to Rotterdam (Europe's actual busiest container port), he was barely speaking to me because he was still furious about my GCSEs. When he had spoken to me it was only to say stuff like 'I expected better from you.' And 'You've not only let me down, you've let yourself down.'

Now it seemed like we were friends again. And when he

said, 'Come on, Little Miss Trouble, I'm going to walk you home,' I didn't point out that I'd only just got my chips or that he was showing me up in front of *le tout* Merrycliffe.

I told Dora and a still pouting Alice that I'd text them, picked up my styrofoam container of chips and let Dad lead me out by the hand like I was six. The only thing I couldn't forgive him for was saying as we walked past Thee Desperadoes' table, 'No socks, Franny? You're asking to catch a cold.'

9

When I woke up on Sunday morning, everything was different.

For one thing, what woke me was the smell of bacon sizzling in the pan. Nose twitching, limbs working independently of my brain, I got out of bed and stumbled downstairs to find my parents in the kitchen.

Dad was reading the paper and drinking tea out of his *Truckers do it long distance* mug, and Mum (I had to blink a couple of times to make sure that I wasn't hallucinating) was up and dressed in something that wasn't a tracksuit but a dress and tights while she literally slaved over a hot stove.

'Morning, sleepyhead,' she greeted me brightly. 'You get the deciding vote. Pancakes or waffles?'

It was like she'd had some kind of intensive therapy overnight. Except her smile was more manic than cheerful and when I sidled nearer and Dad asked how we'd managed without him, she shot me a pleading look.

I stared down at the silver polish on my toenails.

'Sweetheart, will you go and see if we've got any more kitchen roll in the utility room?' Mum asked Dad and with a put-upon sigh he got up, bopping me over the head with the paper as he left the room.

'Please, Franny,' she said once we were alone. 'I haven't been so bad this time. You know that.'

'No, I don't,' I muttered, because bad was relative. She hadn't been as bad as when Dad was away last June, but she'd still been bad and I'd still felt like someone had taken my internal organs and tied them in knots.

'Look, he's only just come back and nobody wants a row and honestly, I am feeling better.' She reached out with the hand that wasn't holding the greasy spatula to touch me, then changed her mind.

'I don't want a row either. It's the very last thing I want, but you weren't feeling better yesterday or the day before that,' I hissed, because I could hear Dad rummaging in the utility room, which meant that he could probably hear us, though I shouldn't really care if he could hear us. In a way, in lots of ways, I *wanted* him to hear us. 'If he knew, then he wouldn't take on the big cross-continent jobs and stay away so long.'

She shook her head. She'd washed her hair, I noticed. She was even wearing mascara. If she could make all this effort for him so she wouldn't be found out, why couldn't she make the effort every day? Until it wasn't making an effort but just part of her routine, part of what was normal. Sometimes you have to fake it, until you make it.

'Look, everyone has their ups and downs. That's all it was. I was just a bit down and only for a little while,' she said, gingerly pushing the bacon round the pan. 'So, did you want pancakes, 'cause the waffles are much easier to make? I can just put the frozen ones in the toaster.'

'Whatever.' I folded my arms and we could both hear Dad coming now, singing a Johnny Cash song at the top of his voice.

'Please, Franny ...'

I hadn't told Dad what had happened the last time he went away, so it was pretty obvious that I wasn't going to now. I wasn't even sure if it was to protect her, or because if Dad knew then maybe it would be too much, and he'd get into his lorry and this time he wouldn't come back.

With Mum like she was and Siobhan at university, there wasn't much of anything to come back to really.

'It's all right. I'm not going to say anything, but will you promise that you'll take your tablets and start going to group again?'

'I took my tablets this morning,' she said and then we both heard the sound of the utility-room door closing. 'So, pancakes or waffles then?'

Dad was back with the kitchen roll and looking at me as if my answer to the pancake/waffle debate might bring about world peace.

'Waffles,' I said. Dad sighed.

'Wrong answer, Franny,' he said and gestured to a carrier

bag on the kitchen table. 'Might not give you your presents now.'

Dad always brought me presents back from all the places he'd driven to. Though when he'd left to go away, two days after I'd got my GCSE results, he was in such a fury with me that I hadn't expected to get so much as a bar of Toblerone.

'It's not fair to withhold when I can see the bag right in front of me,' I protested and he laughed and pushed the bulging carrier bag in my direction.

There was perfume from Hungary, though the writing on the box was in French and promised me that the contents smelled of '*figues et garçons*', figs and boys. Lavender-flavoured chocolate from the Czech Republic. And the mother lode: Dutch *Vogue*, German *Vogue*, French *Vogue*, Russian *Vogue* – lots of lovely foreign editions of the greatest, most beautiful, most sumptuous, most inspiring fashion magazine currently in existence. But the best *Vogue* of all, the *Vogue* all the other *Vogue*s bowed down before and worshipped, was *Vogue Italia*.

'Oh my God! Thank you! Thank you! Thank you!' I gathered *Vogue Italia* to my chest, pressed it against my heart, as if all the ideas and the beautiful pictures of all the lovely clothes would sink through my pores and enter my bloodstream. 'OK, right, I'm going up to my room now. Seriously. Don't expect to see me for the rest of the day.'

They weren't having that. Or Dad wasn't having it. He made me sit down and the three of us ate breakfast together and he must have resigned himself to the fact that I was no longer planning to do five A levels, because he wanted to know how college was going, though mostly he wanted to make sure that I was going to retake my Maths and English GCSEs.

At least there was no shouting this time. Just Dad looking sorrowful and saying, 'You'll never amount to anything in life if you haven't got qualifications in Maths and English.'

'Well, Franny knows that and she's doing fine at college. They put too much pressure on her at that school, expecting her to do *all* those GCSEs. You love it at college, right, Franny?'

She smiled at me desperately, imploringly, so I nodded. 'It's great,' I said, though I didn't love college at all. Not with my GCSE retakes hanging heavy over my head and Barbara on my case and not having any friends. Then I thought about the friend I did have, Alice, and suddenly I couldn't finish my waffles.

Playing at happy families took all morning, until Mum and Dad went out for a long walk along the clifftops because Dad had been stuck in the cab of his lorry for weeks and he wanted to stretch his legs and breathe in the sea air. It was the first time Mum had left the house in days. I waited at the top of the stairs, tense in case she had a panic attack on the doorstep, but all I heard was Dad call out, 'I'll call you when we're done so you can come and meet us at the Golden Dragon for an early tea. All right, kid?'

It was more than all right. The door closed behind them and I gave it two minutes in case they came back but they didn't. It meant I could run up the stairs to my room, jump on my bed and pore over my precious *Vogue*s. It turned out that mostly I lay on my bed and thought about Louis. Thought about last night and the way he'd tilted his head so he didn't miss a single thing as he watched Alice's arse when she walked away from him.

Probably she had only flirted with him because Dora had been hanging out with us all evening and when I let her come to the diner with us and we'd had a conversation that Alice wasn't part of, it had made her mad. Mad enough to exact a tiny but painful revenge by puncturing the little bubble I kept around Louis and stepping inside.

I wondered if Louis had ever checked me out. Not that I was hot or pretty, not like Alice was, but I did have good legs. And Louis didn't have a girlfriend, so it wasn't within the realms of total impossibility that we might get together. I mean, Merrycliffe was a small town – we were always running into each other, hanging out at the same places, there was no reason why I couldn't make this thing with Louis real.

I tried to imagine what it would be like to go out with Louis. How we'd be Merrycliffe's It couple, not that that would be a difficult feat to achieve. I could see myself standing in the wings when Thee Desperadoes played (though The Wow Club didn't actually have any wings) as Louis sang just to me. Though Thee Desperadoes were going to have to improve drastically before they could write the kind of songs that a girl would want them to play just for her.

'Yeah, Louis was a bit of a twat before he started going out with Franny,' people would remark. 'The love of a good woman and all that.'

I hugged myself at the deliciousness of it until I remembered that these were dreams that would never come true because I didn't have the first idea of how to make them a reality. Boys were another country. And Louis wasn't a boy. He was almost a man. A manboy.

It was all right for Alice because she knew how to talk to boys. Alice could make a boy feel like he was the centre of her universe. It was quite something to behold.

Whereas I had one of those faces that are like a mirror to the soul and what my soul was usually saying to boys was stuff like, 'Even though you've doused yourself in Lynx, you still smell of unwashed gym socks.' Or 'Please stop staring at my lack of breasts and, by the way, you're not even a quarter of the man that Louis, my imaginary boyfriend, is.'

It was hopeless. I didn't know how to begin showing Louis that I would make an exemplary girlfriend. Or did I? Maybe it was as easy as picking up my ancient BlackBerry and sending him a Facebook friend request. That was a good starting place. Except, what if he ignored my request or blocked me or reported me for spam? That was the least of it.

There were so many awful repercussions to sending a friend request but before I could explore each one, my treacherous finger had already clicked on Add Friend. Why would my index finger do that?

I stared at my finger in horror. I wasn't strong enough to handle that kind of rejection. I could already hear Thee Desperadoes' mocking laughter as Louis told them he'd got a friend request from the flat-chested girl who gawped at him wherever he went and who had been told off by her father for going out on a Saturday night without any socks on.

Jesus! My day-to-day existence wasn't exactly puppies and chocolate milkshakes and now I'd made things a million times worse. I stared at my phone in frustration and was just about to delete the friend request before Louis got it (there was *no way* he was getting up before lunch on a Sunday) when something dawned on me. While I was on the theme of rejection and having my dreams cruelly dashed on the rocks of life, I realised that my phone had been completely silent ever since I got up.

Which meant that for the first time since I could remember Alice and I had gone ... I glanced down at my mobile ... ten hours without any kind of communication. OK, we'd been asleep for most of those ten hours, but usually I woke up to a text from Alice or I tweeted her like I did every morning to tell her the state of me and she'd tweet me back. This morning I am 70 per cent bedhead, 12 per cent Regina George from Mean Girls, 10 per cent Cheerios and 8 per cent false eyelashes.

It was our thing. It was what we did. But not today.

I couldn't believe Alice had suddenly flipped out on me. Then I came to my senses and got over myself.

It had only been ten hours and we'd been drinking last night and God knows what time *she'd* got in. She was probably still asleep.

Hey U, I texted her. Sorry 2 bail last nite. U get home ok? Shall we hang l8r?

Alice texted me back within a minute. On my way 2 grans 4

church. 4 realz. Just f-ing kill me now. Let's Facetime l8r. Luv U!
xxxxxxxx

I'd been stupid. It was Alice. *Alice!* My Alice. Best friends for ever. I'd put last night's flirtation with Louis down to too much vodka and diet Coke and move on because there was absolutely nothing to worry about.

I loved not having to worry about stuff.

When Dad had done a big transcontinental stint, he was only given local jobs for a while. He'd mutter about the call of the open road and how delivering sacks of sand to Runcorn wasn't really cutting it, but he only worked six-hour shifts and was back home every day in time to cook tea, which meant that Mum was his problem.

Not that Mum was anybody's problem right now. She was pretending to be a fully functioning adult and if she was a bit too thin and a bit too OCD about the housework and had a minor fit when Dad bought non-organic milk, well, that was just because it was her 'special time of the month'. We were all really good at pretending in our house.

And at least now I could get on with my own stuff.

Alice and I were good again too. She'd even bunked off so we could have lunch together on Monday. She didn't mention what had happened on Saturday with Louis so she'd obviously never meant it to be a big deal and I wasn't going to let it become one. It was why I didn't tell her that I'd sent Louis a friend request, especially as it had been forty-eight hours and he hadn't responded. If he hadn't responded in forty-eight hours, then he wasn't going to and I was going to be grown up and philosophical about Louis shunning my clumsy overtures.

Or I was going to *try* and be grown up and philosophical and carry on treating Louis as my own personal sex object until I was old enough to leave Merrycliffe and find a real boy who dressed impeccably and knew who Alber Elbaz was and never ever joked about farts or any other kind of bodily function. Until then, my crush on Louis would just have to do and I could only hope that my friend request was a little secret between the two of us. Please God, let it be so.

Even a few days ago, I'd have been ripped in two over Louis's cruel rejection, but I could deal with it now because Dad was home, Alice was cool and in the little corner of the art block given over to our fashion fiefdom Barbara had given us our first project. It didn't involve filling in an annotated diagram of a sewing machine either. We were going to make an actual piece of clothing!

Before that, we had to suffer three excruciating days of being taught how to follow a dressmaking pattern, which I already knew how to do. I decided not to share that in case Barbara put another black mark by my name, to go with the ten or so that were already there.

So I sat at my table with one of my beloved vintage *Vogue* patterns that I'd bought on eBay and once Barbara was satisfied that we all vaguely knew what we were meant to be doing, Sneering Studio Tech appeared.

'Where do you want them then?' he asked Barbara gruffly. I knew before he'd even opened his mouth that he'd sound gruff.

'Why don't we let everyone choose their dress forms?' Barbara suggested and he sniffed like that was a bad idea, then wheeled in the first dress form.

Everyone, even Krystal with a K, greeted the dress form with oohs and ahs – Paul, who had the workstation next to mine, even clapped his hands in glee. I already had a dress form at home, an eBay purchase that Dad had picked up from Manchester for me, so I had a game plan. While everyone oohed and aahed, I quickly snagged the form that was my size rather than one of the adjustable ones that looked as if they'd fall apart if you tried to adjust them. As it was, the wheels stuck as I rolled it to my workbench.

Sneering Studio Tech gave me a knowing look, but I wasn't sure if it was in acknowledgement of my mad dress-form-getting abilities or if it was because he'd witnessed Louis laughing himself stupid about my friend request. Then I saw him give Paul a knowing look when Paul asked if there were any male dress forms, so I figured that that was just the way his face was designed. It had two settings: the sneer and the knowing look.

'He's in that terrible band. Do you fancy him too?' Dora hissed from where she was sitting behind me.

'No! I'm a one-Desperado kind of girl,' I hissed back, one eye on Sneering Studio Tech. 'All men are somehow *less*, compared to Louis.'

'Yeah, right.' Dora, who was wearing leggings, white shirt and a black velvet tailcoat, what she called a 'casual Wednesday look', gestured at Sneering Studio Tech, who was standing with his arms folded and staring at the ceiling as Sage and

Krystal with a K almost came to blows over the two dress forms that were left. 'He's much better looking than Louis.'

'No, he's not,' I said automatically, because my research had been both exhausting and empirical. Louis was the best-looking boy in Merrycliffe. Sneering Studio Tech was, well, he was ...

I shuffled round on my stool so I could peer at him over my dress form's shoulder. He was tall, but not as tall as Louis. He was thin but not rock-god thin like Louis, just thin. He didn't have Louis's amazing cheekbones either, but he had one of those thin faces that looked intelligent rather than ferrety. His eyes ... well, I couldn't be sure without making it really obvious that I was staring but Louis's eyes were blue and Sneering Studio Tech's eyes weren't blue. He had mousy brown hair that could have done with cutting to stop it falling in his indeterminate-coloured eyes and he was wearing navy overalls and he played guitar in Thee Desperadoes very badly. Definitely not crush material.

'Well, I think he has a certain charm,' Dora said. 'What do you reckon?'

Paul and Mattie, who had the workstation next to Dora, both nodded and Sage, victorious in her battle over the dress form, came over. She gave me a nasty eye flick, because her and Krystal with a K were still fully paid-up members of the hate club. 'Reckon to what?'

'Whether laughing boy over there is fit. Franny says no, but the boys and I think he's a fixer-upper.'

'I'd fix him up,' Sage said immediately. 'He's got really nice hands and he winked at me and smiled when I told Krystal with a K that it didn't matter what dress form she got because she was only killing time until she got a place on a course where she'd learn to make people as orange as she was. So he's got a sense of humour too.'

I didn't think smiling at Sage's bitchy put-down qualified as a sense of humour but then Barbara bustled over with her clipboard. She was rarely seen without her clipboard.'We need to make arrangements for our field trip,' she said. In the morning we were getting the train to Morecambe to go fabric shopping because there wasn't a fabric shop within a ten-mile radius of Merrycliffe. 'I need you at the train station at ten sharp. I will leave latecomers behind.' As she started going on about travel vouchers and how much money we'd need, Sage turned to look at Sneering Studio Tech, who was now doing something with the last rickety dress form and a screwdriver.

'So, anyway, what's your name, then?' Sage asked because she was another girl who had no problem getting a guy's attention.

He didn't say anything at first – probably because he was doing a tricky bit of screwdrivering – then he looked up. 'Francis,' he said.

I wished Alice had been there, because later when I told her that Dora had burst into a shrieking fit of the giggles when we discovered that Sneering Studio Tech HAD THE SAME FIRST NAME AS ME, she wasn't impressed.

'He's Francis with an I and you're not even a Frances with

an e,' she argued, elbows resting on the counter of the Chatter-jee's shop as I sewed on a shirt button. 'Officially you're a Francesca but really you're Franny so it's not that big a deal.'

'Well, it felt like one. I had to stuff my fingers in my mouth to stop myself from laughing and Sneering Studio Tech looked even more sneery than he normally does,' I explained, but Alice shook her head like she just didn't get it. 'I suppose it was one of those things where you just had to be there.'

Alice's face twisted in a scowl that lasted no longer than the time it took to blink. Then she straightened up. 'But I'm not there, Franny, because you abandoned me ...'

'Well, I wouldn't call it abandon and I still can't understand why you don't tell your mum that you don't want to do Business Studies, or go on strike and refuse to do your coursework or something.'

'Oh, please! Don't make out that failing your GCSEs was some kind of cunning masterplan,' she snapped and I gasped in shock. Alice's shoulders slumped. 'Don't look at me like that! It was a joke. I didn't mean it.'

But it wasn't a joke. It was Alice saying something nasty to hurt me. 'I don't know what's going on with us,' I said. 'Look, I'm at college and I spend all day with Dora and the others. What do you want me to do? Not speak to them at all?'

'Yes, that's exactly what I want you to do,' Alice said and she sounded deadly serious.

I didn't know what to say, which was a first, and it was a relief when Rajesh swaggered through the door. 'Franny to the B! Wassup? You feeling breezy, innit?' He finished it off with some weird hand gesture that I was sure was big in da 'hood. Then he saw Alice standing there and his hand stilled in mid-air. 'Oh, you're here.'

'And so are you,' she said without much pleasure. 'Time I wasn't.' Alice gathered up her bag and folders and sniffed contemptuously as Raj made a big deal of holding the door open for her.

'I'll call you later, 'K?' I called out but she was already out of the door.

10

It was bright and sunny for our field trip to Morecambe when we caught the little cross-country train that went from Merrycliffe's tiny station every two hours.

Barbara spent most of the journey suggesting, but really telling us, that we should buy cotton because it would be the easiest material to work with. I was making an A-line sixties shift dress, a very simple design (so it had to be executed *perfectly* because there would be nowhere to hide shoddy sewing) but I'd altered my pattern to add a pair of half-circle pockets, which I wanted to edge in a contrasting band.

My head was full of fabric possibilities as I took out my patterns and made sketches and wrote notes in my *Designers I Have Met And Liked* notebook.

Once we were off the train, it was a short walk to the fabric shop, which was just off Morecambe's seafront. The promenade had been swanked up a few years before, but was still mostly the domain of old people using the new cycle paths to bomb along on their motorised scooters. I kept my eye out for the vintage ice cream van that bore the legend *Every Day Is Like Sundae* because hopefully there'd be time for a walk and a 99 before we got the train home. Morecambe also had several excellent charity shops. I always found that towns full of OAPs had really good stuff in the chazzas because there was nobody cool around to pick over it first.

Morecambe was quite grim and run-down once you left the seafront but at least it had a huge fabric shop. Once we got inside I had a rummage around the cotton but none of it was talking to me. Dora was having a tizzy as she wanted to make a huge billowy skirt but it would take metres upon metres of fabric for full billowyness and she didn't have that much money. Sandra and Karen were discussing something called a colour wheel and saying things like 'I still think you're a Spring, love. You're definitely not an Autumn,' and Paul, Matthew and Sage had disappeared into the furthest reaches of the shop.

I stared up at the bolts of fabric, willing one of them to reach out to me, speak to me, be worthy of being worn by me, but I got a big fat nothing.

'Everything all right, Francesca?' Barbara asked as I disconsolately fingered a bolt of black and white polka-dot brushed cotton. 'That's a fun print.'

'I'm not really feeling it,' I muttered, because I'd done the whole polka-dot thing when I was, like, thirteen. 'Not sure what I'm in the mood for.'

Barbara must have realised I was a hopeless case because she left me to hurry over to Krystal with a K, who was eyeing up some neon-pink velour. 'If she thinks she's making a tracksuit, I will kill her,' I heard Barbara mutter and I was grinning as I wandered further into the depths of the shop, which was actually about six shops knocked together.

There was nothing really lovely that caught my eye, though there was a lot of sparkly spandex to make dance costumes with. There probably wasn't much call for patterned silk or a lovely drapey wool jersey in Morecambe, I thought as I headed for the little alcove where a big red *Bargains* sign was hanging.

I burrowed through grubby polycotton remnants and nasty, shiny lengths of polyester that would burn like a firework if they came within fifty metres of a naked flame. Then I heard Barbara asking everyone to take their fabric to the till because our time was up.

My dreams of a sleek, stylish sixties shift dress were yet to be realised and then I saw a sliver of something grey in one of the bins. I investigated further. It was leather. A thin, buttery soft leather in a beautiful dove grey. It wasn't cotton and . . .

'You can't make something in leather,' Barbara said from somewhere behind me. 'Let's not do a marathon before we can even walk.'

'I'll need to get something for a lining. Polyester would do, don't you think?' I asked Barbara. She looked surprised that I even knew that much. 'I was going to use ribbon for contrast banding on my pockets but maybe piping instead and for the cuffs, maybe the hem. Oooh! This!'

I yanked out about half a metre of leather in a pretty sky blue, which would be a perfect foil for the grey.

'Leather is very difficult to work with even for an experienced seamstress,' Barbara said.

I wasn't experienced but I'd never get to be experienced if I didn't challenge myself.

'But it's very thin, very soft leather. Not like biker jacket leather,' I said, holding it out so she could take it between thumb and forefinger. 'I'm going to get it anyway and I could work on it at home but I'd really like to use it for my first piece so you can get an idea of my design aesthetic. Sharply tailored dresses made of leather are very on-trend. Martin Sanderson did them in his last collection.'

'Martin Sanderson.' Barbara sniffed. 'He might be a successful designer now, but once he was a very silly fashion student with ideas above his skill set who made the most mangled pair of trousers I've ever seen.'

'No,' I breathed. 'What? You ... Martin Sanderson?'

Barbara allowed herself a small smile for rendering me about as speechless as I ever got. 'We were both fashion students at the very same college where you're driving your poor lecturer mad.'

'Shut. Up.'

'No, Francesca, I won't shut up.' Barbara was loving this, I could tell. I was kind of loving it too. I knew Martin Sanderson was about the only Merrycliffe boy to make good but I hadn't realised he'd started out at Merrycliffe Technical College. With Barbara! My brain could not compute. 'Anyway, back to this leather ...'

I might have been almost speechless but I wasn't budging. 'If Martin Sanderson can make a leather dress that isn't slutty then so can I. Or I can try at least.'

'Don't tell me, Francesca, you also read *Vogue* from cover to cover every month,' Barbara said with a sigh, but then she actually smiled at me, like she read *Vogue* from cover to cover every month too. Like, we were totally having a moment.

I nodded. 'And *Vogue Italia* if I can get hold of a copy and any other foreign edition of *Vogue* too.'

'Oh dear, I can see that I'm going to have my hands full with you,' she said, as she gently nudged me out of the bargain corner with the leather clutched to my chest. On the way out I saw some stretchy silver fabric that was just what I needed for my Halloween costume and I grabbed hold of that too. Who would have thought that Barbara and I would have bonded over our mutual love of *Vogue*? I made a solemn vow that I would suck up to her like she'd never been sucked up to before so she'd dish all kinds of dirt on Martin Sanderson. Then she cleared her throat. 'That is, *if* you manage to pass your GCSEs when you retake them.' It was obvious that our bonding moment was gone.

Barbara gave us an hour to amuse ourselves before we got the train back to Merrycliffe, so I hurried off for a trawl of the charity shops. I bought a lined dress for fifty pence – not because I wanted to wear it. No way, it was strictly Mother of the Bride, but I was going to take it apart to see how the lining was constructed. I also found a pair of white kitten heels that I could dye another colour and a really rancid-looking teddy holding a heart that said *Best Friends Forever*. Whenever Alice or I found a particularly hideous piece of best friend tat we bought it for the other one. This was a worthy addition to the pile of shame and it was a much-needed reminder that we *were* best friends forever.

Then, as I was about to head for the station, I saw the *Every Day Is Like Sundae* ice cream van. Clutching a toffee crunch 99 with flake, I had to run all the way back to where the train was already pulling into the platform. Barbara was standing at the door to one of the carriages and waving furiously at me. 'Serve you right if you'd been left behind,' she said, as I heaved myself up on to the train, like it was the only train leaving Morecambe that week, which it so wasn't.

I snagged two seats to myself – Dora, Matthew, Paul and Sage were sitting across the aisle from me. I frantically licked my rapidly melting ice cream and pulled out my phone one-handed so I could send Alice a picture of the bear, and it was then my mind was blown.

Louis Allen has accepted your friend request.

I felt all colour drain from me, as if the blood in my head had decided to plunge to my feet. Then it raced all the way back to the top to heat up my cheeks in the biggest, most painful blush I'd ever experienced.

This wasn't just Louis accepting my friend request. He knew who I was. And who I was was all right with him so he'd added me as a friend. This was huge. It was epic. This was the start of something. I knew it. I could feel it deep in my bones.

Louis had four hundred and fifty-seven Facebook friends but that didn't deter me. Probably half of those were bands or brands and not real people that he knew on a deep, personal level.

I didn't even notice the train stopping and people getting on or getting off because my phone had suddenly become a magical device; a key that unlocked a treasure trove that was full of pictures of Louis. Correction. It was full of bare-chested pictures of Louis, which I pored over. Correction. I perved over them. He had this ridge of muscle on either side of his hips, which made me feel funny. Not as funny as the little trail of hair that disappeared into the low-slung waistband of his skinny jeans.

Alas, once I'd finished staring slack-jawed at the many, many, *many* photos of Louis half-naked, there were many, many, *many* photos of Louis with the gaggle of Desperadettes who dogged his every move. There they were, snuggling up to Louis as they hung out in strange bedrooms in silly hats. Chased after each other on the beach as the sun went down. Drank cider around a bonfire. I wanted to be part of that world, I thought, as I moved on to the next photo.

It was Sneering Studio Tech, or Francis. I'd almost managed to repress the memory that we sort of had the same first name. Unlike Louis or Thee Desperadettes, he did not take a good Facebook shot. He could only look at the camera with arms folded and a scowl.

He did give good scowl though – really committed to his mardy expression and there were girls who liked the sneering thing. Dora seemed to anyway and just as if I'd called her name, she was suddenly standing over me.

'Franny?'

With great difficulty I managed to tear my eyes away from my phone. 'Hey. Did you have enough money to get all the fabric you needed?'

'Mattie subbed me the extra,' she said distractedly, because she was busy pulling a reluctant Sage forward. 'So, this is really stupid because you're both cool and the five of us should be hanging out together and so you two really need to sort stuff out, OK?'

The four of them, Dora, Matt, Paul and Sage, had formed a foursome over the last couple of weeks. They all hung out together and as Sage had made it painfully obvious that she didn't like me, I'd never really moved past the small-talk stage with Matt and Paul. So, none of it was OK, but Dora pushed Sage down into the seat next to me, then she sat opposite us and rested her feet on the armrest nearest to the aisle, effectively blocking either of us from standing up and walking away.

'Any time you want to start chatting this out,' Dora prompted us.

I have to admit I was curious as to what Sage's specific beef with me was. 'Right, who was he?' I asked her.

She scowled. If Sneering Studio Tech had been there, he would have sued for copyright. 'What?'

'Your boyfriend? Your brother? Please don't say it was your dad.'

'What are you on about?' she demanded. Sage was really

beautiful, even when she was giving me bitchface. Not sexy beautiful like Alice. Or pretty like a handful of other girls that I knew. Sage was proper beautiful. She had gasp-inducing cheekbones, elegantly arched brows and a wide mouth that was usually lifted in a glorious, beaming smile to reveal even white teeth. She was tall and thin and elegant and generally looked as if she should be striding down a Milan catwalk dressed in Gucci from head to toe rather than sitting on the Morecambe-to-Merrycliffe train. 'What about my dad?'

Sage was determined to make me spell it out. 'Obviously Alice put the moves on a guy that you were seeing or one of your mates was seeing. But that's Alice. That's what she does. She's my best friend, but you can't hate on me by association, I haven't done anything to *you*. So, you can keep giving me the death glares if you like, but it's ridiculous.'

'This has nothing to do with your friend, Alice, though, quite frankly, yeah, I'm going to judge anyone who hangs out with her,' Sage said scathingly. 'But this has to do with you and me and my gold dress.'

'What gold dress? I've never even seen you wear a gold dress.'

Sage normally wore skinny jeans and big clompy boots, though once she'd totally rocked a jumpsuit. 'Don't pretend you don't know. The gold brocade dress my mum took into your shop for alterations. I'd pinned it. I wrote down really clearly what I wanted done and ...'

This was actually starting to ring some bells. Quite loud bells. I tried to assume a clueless yet innocent expression.

'... when I went in to collect it, the owner said that they had a policy that items that had been in the shop for three months or longer were disposed of. It was barely three months! It was, three months and half a day and then Raj admitted that you'd marked the date on the calendar and taken the dress home with you as soon as the three months was up.'

Oh, yeah. *That* dress. 'OK, well, you didn't want that dress altered. You wanted that dress totally remade. I had to unpick all the seams, take it up, take it in, take off the sleeves and redo the armholes,' I said hotly. 'Mrs Chatterjee told your mum that it was too big a job but your mum begged and pleaded and said that you were desperate.'

'I was! I paid forty quid for that dress from a vintage shop in Leeds!'

'I'd *never* pay that much for vintage. Especially if it didn't even fit me,' I said, because Sage had moved closer and technically she was all up in my face and I hated when people got all up in my face. 'You were ripped off.'

'You. Stole. My. Dress,' Sage growled and Matthew and Paul, who'd been unashamedly listening to every word, held up imaginary handbags and Dora *tsked*.

'Ladies, please,' she said. 'This isn't about blame.'

'Good, because I'm blameless. I spent *hours* working on your dress even though Mrs Chatterjee completely underestimated how much time it would take so I earned twenty-five quid for, like, three days' work, because I get piece rate. That's, like, slave labour. Then you left the dress mouldering in the shop for over three months!' I'd forgotten how angry I'd been about the gold brocade dress but it was all coming back to me.

'Three months and a half-day!'

'That's still over three months, so you couldn't have wanted to wear the dress that badly.' I folded my arms. 'The shop policy was printed very clearly on the back of your receipt.'

Sage looked at Dora imploringly like she was Judge Judy. 'Um, well, I guess possession is nine-tenths of the law,' Dora said. 'Though I don't really know what that means.'

'What do I have to do to get my dress back?' Sage asked sullenly.

I hadn't even worn the dress. It was really scratchy and I'd been planning to put a lining in but I hadn't quite figured out how to do linings. Also gold didn't work so well with my complexion, but Sage was being such a bitch about it and acting like she had the moral high ground when she *so* didn't that I was tempted to tell her that I'd been using it to line the cat's litter tray. But we didn't have a cat and I didn't want to spend every day with Sage all up in my face.

'Pay me a fair rate for the work I did,' I said. She opened her mouth like she was about to protest, but I glared her into silence. 'It was really good work. I had to *hand-stitch* the armholes in the end.'

Sage rested her chin on her chest. 'This is why I'm doing this course; so I can alter my own vintage without being ripped off.'

'I'm not ripping you off. If you'd picked up the dress within three months, you'd have had the benefit of my bloody good alteration skills at a fraction of what they're worth.' I was bored with talking about this. 'But you didn't and here we are and you could have just talked to me about it instead of treating me like I had really terrible BO.'

'Well, it's just ... I've had nights I didn't sleep I was so mad about the dress and I didn't pick it up because I used to go to the grammar school in Lytham St Annes and I spend weekends at my dad's in Leeds and the shop was never open when I was around.' Sage scowled her hardest scowl yet. 'When I asked my mum, she said I treated her like a lady's maid.'

'God, mums always say stuff like that,' Dora remarked and Matthew and Paul agreed with her and I made similar noises, though it was the other way round with my mum. I felt more like staff than a daughter.

Finally, after some tense negotiations, we agreed that Sage would give me an extra twenty-five pounds for the dress, a fiver a week, and I would hand over the dress once payment was complete. 'Most bloody expensive dress I've ever bought,' she muttered, then she asked me if I'd made a whole item of clothing before or if I just knew how to alter things.

'Well, I made this,' I said, gesturing at the miniskirt I was wearing. It was nothing special. Just two pieces of denim sewn together, hemmed and ...

'Oh my God, you put a zip in? How do you even know how to do that?'

'It's easier than you'd think.' Then I told them that there were videos on the internet of people doing all sorts of complicated sewing stuff and we talked about making clothes all the way back to Merrycliffe.

110

It was amazing. It was liberating. I was finally with people who spoke the same language as me. Who knew that when I said YSL, I meant Yves Saint Laurent. Who got the difference between being on-trend and being directional. And they were as confused about seam allowance as I was.

Alice understood me in the way that you only could when you'd been best friends with someone for as long as we had. When their face and their dreams and their secret fears were as familiar to you as your own, but I'd never had any fashion friends before and I thought that I might just have found some. Alice was going to kill me, but if I kept my college stuff separate from my Alice stuff, then maybe she never had to find out.

'See you tomorrow then,' Sage said and as we walked up the road from the station, Dora asked for my phone number and Matthew and Paul had already added me on Facebook.

I'd been down for so long that being up and positive felt strange but it also felt really good. It felt good for the time it took to check my phone and see that Louis had added another new friend on Facebook.

It was Alice.

11

'I don't know why you keep going on and on about this so-called best friends code,' Alice said, after admitting that she'd sent Louis a Facebook friend request. Even worse, by the time I rang her to ask her what the hell she was playing at she'd written, Hey handsome, thanks for the ketchup. Must do it again some time, on Louis's wall. 'I should think it must be against the best friend code that you've just made up, to rub my nose in it that you've got a whole bunch of new friends who you'd rather hang out with.'

'What new friends? What am I rubbing your nose in?'

We were sitting on the wall outside the sandwich shop, which was an equal distance from our two houses. It was starting to get too cold to sit on walls, but when I shivered but it was nothing to do with the chill, but more to do with Alice waving her iPhone in my face. 'These four new friends you added on

Facebook! And the hilarious in-jokes on your wall about seam allowance. I don't even know what seam allowance is but it sounds really, really boring.'

'It is really boring.' I paused. Shut my eyes. Took a deep breath. 'You can't expect me to spend all day sharing a workroom with people and refuse to interact with them. It doesn't mean I like you any less. What you and me have is special, so stop being so stupid.'

It was Alice's turn to not say anything. I could see all the emotions slugging it out on her face; fear, doubt, sadness and finally she ended up at defensive, stuck out her chin and decided to stay there.

'No, what's stupid is that you've had a crush on Louis for four years, but you've never done anything about it and that makes Louis fair game.'

'He's not fair game and you *know* it,' I said to her in a low voice because I didn't trust myself to turn up my volume knob. 'OK, maybe I'm overreacting if this is never going to go any further than you and Louis being friends on Facebook but be honest, do you want to take it further?'

Alice shook back her hair. 'You're being really unreasonable about this, Franny. You've never gone out with Louis or got off with him, or snogged him.' She counted off on her fingers all the ways that I'd failed to connect with Louis on a meaningful level. 'You can't just place indefinite dibs on a guy, Franny. You've had *years* to make a move.'

'I could hardly make a move when I was twelve, could I? That would have been wrong and gross.'

'Yeah, but you could have made a move at any time over the last two years and you didn't,' Alice pointed out, like making a move on a boy was the easiest thing in the world, which it was ... to her.

How could you explain your irrational but crippling fear of rejection to someone who had never been rejected? But it wasn't just about that. It wasn't even about me and Louis, or, God forbid, Alice and Louis. It was about me and Alice. It was about *us*. Our friendship.

'You know how I feel about Louis.' I put my hand on her arm, because I had to get through to Alice, reach out to her, remind her that this was me. 'There's a whole town of older boys, why do you have to pick *him*?'

'Because practically all of the boys in Merrycliffe are complete losers. Hello! Eleventh largest container port in Europe! That doesn't exactly bring in the foxes, does it?'

'But it's *Louis* and I know you think it's just a dumb crush and I'm just a dumb girl who hasn't even kissed a boy ...'

Alice patted my hand. 'Of course I don't think you're dumb and *what*? You *so* have kissed a boy! What about that time when we pulled those lads on the exchange trip to Cracow?'

As if things weren't bad enough, I then had to remind Alice that the boy I'd paired off with had wanted to kiss Alice, not me. Just like every other boy on the planet. Just like Louis would want to. 'You of all people should understand how things are at home. It feels like they're never going to get better. But then I see Louis in town and he smiles or the sun's hitting his face and he looks amazing and for five minutes everything isn't rubbish. Why do you have to go and ruin it?'

'Please do not play the mentaller mum card just this once! My life isn't exactly going the way I want it either.' Alice tossed her hair back again. 'It's all right for you. You're swanning off to college and making all your fancy new friends, but what about me? I'm stuck exactly where I am. Worse than that, I'm getting left behind.'

'I'm not leaving you behind. I want to take you with me.' It should have been a relief to know that Alice was having a bad dose of insecurity – that she hadn't suddenly gone for an evil upgrade. Usually Alice was stuffed so full of confidence that I always secretly wished that she had a bit left over for me. I knew exactly what it was like to feel as if you weren't good enough but Alice wasn't putting a brave face on it. She was putting on her fight face and it was making it really hard for me to feel sorry for her. 'Is that what this thing with Louis is all about? Really? Because you know . . . '

'Look, what do you want to do?' Alice asked, cutting right across what I was trying to say. 'Are you going to go for it with Louis then?'

I knew that if I said yes, Alice would back off. I was 95 per cent sure of it. Though a couple of weeks ago I'd have been 110 per cent sure of it.

'The thing is, I'm not sure that I'm ready to go for it,' I admitted, because going for it felt like jumping off the highest diving board at Conley Road pool and I hated getting my face wet. 'Why are you being like this? You're acting like you care more about getting with Louis than our friendship.'

'Of course I don't, but if you're not going to go for it, then I am!' Alice said quickly and defiantly, like she'd lose her nerve if she didn't get the words out as fast as possible.

I hated her a little bit then. Just a little bit. 'What's that meant to mean, then?' I demanded. 'Like, a declaration of war or something?'

Alice recoiled, like she was shocked that things had gone this far. But only for a second, then she sat up straighter and stiffened her spine. 'Not war, not at all, but if you don't want him, then you can't bogart him just because someone else does.'

'But you never stick with a guy for longer than five minutes. You know it! Are you going to risk our friendship for a week going out with Louis?'

'It might not be a week. Maybe the fact that guys bore me is because you were right and I was aiming too young.' Alice had some colossal nerve; throwing my own words back at me. I looked at her. She refused to meet my eye. 'Louis is older and he's in a band and he's been to London. And he's really fit and he's totally been flirting with me and if our friendship is strong enough to survive you having all these new friends, then it can survive me hanging out with Louis.'

'You have nothing in common with him,' I snapped. 'Nothing!'

'And you do, I suppose?'

I had loads of things in common with Louis. Or, to be more accurate, I had a list of things that was a bit pathetic when I catalogued them in my head; we both liked the same pasty from the very sandwich shop that I was sitting outside. We both ran to the dance floor whenever they played the Beatles at The Wow. And before he started bleaching it, our hair was almost the exact same shade of mousy blond and actually, yeah, it was a really sad list, but I wasn't going to tell Alice that. That was a first too, because we told each other everything.

Her chin was still jutting out the way it did when she argued with her mum or was telling me about the argument that she'd just had with her mum. As if I was against her too. Alice hated it when things didn't go her way.

Spoiled, my mum called her, so did Siobhan and even Alice's dad, who was the one who did most of the spoiling. Alice was so used to just snatching anything and anyone that took her fancy. She knew that she could always rely on her looks and her big blue eyes. And that she could get any boy she wanted just by thrusting out her tits and licking her lips.

Alice might be sexy, but I was way cooler than her and maybe it was time I started working that. I'd been trailing in Alice's shadow for too long. I hadn't expected Louis to friend me back on Facebook but he had. And Dora and Matthew and Paul and even Sage were on the way to becoming my friends. I had things going for me and it was about time that Alice realised that. Hell, it was time that I realised that.

'Me and Louis have tons in common.' I didn't recognise the sound of my own voice. It was chippy and hard. 'And so, yeah, I'm going for it.'

'No! You already said that you weren't.' Alice jumped off the wall so she could stand there with her hands on her hips. 'I said that I'm going for it.'

I was fed up with people thinking that what I wanted wasn't important. 'Well, we're both going for it then, I suppose.'

'Fine!'

'Fine!' I snapped back, though if either of us were thinking clearly we'd have known it was not fine. 'You're on.'

'You're *so* on!'

The next morning I really felt like skipping college. Only the thought of Dad telling me in his sad voice that he was disappointed with my commitment to retaking my GCSEs and making something of myself had me packing my bag, slapping on some heavy-duty concealer and wearing my mint-green skinny jeans so at least my legs looked bright and cheerful.

I'd hardly slept at all. I kept thinking about how, for one moment yesterday afternoon, everything had been great, anything had seemed possible. Dad was back. Mum was taking her pills and functioning. I had all I needed to make a killer dress. I was making new friends. I was connecting with Louis. And then I'd fought with Alice and now nothing felt right in my world.

All night I'd replayed the argument we'd had, working it around and around like an aching tooth that you keep worrying with your tongue even though you know that makes it hurt even more.

It wasn't until it had started getting light outside that I came to the realisation that if I had to choose between Alice and Louis, I'd choose Alice every time. I would. Even if Louis was coming round every day and phoning me all the time and pledging his eternal love, even constant Louis kisses, couldn't compare to hanging out with Alice. Louis would never make me laugh so hard that the diet Coke I was drinking spurted out of my nostrils. Even if I went out with Louis for five years. I couldn't imagine ever being so comfortable with him I'd let him see me without make-up or in the grungy pyjamas I always wore when I had period pain.

But I still didn't see why I couldn't have them both. If my friendship meant as much to Alice as hers did to me, she'd let me have Louis because whatever she said, I did have first dibs on him.

I was so late getting downstairs that there was only time to grunt 'Good morning' at Mum and Dad as I grabbed a banana, then I opened the front door and there was Alice.

'Oh . . .' She should have been on her way to school. 'Um, hi.'

Alice bit her lip. It was a very unAlice gesture. 'Look, Franny . . . I didn't sleep, like, at all last night,' she burst out. 'I couldn't bear it if we stopped being friends. Really couldn't bear it. I know I sound like some awful song on Heart FM but you're the best thing that ever happened to me.'

Whatever angry thoughts I still had about Alice went . . . like they'd never existed. 'Well, same here. We are too good to fall out over a boy.'

Alice nodded vigorously as we fell into step and started walking up towards the town. 'Right. Not just any boy but Louis Allen! He doesn't deserve either of us really.'

'I know. If only he wasn't so pretty.' I couldn't help my wistful sigh.

'Yeah,' Alice agreed. It sounded as if she'd finally come to her senses because I totally had prior claim on Louis. 'So, I couldn't sleep and I think if we're going to both have a crack at him, we should keep it civilised.'

'Say what?' I nearly walked into the road on the red man. Alice yanked me back. 'I thought ... you said ... What do you mean, keep it civilised?'

'That we have some rules so things don't get out of hand,' Alice explained. She came to a stop outside the one coffee shop that did coffee in fancy cardboard cups with the little cuffs to stop your hands getting burned. 'Shall we work on them now? I've a free first period.'

'I don't,' I said, because I had my English catch-up class and even if I had had a free period, I needed time to process this. Also, these rules. She'd had all night to come up with rules. I'd had one minute.

'Can't you bunk it?' Alice asked. 'This is important.'

'So are my retakes,' I said, hoisting my bag more firmly on to my shoulder. Alice pulled a face like she was bored with hearing about my GCSE retakes – not as bored as I was of studying for them. 'What about lunch?'

'I have Politics right after lunch. I can't be late back.'

'Can't you bunk that?' I asked, because Politics wasn't that important in the grand scheme of things.

'Well, not really.' Alice looked torn. 'Though I haven't done the reading on the Corn Laws. OK, yeah. Let's meet back here at one.'

12

In my *Designers I Have Met And Liked* notebook were what Alice and I called our Rules of Engagement. 'Though I'm not expecting either of us to get engaged to him,' she'd said before we got down to business.

The Rules

No pretending to like crap bands just because he does.

No laughing at his jokes like a saphead, unless he tells a
   really funny joke and laughing is inevitable.

No private messaging. That includes using technology to
   send pictures of your body parts.

No flashing of said body parts in a real-life situation.

No nudity. (This should really go without saying, but it has to
   be said.)

No sexual contact, including grinding up against him on

the dance floor of The Wow or anywhere else for that
matter.
No dirty talk.
No getting him drunk.
No getting yourself so drunk that shoving a tongue down
Louis's throat seems like an acceptable tactic.
No offering to cut his hair for free or make him an item of
clothing.
No slagging each other off or running each other down to
Louis.
When one of us gets him, the other one has to back off
immediately with no hard feelings and no pass-agg
tweeting.
The winner is declared when Louis changes his Facebook
status to: 'In a relationship with ____ _____' (insert the
victor's name.)

'The important thing is that we're not going to fall out over
this,' I'd said once we'd finished. 'It's just a bit of healthy
competition, right?'

'Right,' Alice had said. 'It might even get you to take the
training wheels off, Franny. Then no man will be safe from your
charms.'

'I'm not interested in anyone but Louis,' I insisted, as we got
to the corner where Alice went left and I went right. 'But if
some other foxy boy catches your eye in the meantime, feel free
to go for it.'

'Well, if Ryan Gosling decides to relocate to Merrycliffe then you can have Louis. I'll even arrange to have him gift-wrapped,' Alice decided and I never expected that we'd both be giggling as we went our separate ways.

Drawing up the rules had taken all of our lunch hour and a little bit of flouncing and I was really late back for yet another tutorial on how to follow a dressmaking pattern, but I muttered something about women's problems and needing a chemist and Barbara let it go.

'You all right?' asked Sage, as I hauled myself up on my stool. She was perched on Paul's workbench and leafing through one of Barbara's big binders full of patterns. 'I've got some parac- etamol in my bag if you've got period pain.'

The other thing I'd decided during my long, dark night of the soul was that I'd been kind of unreasonable about Sage's gold dress. It *had* only been half a day and it wasn't her fault Mrs Chatterjee had undercharged her. Besides, the dress was wicked itchy so I'd given her back the frock that morning.

'But we agreed I'd give you the first five pounds on Monday,' she'd said.

'Just have the dress.' I'd shoved it at her so she had no choice but to take it.

'At least let me buy you lunch,' she'd insisted, but Alice and I had a prior arrangement so Sage had said we'd take a rain check.

Now she was rooting in her big slouchy tote that proclaimed the legend *My other bag's a Birkin* and pulled out a Crunchie. 'I always need huge amounts of chocolate when Aunt Flo's in town.'

'Aunt Flo isn't due for another week,' I whispered because Barbara kept glancing over in our direction to see if we were engrossed in the finer points of pattern reading. 'I just took a long lunch.'

Barbara really was looking over at us now so we both shut up and gave our patterns our full attention. I was meant to be working out seam allowance, but my mind was on other things. It was on Louis. Or rather it was on Alice, who was the immovable object blocking my path to Louis.

It was meant to be a clean fight, but Alice was a Jedi master when it came to pulling and I was the absolute opposite of a Jedi master.

What I needed was a secret weapon (I also needed to stop using all this battle lingo) and that was when I saw him as I was swapping phone numbers with Sage.

It was Sneering Studio Tech, not in his overalls but jeans and a plaid wool jacket, canvas satchel slung over his shoulder, walking towards the big double doors.

It was obvious what I had to do.

I hurried after him. Francis. (Oh God, I kept repressing the knowledge that his name was Francis. Sneering Studio Tech suited him much better.) He was walking superfast like he couldn't wait to get out of the place.

'So, hey, hi!' I panted when I finally caught up with him. He pulled back one of the doors. 'Great gig on Saturday night. One of your best.'

He froze and gave me the oddest look, like I was speaking in tongues or had dyed my hair purple since the last time he saw me. Not that he'd ever acknowledged my presence outside of the fashion studio. He indicated the open door with a jerk of his head.

'You're Francis, right? I'm Frances too. Well, I'm a Francesca, but everyone calls me Franny. Franny B.' I could be quite tongue-tied with boys I didn't know but this running of my mouth was an entirely new experience, especially as Francis wasn't giving me anything to work with.

He'd marginally slowed his steps so I didn't have to scamper to keep up, but that was all the encouragement he was prepared to give.

Still, I persevered. 'Yeah, so great gig. Really good sound. Those new songs are coming along, aren't they? And Louis . . . well, he always puts on a show, doesn't he?'

I ground to the grindingest of halts because there really weren't many positive things to say about Thee Desperadoes' show on Saturday night and I'd said them all. I smiled. I could tell it was a very cringing smile.

Up close, even obscured through a mop of brown hair, his thin face was even frownier than I'd previously thought.

We'd reached the college gates by now and the thing was I'd come this far – these were HUGE steps for Frankind – so I couldn't back down now.

'Which way are you going?' I asked brightly, though on the inside I was dying.

'Whatever way I'm going is going to be the way you're going too,' Francis said drily. He folded his arms and leaned back against the railings. 'I suppose you fancy Louis.'

'No!' But I couldn't deny it, because if I denied it then I was never going to get anywhere with Louis. Louis was the reason why I was having this torturous conversation with Sneer—Francis. Francis! His name was Francis. 'Well, yes I do fancy him. A little bit.'

Francis looked me up and down. I got the impression that he found me wanting. Like, my hair was too stringy and my face was forgettable and mint-green skinnies weren't fashion-forward but a terrible idea that should have never made it to the cash register, let alone out of the shop, back home with me and worn on my actual body.

'He eats girls like you for breakfast,' Francis informed me flatly. 'Not even for breakfast. As a light snack between meals.'

Great. It sounded like Louis and Alice had so much in common already. 'I'm sure that's not true. He doesn't know me, you don't know me that well either.' I attempted a winsome smile. 'Louis probably hasn't met the right girl yet.'

'I don't think the right girl for Louis exists.' Francis wasn't being at all encouraging. He was being completely *dis*couraging. 'Unless there's a girl somewhere in the world who turns into a curry and a six pack of lager after she's spent a few hours shagging.'

Ewwwww! Louis wasn't like that at all. Francis was probably trying to throw me off because he was fed up with all the girls wanting to get with Louis and not with him. I could empathise, except if Francis wanted girls to get with him then he needed to lose the attitude and the slouching like he had advanced osteoporosis, and the emo fringe, which was so three years ago.

'Well, for all you know, I could be the right girl for Louis,' I said with a slight edge to my voice.

Through the fringe I could see his eyes widen. Close up, they were a nice shade of greeny hazel, I'd give him that at least. 'Wow! So you have the ability to transform yourself into a tikka masala and six bottles of Stella? Have you told the British Medical Council about that?'

'No, because I'm worried that they wouldn't use my powers for the greater good,' I snapped, before I remembered that I was trying to be winsome and charming and totally getting Louis's bandmate and friend on side. 'So, anyway, you could put in a good word for me . . .'

Wide eyes again. 'And why would I do that? What's in it for me?'

In a way this would be a lot easier if it were a straight swap: Francis's talking me up to Louis in return for goods and services, because being charming and winsome really didn't seem to cut any ice with him.

'Well, um, I could make you something. Like a piece of clothing,' I explained, because that would only be against the rules if I were offering to make Louis a piece of clothing. 'I've never made anything for a boy before but it can't be that difficult – just broader and with buttons on the other side. I could make you a shirt. Or embroider your name on your work over-alls in a retro American sort of style.' No way was I making him trousers and having to deal with crotch issues. No freaking way.

As it was, Francis was looking distinctly underwhelmed at my offer. His lip was curling. 'Or . . . or I'm really good at making dresses and skirts. I could make something for your mum or your girlfriend.'

I couldn't believe that Francis had a girlfriend. Someone so objectionable could not have found a girl who was happy to kiss him at regular intervals.

'God, just stop talking,' Francis said, which proved my no-girlfriend theory, then he peeled himself away from the railings and walked off.

Which was very rude and completely unhelpful.

13

Usually if I wanted boy advice, which wasn't often, I asked Alice, who had a never-ending supply of interesting facts and useful tips. 'They think about sex every six seconds, unless the footie's on,' she'd announce out of the blue. 'Then they only think about sex every ten seconds.'

This time Alice was not going to be my go-to guru on matters of the heart, as both our hearts were yearning for Louis. Well, mine was. Alice was more concerned that there was someone under twenty-five in Merrycliffe yet to fall for her very obvious charms.

Luckily, Siobhan was coming home for the weekend – for once. She never came home during the university holidays, though when we'd left her two years ago at Manchester University in her little room in the halls of residence that had been the general idea. But then Gran had died and Mum got made redundant and everything was ruined. Mum wouldn't stop crying and washing her hands so much they were rubbed raw and bleeding, and Dad was away all the time on the big-money transcontinental jobs because we were relying on his pay packet. Siobhan didn't come home for a whole year. She said it was because she'd got a part-time job in Whistles, but even once Mum was kind of better Siobhan would never come home if Dad was away. Obviously, it was less about her part-time job and more to do with her completely not wanting to deal with Mum.

I sort of hated Siobhan for that when she wasn't here, but as soon as I walked through the door on Friday evening and she jumped on me with a gleeful cry, I went back to loving her so much it hurt.

'Franny B, light of my life,' she cried, because yes, even my own sister calls me Franny B. 'I've missed you, you funny-faced little freak.'

Although I was ten centimetres taller than Siobhan and she had long, dark brown hair with a new Zooey Deschanel-style fringe cut in, we could have been twins. 'I know you are but what am I?' I demanded.

'Oh, I'm sorry, are you still ten?' Siobhan asked me with a smirk. 'So, what's been up with you?'

There wasn't time to tell her anything because then Dad came in. He'd been to get fish and chips in Shuv's honour and he even let me have a glass of shandy, like I hadn't been guzzling vodka and various mixer drinks every Saturday night for the last two years.

130

Dad wanted to know all about Shuv's course and her exams and if she was doing any work placements and what her tutors said and what she'd need to do for her post-graduate studies if she wanted to be a barrister and no one else could get a word in edgeways. He hadn't even been a fraction interested in what I was doing at college once he'd made sure that I was signed up for my GCSE retakes, but Shuv was the brains of the family. I always suspected that she was Mum and Dad's favourite too, which was hard to take but at least I didn't have Dad trying to mastermind my future career plans.

Even Mum was interested enough to ask Shuv about her exciting life away from Merrycliffe. 'But you do have time to go out and have some fun, don't you?' she asked as she slowly and torturously removed all the batter from a tiny piece of cod. 'You can't work all the time, love.'

Shuv could barely bring herself to even look at Mum. 'Yeah, whatever,' she said brusquely and because it was Shuv, neither Mum nor Dad called her on her borderline rudeness. Sometimes I wished that Shuv and I could change places.

But then again, maybe not because Dad was still rabbiting on about the Law Society and chambers and boring legal stuff at 10 p.m., when I ignored Shuv's desperate, pleading look and said I was going to bed.

The next day I was working in the Chattterjees' shop and poor Shuv was scheduled for some mother/daughter bonding so it wasn't until she came to meet me from work that we could get down to business.

'I'm not going down The Wow,' she said before I'd even shut the door behind me. 'Not while I still have breath in my body.'

'But it's Saturday night . . . '

'Yeah, that's why we're going to the Pizza Express in Lytham St Annes, my treat, so we can have a proper chat. Dad lent me the car. I'll even let you have both kinds of doughballs.'

It was a tradition that we always went to the Pizza Express in Lytham St Annes when Shuv did bother to come for a visit, and that we had the garlic doughballs for a starter and the doughballs with Nutella for pudding. Two kinds of doughballs and quality time with Shuv just about won out over The Wow Club, just about – though Alice wasn't happy that I had to bail on her.

Jeez, Franny. I hardly ever see u & now ur a wow no-show. U r out with Shuv, not any of ur new college m8s, rite?

Not only was I worried that Alice was in a mood with me, *again*, I was also worried about what Alice might get up to with Louis in my absence. I had no choice but to text Dora and ask her to keep an eye on Alice, but she didn't know about Alice and me doing battle over Louis and it was very hard to explain it via text message.

It wasn't until we were in Pizza Express with the garlic doughballs in front of us that I was able to give Siobhan my undivided attention and a brief explanation of what was up with me. There was quite a lot up with me for once: Alice and me fighting all the time, college, Dora and Sage, my leather dress and Louis.

Finally I got to the end of my monologue and asked Shuv for

some big-sisterly advice. She'd actually had boyfriends while she was at school and though she swore she wasn't dating right now, there were a lot (like, really a lot) of pictures of this geeky, hipster-ish boy all over her Facebook. In two of them they were even kissing.

'Come on! You have real world boy-getting experience. Hit me up with your best tips,' I said. 'What do I need to do to have Louis begging to spend time with me? Dying to snog me? Pining for the touch of my hands?'

'Oh, where to begin,' Shuv sighed. She leaned back in her chair like she was settling in so she could impart all her wisdom.

It turned out that Shuv's wisdom wasn't all that and a bag of Hula Hoops. While we worked our way through two huge pizzas, she told me that the boys in Merrycliffe were so emotionally stunted that I might just as well not bother.

'But, Louis . . . '

Shuv rolled her eyes. She could pack the entire works of Shakespeare into one of her eye rolls. 'If you're intent on bagging your precious Louis, who was in the year below me at school and was a total twat even then, all you have to do is listen to him jaw on about all the stuff that Merrycliffe boys usually jaw on about and laugh at his pathetic jokes.'

'At school the boys were obsessed with fart and knob jokes.' I waved away the waiter and his gigantic pepper grinder. 'I'm sure Louis isn't like that. Also, when you are interested in someone, how do you strike a balance between being known as tight and being known as a slag?'

'Ah, the age-old conundrum that women everywhere, forced to conform to patriarchal standards of so-called acceptable female behaviour, struggle with. Let me know if you ever figure it out,' Shuv said tartly.

'Don't go all Studies in Feminism on me,' I whimpered. 'I need practical help, not a lecture.'

'The only practical help I can give is to tell you to give up on boys until you move somewhere that's not stuck in a total timewarp.'

'When I move to London, I'll be too busy to have time for boys. *If* I get to London and *if* I get into Central St Martin's and *if* I get to be a famous fashion designer.' It all seemed so daunting when I said it out loud. 'Though I'd be happy just to work for a famous fashion designer.'

'But there's no reason why you can't be a successful fashion designer. I'd rather buy one of your dresses than anything made by Karl Lagerfeld. How did he ever get anyone to take him seriously?' Shuv mused. 'Don't give up on your dreams, Franny. You let them burn bright, you hear me?'

'I will,' I assured her and I saw my dreams as a glowing pile of silver and gold paillettes, then they stopped glowing and my shoulders slumped. 'But Martin Sanderson is the only person to ever get out of Merrycliffe and achieve global success. It's like basic probability, isn't it, that a dump like Merrycliffe wouldn't produce two fashion superstars?'

'What about that designer you like, Henry Holland, and Agyness Deyn, who just happens to be a supermodel? They've been friends for ever and they both come from a Lancashire town even smaller than Merrycliffe.' Since she went to university, Siobhan likes to pretend that she never used to read *heat* from cover to cover, but her knowledge of celebrity is still encyclopaedic. 'Anyway, what about your precious Louis? Isn't he destined for the big time?' she added with a sly smile.

It was my turn to roll my eyes. 'Not with Thee Desperadoes, but I suppose he could always go on *X-Factor* or get spotted and become a model. You have to admit, Shuv, he is really fit. Proper foxy.'

Siobhan would admit no such thing but she let me have a shot of Baileys in my coffee so I couldn't hate on her too much.

'You have to come down to Manchester for the weekend once you've rocked your retakes,' she said when we were driving back to Merrycliffe. We never went into the real reason why I had to retake them, though I was sure Siobhan had figured it out. The thing with our family is that there's stuff that we never really talk about. It was there and everyone knew it was there, but talking about it would make it real and something that had to be dealt with and so it was always left unsaid.

We left it unsaid this time too. Instead we talked about the boys in Manchester. Siobhan said that some of them even described themselves as feminists though I wasn't really sure I wanted a boy like that.

The boy I wanted was Louis and Dora had texted me late on Saturday night to report that although there had been no grinding, there had definitely been some low-level flirting. Ur m8 tosses her hair back a lot, doesn't she?

It was one of Alice's signature moves, along with licking her lips and staring at a boy's mouth like she hadn't had a square meal in months. There was also the running of her hands down her body in this absent-minded way that drew attention to what Alice called her three B's, 'boobs, belly and bootie'.

How could I compete with Alice's three B's when the only B's I had were my 32B's? Now it was Sunday lunchtime and Alice hadn't responded to any of my texts from Sunday lunch at the Brewer's Fayre. Whenever Shuv did come home for the weekend, all of us – Mum, Dad, older sister Anna, her husband Steven, Jayden and Aiden, the nephews from hell – would gather to eat lots of meat.

Jayden and Aiden spent most of their time hitting each other over the head in the kids' playzone, Mum kept getting out her hand sanitiser and Siobhan pulled such awful faces at me every time Anna or Steven spoke that I was worried she was going to dislocate something. Quite frankly, I'd had better Sundays.

Much better Sundays. The reason Alice had gone silent on me became obvious when I got home. There on my computer, on Twitter, were Alice and Louis flirting up a storm.

@LouisDesperado Great hanging out last night wit U :D That thing with your tongue. Rude!

@WorstGirlfriendInTheWorld U loved it! (Ur Twitter name 2 long but is it fair warning?)

@LouisDesperado U better believe it hun! U man enough to take me on?

@WorstGirlfriendInTheWorld Babe, can write backwards on windows with my tongue. Can easily handle U!

I was appalled! Fucking appalled. The war was already won and I was yet to fight a single battle. God, I was thinking in war lingo again.

I didn't even follow Louis on Twitter (though I Twitter stalked him) and the Facebook friend request had been traumatic enough, but I leapt straight in without even looking to see where I was going to land.

@LouisDesperado @WorstGirlfriendInTheWorld That's nothing. I can make my elbows go back to front.

Inevitably, there was silence. I'd killed the conversation stone dead. At least I'd managed that, but maybe they'd moved to direct messaging instead. Arranging to meet. Exchanging rude pics. Even though the rules clearly stated that private messages were forbidden. Oh God . . .

@FrannyB Yo! Franny! Where U at last nite? Hope U weren't seeing another band??!!!!!!!

I genuinely had to shove my head between my knees because I thought I was going to pass out. Louis had just tweeted me. Like he knew me. And not only did he know who I was but he'd noticed that I wasn't at The Wow. OK, he used a lot of unnecessary exclamation marks but like *that* was a dealbreaker.

@LouisDesperado Went to dinner in Lytham with my sister. (That didn't sound cool, even though Siobhan was one of Merrycliffe's coolest exports. I thought for a second.) Shuv says hi by the way.

Just as I was known as Franny B, it was Siobhan's lot in life to be called Shuv by everyone who knew her.

Louis had just replied (@FrannyB OMFG every1 @ skool was in luv wit Shuv. She still hot?) when Alice rang.

'That is really rude,' she said as soon as I answered. 'Like, to just take over someone else's Twitter conversation.'

'I tweeted both of you and it's a public forum,' I said defensively. 'Anyway, so how was it last night?'

'Oh, it was fine. It was The Wow. Nothing new to report.'

Nothing new except Alice flirting up a storm with Louis. 'Right, so did you ... I mean, how ... You didn't hook up with him, did you?'

'No! I just hung out with him a little bit.' I heard her sigh. 'There wasn't really anyone else to hang out with, apart from your friend Cora ...'

'Dora.'

'Yeah, whatevs. Anyway, I hung out with Louis for fifteen minutes tops, then Thee Desperadettes descended and your namesake, that Francis boy, said that it was time that Louis finally got a round in and he went to the bar and that was the last I saw of him.' Alice sighed again. 'I missed you. There was no one I could laugh about Mark the mad dancer with.'

I felt better on so many counts. 'Promise I won't be a no-show next week. Then the week after that it's the Halloween party. I wouldn't miss that for the world.'

'No way! Highlight of the Merrycliffe social season. Actually I wanted to talk to you about that ... about my costume.'

'Right. Well, I got some slinky silver material for my dress; it's almost rubbery and I've done a Google Image Search and

I was thinking I'd make you a floor-length black dress with a slit up the side like—'

'Well, yeah, that's the thing, I'm not really sure that I want to go as Audrey Hepburn in *Breakfast at Tiffany's*, it's kind of random.'

'No, it's not! It's an iconic look with the beehive and the two blonde streaks and I'm going to make you a long cigarette holder,' I reminded her. 'We agreed this ages ago. We were dressing up as two sixties superstars; you as Audrey Hepburn, me as Edie Sedgwick.'

'Look, Franny, I get your whole Edie thing but nobody knows who she is and nobody knows who Audrey Hepburn is either. I only know who she is because you've made me watch *Breakfast at Tiffany's* about a gazillion times. Besides, that dress is going to be really difficult to dance in ...'

'I just said that it would have a slit in it!'

'... I could have someone's eye out with a cigarette holder. I know you're busy with college and stuff so I'll sort out my costume.' Alice finished in a breathless rush like she'd been steeling herself to have this conversation with me. Like I was going to take it badly.

'For God's sakes, Ally! We always do a themed double act for Halloween. Always!'

'When we were six and thought it was cool to dress up as Elizabeth the first and Queen Victoria, but we're not six any more. I'll wear something slinky and black, buy one of those hair bands with ears attached, paint whiskers on my face and go as a cat. A sexy cat. Job done.'

'You know how I feel about those non-costumes that are just an excuse to look sexy.'

'That's how *you* feel, Franny,' Alice sniffed. 'I don't think there's anything wrong with looking sexy.'

'Well, I'm not going to go as Edie then,' I said, though every fibre of my being yearned to go as Edie. 'One sixties superstar on her own is just going to look weird.'

'Oh, you should totally go as Edie – or go as Twiggy. More people know who she is. Oooh! A zombie Twiggy!' Alice suggested. 'Let me make this up to you by cutting your hair. You've been talking about having an urchin crop for ages and it would look wicked with your cheekbones.'

'I don't think I'm ready for such a drastic step,' I protested, craning my neck to see my hair in my dressing-table mirror. It wasn't doing anything much – just sitting on my head in a limp kind of way. Cutting it would be edgy and hipster-ish. Might even make some people realise that I was different to all the other girls. 'You know what? I'll think about it.'

Normally Alice and I hung out on a Sunday afternoon to watch one of the six films we always watched and work our way through a mound of crisps and chocolate. But I'd had a big lunch and Alice said that she still had an essay to finish, so I wound up on my own late Sunday afternoon with that back-to-school feeling even though I didn't go to school any more.

After I'd said goodbye to Shuv who was getting a lift to the station from Dad, I could have worked on my Halloween costume but my heart wasn't in it now. Without Alice at my side to gee me up, I wasn't sure I had the guts to walk into The Wow dressed as Edie. Not when it involved spraying my hair silver and wearing a dress that was really a T-shirt.

Gloom was settling around me like a bad smell as I checked Twitter to see if Alice and Louis had gone back to flirting with each other so my misery would know no bounds, and then I saw that Louis was now following me.

He was following me. I wasn't following him.

Repeat, Louis was following me.

I quickly followed him back and before I knew it, Sunday evening flew by as I LOL'ed his tweets and then when Louis tweeted a pic of a cat wearing sunglasses, I spent long minutes searching for the perfect picture of another cat wearing sunglasses so I could tweet it to him.

@FrannyB Yeaahhhhh! Nice 1, he tweeted back and I should have been pleased at Louis's acknowledgement of my mad Google-fu skillz, but I was still too pissed off with Alice to care that much.

14

I was the only fashion student in on Monday mornings as I had a Maths catch-up lesson at nine-thirty, which was cruel and unnecessary.

At least my tutor said that short of not turning up for the retake or completely forgetting about Pythagoras and his freaking theorem, I was guaranteed a grade C or higher.

By eleven-thirty, I was done with Pythagoras but instead of hanging out in the canteen by myself, I slipped into the work-room to spend a couple of hours on my grey leather dress.

I had my pattern pieces laid out but before I cut into my leather, which I didn't have enough of to make any mistakes, I wanted to do a test run using muslin first – what we fashion peeps called a toile.

As soon as my pinking shears cut into the fabric with a satisfying crunchy sound, nothing else mattered. I was calm. I was centred. I knew exactly what I was doing. Any problems were technical problems I could figure out by poking around on internet dressmaking forums.

Time slipped away. It was only when I looked up from my sewing machine and stretched my hunched muscles that I realised it was lunchtime. Just as I thought it, I saw someone hurry past the half-open door.

It seemed much easier in films to follow people but at least Francis had his head down as he hurried through the college grounds. Once we were out on the street, he kept to the same fast pace and didn't even pause to check out the fashions in the really hideous gentlemen's outfitters, which hadn't changed its window display since God was a boy, or the attractive array of plastic crap outside the newly opened 59p shop.

Francis stopped outside the Chicken Hut, the closest Merrycliffe will ever come to having a Nando's, and I blessed the gut instinct that had made me follow him because there was Louis slumped over one of the tables. Francis tapped on the window. Louis sat up, grinned and waved.

I felt as calm as I had when I was cutting out my muslin. This felt right. If it felt right, then it couldn't be wrong. Francis was now inside the Chicken Hut and before I could talk myself out of it, I took a huge breath and didn't let it out until I'd walked the ten metres to the door and opened it.

Louis was eating barbecue wings. He looked foxy even with a little barbecue sauce round his mouth. It was the incentive I needed to walk over to them with a look of feigned surprise that

I was sure Francis wasn't buying for a second. His top lip was starting to curl again.

I should have thought this out better because all I could think of to say was, 'Fancy meeting you here,' but before I could get the words out, Louis looked up, caught my eye and smiled. 'Hey! Franny B! Never seen you in the Hut before,' he said.

That was because I'd shunned the Hut since the time Siobhan had come here in Year 11 and spent the rest of the week with either food poisoning or the vomiting bug. We'd never known which. 'Oh, I was just passing,' I said vaguely. 'Thought I'd pop in and say hello.'

'Hello,' Francis said flatly. He folded his arms. I didn't know him very well but I did know that sneering and folding his arms were two of his favourite things in the world.

I decided it was best to ignore him, but not in a hostile way because he was still Louis's mate. So I smiled briefly at him and turned my attention to Louis, who was wiping the barbecue sauce from around his mouth with the back of his hand.

'Sit down. Have a fry,' he said. I gingerly took a small fry from the bag he was offering and held it near my mouth to show willing. 'Weird, isn't it? Like we hardly ever talk, then we're Twittering it up yesterday. Now it's like we've known each other for ever.'

'Yeah, it's strange, but like good strange.' Of course, I already knew loads of things about Louis from years of admiring him from afar – it was hard to admire someone from afar and not get a bit stalker-y – but I couldn't tell him that because he'd take out a restraining order. And really, he didn't know that much about me, except he thought that I liked pictures of cats wearing sunglasses when I wasn't that much of a cat person.

Francis had gone to the counter to order some chicken dish that probably came with a side of salmonella and Louis seemed quite happy for me to stay, so I perched uncomfortably on the edge of the plastic chair. I didn't want to make myself too comfortable because as soon as I sensed that I'd outstayed my welcome, I'd need to make a speedy getaway.

But it turned out that Louis was really easy to talk to. He kept up a constant stream of chatter and when Francis came back to the table with a chicken burger, Louis was listing all the really gross things *in* a Chicken Hut chicken burger.

Francis sat down next to Louis, shook his head and took a decisive bite of his burger. 'You don't want to do that, man,' Louis told him. 'They get the chickens, take off all the nice bits and give them to Waitrose, then they take everything that's left and shove it in a mincer. Like, *everything*. Nipples, eyelashes, toenails, testicles . . .'

'Louis, chickens don't have testicles,' Francis said mildly and I'd just been thinking that myself and I couldn't help but smile. Francis smiled back.

It looked weird on his face, like he mostly used it for sneering. 'I don't think chickens have nipples either,' I said and I didn't even blush . . . much. 'But I've never got that close to one to be able to know for definite.'

'Still, reckon that burgers have got chicken toenails in them . . .'

'They have claws, dickhead.'

'. . . and hair and teeth,' Louis insisted quite happily. He was one of those people who didn't seem to ever take offence. 'You start growing extra nipples you're out of the band, laughing boy.'

'How will I ever get over that crushing blow.' Francis shook his head again and carried on eating his burger, while Louis told me that Francis had been kicked out of the band when he'd got a place at an art college in London and they wouldn't let him rejoin when he came back after a year until he really grovelled.

'I don't remember grovelling. I do remember you begging me to join again because the new guitarist only knew two chords and I know three.'

'You came back to Merrycliffe after escaping to London?' I heard myself ask in scandalised tones. 'Christ, I would never come back here if I made it to London. Never. Not even for public holidays.'

'Yeah, I thought that too but here I am,' Francis said. He looked pretty gutted about it. I couldn't blame him. I was dying to know why he'd come back, but it was probably because he'd been kicked out of art college so I didn't want to pursue it. 'You have been to London though, haven't you?' Francis asked me. 'To see the Christmas lights or on a school trip or something?'

I could have bluffed but Francis had lived in London so he'd know that I was lying. 'Nope. Barely made it south of Manchester,' I admitted sadly.

'We can't have that,' Louis exclaimed and now that I wasn't

simply admiring him from afar, he was even better than I'd ever imagined. Friendly and funny and not at all up himself. 'We're playing a gig in London in November. In Camden!'

'Camden,' I echoed a little wistfully. 'I'd love to go to Camden. And Hoxton and Shoreditch and Selfridges and Liberty to buy fabric.'

'We're hiring a minibus to take us down. There'll be room for you if you fancy it,' Louis said casually. He didn't seem to realise he was offering me the keys to the kingdom. Louis and London. Louis in London. Me and Louis in bloody London. 'You just have to chip in a tenner for petrol.'

'Really? Are you sure? Is this some kind of elaborate piss-take?'

'No!' Louis looked quite hurt at the suggestion. 'Franny can come up to that fancy London gig with us, right, Francis?'

Even Francis didn't look too horrified at the thought. He did look a little put-upon, but I was starting to think that was just how he looked when he wasn't sneering. 'Yeah, sure, come. Just promise you won't drink too much, then get a kebab from a dodgy place in Archway on the way home and throw up all over the minibus like Louis's done twice.'

'I would never do that! I hate kebabs!' I said and they both grinned and I was in. I was *so* in.

I floated back to college on a little cloud made of euphoria and stardust. Then, as if the day couldn't get any better, Barbara praised my hard morning's work and was really impressed that I was mocking up my design on a toile first. The others all glared at me.

'Teacher's pet,' Matthew hissed when Barbara was busy berating Krystal with a K, who'd managed to get fake tan on the pink velour she'd insisted on buying. 'How did you even know what a toile was?'

'I illegally download episodes of *Project Runway*,' I whispered back and Sage said that she did too and as we worked, we talked about the last season and a designer we'd both particularly hated and loved in equal measure. And all the time I was thinking about Louis and going to London and the only little black spot was that I really wanted to tell Alice about it.

Not in a gloating way but because I was used to telling her everything and it used to be that we cheered each other's good times and helped each other through the bad times. And also, I kind of wanted Alice to come to London in Thee Desperadoes' minibus because she would automatically make it ten times more fun.

15

Because I felt so guilty about not telling Alice I'd hung out with Louis, I agreed to let her cut my hair.

I hadn't been going to. I still wasn't convinced that I had the bone structure or the balls for an urchin crop, and an urchin crop wasn't necessary since I'd decided not to dress up as Edie Sedgwick for The Wow's Halloween party. I was going to do what everyone else did: wear what I'd normally wear and shove a witch's hat on top.

Then Sage found my rubbery silver T-shirt dress scrunched in a heap on my work table when I said she could borrow my tape measure. 'What's this?' she asked, holding it up. 'One of your seams is puckered.'

'It's hard not to pucker stretch material,' I said, barely glancing at my abandoned dress. 'It was part of my Halloween costume. I was going to go as Edie Sedgwick, but now I'm not.'

'Oh, that druggy heiress who used to hang out with Andy Warhol?'

I promptly stabbed myself in the finger with a pin. 'Ow! Wait! You know who Edie is? How do you know who Edie is? No one ever, ever does!'

Sage blinked. 'I saw that film about her with Sienna Miller, *Factory Girl*. It was amazing. She was gorgeous but so doomed ...'

'I know! Like, the world should have been hers but she was surrounded by people who fed off her beauty ...'

'Right! I read this book about her after I'd seen the film,' Sage said and I was all set to bombard her with a thousand questions but then Paul stuck his hand up and asked who Edie was.

Nobody could ever ask me who Edie was and expect me to give them a brief one-sentence reply. I had to stop what I was doing and give Paul Edie's potted biography and make hand gestures as I said things like, 'And then after she'd come out of the menty hospital before she went to live in New York and became an artist, she went to this clinic where she *literally* had her legs pummelled into shape. *Literally*.'

Sage pulled up some pictures of Edie on her iPad, then she found a YouTube clip of Edie that I'd never seen before. We watched Edie and Andy Warhol appearing on a sixties American chat show – him refusing to speak because he was too cool and Edie being funny and charming and it must have been the most inspiring thing you'd ever seen if you were stuck in a small boring house in a small boring suburb – it would have totally made you want to move to New York and become an artist too.

The way I felt about Edie, the way she moved and fascinated me, was the feeling that I wanted people to have when they wore my clothes, and then I really wished I was still going as Edie for Halloween.

'You so should,' Sage said when I told her. She looked round the workroom. 'Hey, Mattie, do you fancy dressing up as Andy Warhol for Halloween?'

I clasped my hands to my heart. 'Oh, please say that you will.'

Dora was busy scrolling through photos of Edie and Andy and the other 'Superstars' who'd hung out at Andy's studio, the Factory. 'I've been really stuck for a Halloween costume.' She gestured at her black crinoline. 'It's hard when you wear ball-gowns on a daily basis to up your game for Halloween, but I'd quite like to dress up as this Ultra Violet woman. I might even dye my hair purple.'

Then Sage said that if we were all going, she'd skip spending the weekend in Leeds with her dad and come to The Wow's Halloween party. 'I'll go as Nico from the Velvet Underground,' she decided. 'If anyone says a black girl can't be a blonde German then I pity them. I'm going to rock the hell out of a white trouser suit and wear a blonde wig and a big hat.'

Obviously Paul didn't want to be left out so he said he'd dress up as Lou Reed, the Velvet's lead singer, and being part of a gang all with a common Halloween theme was so much cooler than wearing a witch's hat and being done with it.

But if I was going to do Edie justice then I had to cut my hair. When I texted Alice to ask if she was up to the job, she texted back, YES! YES! 1000xYES! Best news I've had all week! YAY!!!!!!!! Cutting my hair would also make Alice happy, which was good, because stuff between us wasn't as great as it could have been.

'You won't regret this,' she promised when I turned up at her dad's salon on Friday afternoon. She pulled me through the salon, which had black walls and floor and these cream-coloured, French-chateau-style chairs and cabinets. It was very cutting edge for Merrycliffe. All the girls who worked there wore black too. They looked up from highlighting and blow-dries and manicures and smiled as Alice hurried me past them. 'Now I know it's an Edie look but I've also got these pictures of Carey Mulligan in *Vogue* so I've got something really detailed to work with.'

I didn't want to look like Carey Mulligan even on the front cover of *Vogue*, but I nodded as I waited by the sinks while Alice wrapped me in a huge black robe. 'Just remember to keep it long and messy in the front, OK?'

'You got it,' Alice said brightly. Then she cracked her knuckles like she was about to have a fight, which worried me a lot, but soon I was leaning back against a basin while she washed my hair and gave me a head message as she worked the conditioner through. 'Your head actually has all these pressure points that relate to different parts of your body.' Alice sounded like she was reading from a textbook.

'Oh really? I thought that was your feet,' I said.

'It's your head too,' she said firmly as she kneaded her fingertips against my temples, then made circular motions towards the crown of my head. It felt amazing. 'I forgot to ask, was the water too hot?'

'It was perfect.' In fact, it was probably the best hairwashing I'd ever had.

Alice did the hairdresser thing of carefully arranging a towel around my wet hair instead of making a turban like you'd do at home, then led me to a screened-off area, away from the hair-spray-scented hustle and bustle of the salon. I saw her dad, Sean, busy with his scissors but before I could wave, Alice yanked me behind the screen and pushed me into the chair.

'I thought we'd be more private here and we can have some of this, like my dad's favourite clients.' This was a bottle of Prosecco chilling in an ice bucket along with two glasses.

I was completely down with drinking some really posh sparkling wine, but I wasn't sure that I wanted Alice going anywhere near alcohol when she was meant to be cutting my hair. After all, she refused to drink booze when she was doing her nails 'cause it made her brushwork go wonky. 'Maybe you should wait until we've finished,' I started to say, but Alice had already downed a glass of Prosecco in one.

'Don't you trust me?' she asked in a hurt voice, as she finally handed me my glass. 'I'm not going to make you look anything less than gorgeous.'

Alice seemed really jumpy and kept picking up a pair of scissors and then putting them down again. But I wanted things to be right between us, even though I still hadn't told her that

I'd been hanging out with Louis. I also wanted to differentiate myself from her and Thee Desperadettes by embracing my edginess. And I really needed to get in touch with my inner Edie, leech a little of her cool and daring – well, when she wasn't having nervos and doing a shedload of drugs.

'OK, let's do this!'

'OK!' Alice picked up a wide-toothed comb and ran it through my damp hair, then she gathered it into a loose ponytail and secured it with a scrunchie. 'You ready, Franny?'

'I'm ready!'

'Here goes!' She picked up the scissors and cut my ponytail right off!

'Christ, some warning would have been nice!' I cried as I jerked my head, which wasn't very clever when Alice was still holding the scissors and nearly sliced into my ear.

'Don't panic. That's how we always start,' Alice soothed me. 'Have another drink.'

It didn't help that I was facing away from the mirror as Alice combed, then cut, then looked at me with her face screwed up either in concentration or consternation – it was hard to tell which.

We talked about *Strictly Come Dancing* and I moaned about Mr Chatterjee, who'd told me off for chewing gum while I was stuck in the window doing alterations because I was 'an ambassador for the shop'. And Alice talked about school and how one of the Year 13s was definitely pregnant but everyone was too embarrassed to come right out and ask her.

It was as if we'd both decided that the topic of Louis was out of bounds but as Alice carried on cutting – lots of little snips now, much combing and a lot of frowning – she got quieter and I talked more and more to cover up what was turning into a tense silence.

I found myself telling her that I was now going to The Wow Halloween as part of a themed group of Warhol acolytes. 'I'd have been happy just to have Mattie come with me as Andy Warhol but the others decided they wanted in too.'

Alice's frown became even more ferocious. 'I thought we were going together. We *always* go together.'

'We are. We will. But they're coming along too. Sage is really cool now we've got over that business with the dress. You'll love her.'

'Great. Everyone will know that you lot are a group and I'll be stuck on my own,' Alice complained, as the combing and the cutting speeded up. 'They'll think I'm totally lame.'

I'd been so excited at the thought of recreating the Factory at The Wow and bonding with Sage over Edie that I hadn't spent even one minute thinking about how it might make Alice feel. Now I did think about it and I knew that if she'd suddenly become best mates with Ash and Vicky and wanted to go to the Halloween party as Destiny's Child or Charlie's Angels, I'd have been jealous and felt left out and rejected too.

This whole *thing* with Louis had started because Alice got in a strop that I was hanging with Dora and I needed to be a bit more sensitive about Alice's feelings. Especially when she was currently armed with a pair of very sharp scissors.

'Nobody could ever think you were lame. Everyone knows

we're best mates and we're going to have a great time tomorrow night. It's Halloween! We love Halloween! And it's still not too late to go with the whole Factory thing we're doing. You could come as, um, well, like Ingrid Superstar?'

'Who the hell is Ingrid Superstar?' Alice demanded and she did have a point. Despite her name, Ingrid Superstar was the most forgettable of the Warhol Superstars. Sage had already bagsied Nico so only Brigid Berlin was left, which meant Alice would have to wear a fat suit. 'Jesus!'

'I'm sure there's someone else you could go as. Lots of famous people hung out at the Factory all the time. I'll Google it in a minute. Please calm down.' I wasn't very calm myself. I was trying to see things from Alice's point of view but I was a little fed up with Alice getting hissy every time I dared to mention college – and she'd been cutting my hair for ever and now my head felt suspiciously light. 'Are you done yet? Can I see?'

'No!' It was a scream. 'Don't touch it!' Alice slapped my hand, which had crept up to assess my new do. 'Just don't fucking touch it, OK?'

'Language!' Sean, Alice's dad, poked his head round the screen. 'What's going on in here?'

'Nothing,' Alice said and she actually hid the scissors behind her back, which made shivers run up and down my spine. Not the good shivers. The very, very bad shivers.

'Alice is meant to be giving me a sixties urchin crop.' My voice was perilously high. 'That's the plan anyway.'

'Shut up,' Alice hissed at me. She cleared her throat. 'We're just hanging out. I pinched some Prosecco. Hope that's OK.'

It was obvious that we were not just hanging out. There was a huge pile of my hair on the floor and from the horrified look on Sean's face there was not a sixties urchin crop on my head.

'What the hell do you think you're doing?' he boomed at Alice. Usually Sean was affable and chuckly and the coolest of dads but as he marched over to us, red-faced, eyes actually bulging, he didn't seem so cool any more. 'You're not even allowed to blow-dry without supervision!'

I put my hands to my head. I had no hair! What had she done?

I jumped up from the chair and whirled round so fast that I nearly tripped over. 'Easy there, Franny.' Sean took hold of my arm. 'We'll fix this.'

'It doesn't look so bad,' Alice said, but she looked like she was about to throw up. I tore myself out of Sean's grasp so I could go crashing through the screens and race to the nearest mirror.

I burst into tears. I went from not crying to full-on weeping with added snot in the one second it took to assess the damage. Boy, was there damage.

My hair was short. Really short. About as short as you can go without using clippers and instead of leaving it long and messy at the front as I'd asked her to about a gazillion times, Alice had left me with one forlorn strand of hair. I don't know how, I don't know why but Alice had given me a comb-over, like how baldy old men drape their one good piece of hair over their scalps and hope it will fool the world.

'I'm sorry, Franny,' Alice said, her hands on her face like she wanted to shield herself from the horrific vision she'd created. 'Your hair is really weird. It doesn't lie flat.'

'My hair? Weird? You ...' I couldn't speak in sentences, only sob out the odd word. Sean marched out from behind the screen holding my sodden ponytail.

'You are in a whole world of trouble!' he barked. Alice shrank back. 'Look what you've done to her! What were you thinking? Your mum will be here in five minutes to pick up the books. She's going to kill you.'

That was when Alice burst into tears. Not because she'd butchered my hair, but at the prospect of her mum getting all wrathful on her arse. If Sean was normally a lovely teddy bear of a man, then Tania was a Rottweiler.

'I'm sorry,' she sobbed to Sean. By now Chloë, Sean's senior stylist, had come over and was staring at the back of my head.

'I think I can see a bald spot,' she said in a loud stage whisper.

'You did this on purpose!' I would have shouted but I was crying too hard. 'You did this to sabotage me with Louis.'

'No, I didn't ...'

'And because I dared to maybe make some new friends.'

'That's not true ...' Alice was wringing her hands now. Her face was red and wet and distorted. I'd never seen her look so ugly.

'Well, you know what? I'm going to take my new friends and keep as far away from you as possible. I never want to see or speak to you again,' I spat and only then did I let Chloë and Sean guide me back into the chair.

It was another hour before I left the salon. I had to give up my dreams of having Edie hair and go for what Sean called a Mia Farrow. Chloë showed me pictures of a blonde actress from a sixties film called *Rosemary's Baby*, who'd had very, very short hair with a very, very short fringe but she was gamine and beautiful and had adorable freckles and eyelashes. I didn't have adorable anything. I just had a bald spot and a comb over.

Tania had arrived halfway through, stood in the doorway and said nothing. She'd simply watched as I cried in the chair while all Sean's stylists gathered around and told me not to cry, and as Alice wept as she swept up the hair she'd cut even though it turned out that she'd never, ever, not once, cut anyone's hair before.

'What's been going on?' Tania had eventually asked and even when she shouted at Alice and grounded her until she was eighteen, it didn't make me feel better.

Neither did the complimentary silver gel nails and the eyebrow threading or Chloë telling me to come back for free eyelash extensions. They couldn't do them then because I was still crying and Chloë said they wouldn't take.

By the time I got home, the wind viciously whipping against my exposed neck and ears, I was exhausted. Emotionally drained. It was all I could do to drag my feet up our path and lift my arm to put my key in the lock.

Mum was coming down the hall as I stepped through the

front door. 'I'm going to bed,' she said defensively before I'd even opened my mouth. 'I'm really tired, OK?'

It was then I remembered that Dad had an overnight job delivering some slate tiles to Cornwall. With him out of the house, obviously Mum had decided that she could take a break from pretending to be a fully functioning adult.

Not for the first time, I wished that she'd be my mum. Be a mum. Stop being so colossally self-involved and concerned with how she was feeling so that she could notice how *I* was feeling. That my eyes were red and swollen because I'd been crying for hours and that I actually had very little hair and what hair I did have was now what Sean and Chloë kept calling a pixie cut but looked more like that Katy Perry video where she joins the army and they razor off her hair.

I couldn't help it. I started to cry again and she sighed. Not a sympathetic sigh, but an impatient sigh like she didn't have time for my tears when she was holding it together just long enough to get up the stairs and shut herself in her bedroom.

'What's the matter?' she asked in a tired voice.

'Look what Alice did to me! Look at my bloody hair!' As I sobbed, I realised that it wasn't just about my hair; it was about me and Alice.

When she'd picked up those scissors and started cutting, she'd cut into our friendship too. Yeah, my hair would grow back eventually (and eventually was going to take a long, long time to come) but I wasn't sure if Alice and I would grow back. Or if I even wanted us to.

I couldn't begin to explain that to Mum, not when she already had her foot on the bottom stair and was giving me a long, hard look.

'Jesus, Franny,' she said in the flat, resigned voice that I hadn't heard for a couple of weeks and really hadn't missed. 'If a bad haircut is all you've got to cry about then you're a really lucky girl.'

16

My plan was to never leave the house ever again. Except morning rolled round as it always did and I had no choice but to go to work.

The only hat I could find was a red and blue knitted number with a bobble on, but there was no contest between wearing a stupid hat and having stupid hair.

It was very hard to sit at my sewing machine and not spill tears over a pile of shirts that needed buttons sewn on. Only the fact that I was sitting in the window and Rajesh was working that day (Mr and Mrs Chatterjee had gone to a wedding and he'd threatened to leave home if he had to spend all weekend at his auntie's house in Walsall) kept me dry-eyed.

Raj spent two hours trying to get me to lose the hat. Even made me coffee though I would've sworn he didn't know how to operate a kettle, but I refused to take it off, even though dry-cleaning shops are hot, stuffy places and I was tempting heat-stroke by lunchtime.

I did tell him why I was wearing a hat and if misery loved company then Raj was the perfect companion for someone who never wanted anything to do with Alice Jenkins ever again.

'She's a bitch, innit,' he said when I'd finished my sorry tale of hair loss and betrayal.

'Total bitch,' I agreed. I didn't feel a single pang of disloyalty. Not one.

'Is one thing to break someone's heart, but to do that to her best friend's hair is not right.' Raj was meant to be putting dry-cleaned clothes in plastic garment bags but he was too busy shaking his head. Actually there was something I'd always wondered but never asked about before, and now I didn't owe Alice one itty bitty little morsel of girl solidarity.

'So, Raj, was it you who wrote *Alice Jenkins Is The Worst Girlfriend In The World* in the Burger King loos?'

He pulled down his baseball cap so I couldn't see his eyes. 'Like I'd give her that satisfaction,' he mumbled. Then he became very interested in getting busy with the garment bags and I kind of had my answer. One thing to call out your ex-girlfriend, quite another for your ex-girlfriend to adopt it as her Twitter bio and get her best friend to spell it out in sequins on a T-shirt because she was so proud of the accolade. 'Anyway, you're better off without her, Franny, 'cause girl you fly and she be dragging you down, yo.'

I did feel dragged down, like I was in a hole that I couldn't climb out from. I now had some understanding of why my mum took to her bed so frequently. That was where I was heading as soon as I got home. There was no way I was going to The Wow Halloween party, even though theoretically with Alice grounded I had free access to Louis all night. I was deluding myself if I ever thought he'd go for me, not when he had Thee Desperadettes as his own personal entourage and I had my shit hair.

Sorry 2 let U down but not coming out 2nite, I texted Dora and Sage.

I refused to be drawn on the details of my no-show. They'd find out on Monday, if I decided to get out of bed and go to college and if I decided to forgo my woolly hat, which was highly unlikely.

I was all set for a top night moping under my duvet. I had *Steel Magnolias* and *Beaches* on the Sky planner because Mum watched them over and over again. I had loads of corn-based snacks and Polish chocolate from the 59p shop and I had a bottle of Lambrini that had been at the back of the fridge since last Christmas.

Even my mum had realised the Halloween party was kind of a big deal and expressed surprise that I wasn't going. 'I think I'm coming down with something,' I insisted when she and Dad, who'd got in from Cornwall at the same time as I arrived home, wanted to know why I wasn't heading straight for the bathroom. Normally I needed at least three hours' prep to get ready for a Saturday night.

Going to bed yesterday had obviously done her a world of good because she even put a hand on my forehead to check my

164

temperature in a maternal gesture, which didn't come naturally to her. 'You do feel a bit hot but that's no surprise if you will wear that hat indoors.' She folded her arms and tried to look sympathetic. 'Tania called and told me what happened at the salon yesterday. Said to give her a ring and fix a time to come in for the eyelash extensions.'

'I'm *never* setting foot in that place ever again,' I muttered.

Dad, who was watching the football highlights in the lounge, shouted, 'It's only hair, kid. You'll look back on this in a couple of years and laugh about it.' That only went to show how little he understood.

'Have you spoken to Alice?' Mum asked and I hadn't because after I'd been getting texts from her every five minutes saying that she was sorry and wanted to make it up to me, Raj had shown me how to download this app so I could block her number from my BlackBerry.

'No! Stop asking me questions. I don't feel well. I'm going to bed. I'm not home if anyone calls or comes round,' I snapped and Dad told me not to use that tone of voice but whatever, I was halfway up the stairs by then.

I was lying on my bed in my leopard-print onesie watching *Beaches* and not even able to choke down any corn-based snacks when there was a gentle tap at the door.

'I told you that I didn't want to be disturbed,' I bellowed, not that either of my parents ever listened to a single word that came out of my mouth, because the door slowly opened and then, to my horror, Sage and Dora were in my room.

Corn-based snacks flew everywhere as I yanked the quilt over my bare head. 'What the hell! Get out!'

'I'm not getting out,' Sage said. 'And you are not bailing on us. Have you any idea how much my new blonde wig cost me?'

I did feel a bit guilty about that but not enough to come out from under my duvet. I was also embarrassed that I had a Cath Kidston-style duvet cover that wasn't actually Cath Kidston but a poor imitation from BHS.

'Oh come on, Franny B. We have vodka and a choice of mixers and I bought the silver spray we talked about,' Dora said cajolingly. 'Your mum said you had hair issues but once you've got a metric arse ton of silver spray on it, who's going to notice?'

Dora had a point, but mostly she had vodka. 'It looks awful. I have a bald spot.'

They both pretended they couldn't hear me with my voice muffled by the duvet and I knew for certain that Sage would drag me bodily out of bed. I took a deep sigh and shucked off the duvet. 'Honestly, would you want to go out in public with this?' I pointed at my head.

To their credit, neither of them pretended that I was making a fuss about nothing.

'That Alice girl did this to you?' Sage asked and she pulled a face that encapsulated exactly what she thought of that Alice girl and it wasn't anything good. 'You need to get some new friends.'

'You *have* got a bald spot,' Dora announced sympathetically. 'But it doesn't look so bad from the front. You look gamine.'

'I'm meant to look like Mia Farrow,' I told them. 'I Googled her. She married two really old blokes and adopted loads of kids from different countries way before Angelina Jolie did.'

'You have cheekbones. When you have cheekbones you can get away with anything,' Sage said, peering critically at my face. 'And you've had your eyebrows done and they look amazing. When my mum gets her eyebrows done, she says it's as good as having a facelift.'

They coaxed and flattered and bullied me in an effort to get me out of bed. 'Between the four of us we've spent loads of time and money getting our outfits together and so you have to stop being so lame.'

By then I was almost at the end of my first vodka and Red Bull and the world was looking like a slightly better place, but only slightly better. Sage drew herself up so she was suddenly taller and fiercer and pointed a finger at the leopard-print one-sied heap that was me. 'It's at times like this that you have to ask yourself what would Edie Sedgwick have done if she'd suffered some kind of style malfunction,' she said sternly.

'If it was later Edie, she'd have done a huge amount of drugs and attempted suicide,' I said grumpily because this was not the time to summon the spirit of Edie.

'Yeah, and if it was early Edie, she'd have styled it out big-time,' Sage rapped back. 'Like, like ... like that time she broke her leg and she went clubbing with a whopping great plaster cast and crutches and took to the dance floor and worked it.'

'Really? Did she?' Dora looked very impressed. 'She sounds awesome. I need to Google her.'

'I'll lend you my Edie biography as long as you promise to give it back,' I told her.

Sage was right. Edie wouldn't moulder in bed because of a bad haircut. I was behaving more like my mother and that could never, ever happen. I jumped off my bed. 'Right. OK. I'm up. Let's make this happen.'

We made it happen. I showered and got dressed in the stretchy silver T-shirt dress I'd made, black opaque tights and the kitten heels I'd bought in Morecambe, which I'd spray-painted silver.

Then while Dora was working on my hair, adding mousse to make it look thicker and give it texture then applying the silver spray, Sage helped me with my make-up. We painted two thick stripes of black eyeliner over each eye and then applied not one set of false eyelashes, but two. I felt like I needed a hoist to blink because my eyelids were so weighed down, but I was happy to suffer when my eyes looked so fantastic.

Staring back at me from the mirror was a slinky silver sprite of a girl who'd stepped from another time and place. I looked like I should be frozen and photographed in black and white and pinned to a Pinterest board. I was the past and the future and actually, yeah, maybe I needed to go easy on the vodka and Red Bull.

'Well, I think I'll do,' I said, stepping back from the mirror. 'Thanks for helping me out and you two ... you're looking pretty fine, ladies.'

Sage was wearing a tight white trouser suit, black shirt and black fedora over a long blonde wig with a fringe. She could have stepped out of the pages of a 1969 edition of US *Vogue* and Dora, well, she didn't look much like Ultra Violet, she just looked like a more purply version of herself but she'd made the effort.

I knew then that Sage and Dora were my friends. Not people who were friendly to me when Alice wasn't around but people who liked me for me, even though they'd witnessed the part of me that could be an absolute mardy bitch.

'We all look amazing,' Sage said with satisfaction. 'We are going to walk into this so-called Wow Club and rule the school.'

17

I'm not sure that we ruled the school, or that I'd ever want to become supreme monarch of anywhere as crap as The Wow, but when the five of us strutted in, everyone turned to look.

We'd picked up Paul and Matthew at the Red Lion en route. They both looked the part in tight jeans, black leather jackets and shades. Matthew had borrowed one of my stripy T-shirts and we'd found a really bad grey wig in a charity shop. Andy Warhol had been known for wearing really bad wigs so it was fate or something. I just hoped that my hair didn't look like a bad wig too, but I got the feeling that Sage and Dora would smack me if I mentioned my hair again.

It felt weird to sit at my usual table without Alice, but Sage was a Wow virgin so I was busy pointing out who everyone was, from Mark the mad dancer to Thee Desperadettes to Louis. Thee

Desperadoes weren't playing but Louis was there, because where else would he be?

'Oh, so that's him,' Sage said doubtfully. 'I thought he'd be much ... Well, that he'd be, y'know ... '

'What? You can't deny that he's foxy.' She couldn't deny it, but then I didn't want her to agree with me too much.

'He just doesn't look like the sharpest pencil in the box,' Sage said, flicking a glance in the direction of Louis, who was attempting to balance a bottle of lager on his nose. He was wearing a pair of flashing red devil horns but even they couldn't eclipse his beauty.

'He has a sense of humour, what's wrong with that?'

'I don't think it's his brains that Franny's interested in,' Matthew said drily and then we had one of those conversations about fashion (specifically how we all agreed that Lady Gaga wasn't a style icon because she wore costumes rather than clothes) that thrilled me until, unbelievably, the DJ put on a Velvet Underground song, 'I'm Waiting for the Man', and the five of us took to the dance floor.

I danced with Mattie because we were a matched pair and we danced in character. He stood there stock still with his shades on and I flailed my arms and shimmied the way I'd seen Edie dance on clips I'd found on YouTube. It wasn't *that* different to how I usually danced.

It seemed as if everyone in the club were suddenly gathered round the five of us, not dancing, just staring. But the really weird thing was that I didn't care. It wasn't just Alice and me against the world. I had four people who had my back. I was part of a gang. I was part of a larger something. It was a relief not to have to rely on only one other person.

It was also a relief that I didn't have to make my own fun while Alice copped off with someone she wouldn't even acknowledge a week later.

Not that any of us were likely to cop off. Matthew and Paul could hardly start snogging; Merrycliffe wasn't ready for that. Sage had already said that every lad in the place was a loser compared to the lads in Leeds and there was no one at all like Dora. That left me. There was only one person I wanted to cop off with and though he was no longer trying to balance a bottle of lager on his nose, Louis was hemmed in by an adoring throng of Desperadettes. They never left him alone for a minute.

'I need to adjust my eyelashes,' I said, when the DJ started playing Coldplay and we all decided as one to go back to our table. 'I think one's coming untethered.'

The Wow Ladies bathroom was its usual grotty self. The floor was wet and covered in grimy loo roll. You had to hold your breath so you didn't breathe in the stench of toilet, twenty different body sprays and something really fetid and undead. There was a massive queue for the one loo out of three that a) flushed and b) had a lock on the door.

Mouth clenched shut, I fixed my eyelash and hurried out, gulping in huge lungfuls of air as soon as I opened the door.

'Hey, Franny B, where's the fire?' Louis asked as I barrelled right into him.

'Oh, sorry,' I gasped. The shock and lack of oxygen became

too much and I started coughing. Technically, it was more like a choking fit.

'You all right?' Louis patted my back with so much enthusiasm that for one terrible moment I thought I'd throw up on his pointy-toed, Cuban-heeled boots. I didn't, but only because one of Thee Desperadettes suddenly thrust a bottle of water at me.

I was red and my mascara and liquid eyeliner were running as I glugged down the water, which always tasted of dry ice in The Wow. 'Er, thanks.'

I didn't know any of Thee Desperadettes' names but she had red hair and like most of the girls in The Wow was wearing black leggings and top, cat's ears and had painted whiskers on her face. She looked me up and down. 'You and your mates, don't know who you've come as but you look really cool.' She was right up in my face. 'Two pairs of eyelashes. Aces!'

'They hurt like you wouldn't believe,' I confessed, because what with the itchy eyelash glue and the strain of keeping my eyes open, it was all I could do not to rip them off.

'Kirsten, you must know Kirsten,' she gestured towards a blonde girl at the bar. 'The only time she wore false lashes, it turned out she was allergic to the glue and her eyes swelled up like golfballs.'

'That sounds horrific,' I said in alarm. Maybe the itch wasn't due to the eyelash glue. 'Do my eyeballs look normal-sized to you?'

She laughed. 'They look fine. You're Franny, right? Friend of that Alice?'

I stiffened at the mention of Alice's name. 'I suppose,' I said unenthusiastically.

'So do you think you'll be making more of those sequinned T-shirts that you made last year? My sister got one.'

Lexy was the older sister of a girl in the year below me at school who'd asked me to spell out *Hot Bitch* in sequins on one of the American Apparel T's I'd bought in a job lot on eBay. Her mum had pitched a fit and forbidden her from wearing it outside the house. I still had loads of T's stuffed in a box so we swapped deets and Lexy said she'd think about what she wanted written on her shirt.

Lexy was doing the art foundation course at college and she casually invited me to hang with her and the other Desperadettes (though she called them 'my mates') during breaktime. 'Been meaning to say hello to you at college,' Lexy told me. Alice and I had always imagined that Thee Desperadettes were really stuck-up but Lexy wasn't a bit like that. She looked back towards her friends and it was my lucky night because Louis was heading our way again. 'I'd better go to the bar before I get shouted at for not getting my round in. Love your hair, by the way. Like Rihanna's when she cut it all off.'

'Yeah, Franny B, thought there was something different about you,' Louis said, looking at me closely as if he could see all the way down into the depths of my soul. 'Your hair! Dude, it's really short. It looks like that haircut that Gazza and all those footballers had. You know, the one that Roman emperors had too.'

I thought I might burst into tears. '*What?*'

'Oh, don't worry, Franny, you can pull it off,' Louis told me, like it was a good thing that I could pull off a haircut that loads of naff old footballers had had in the freaking nineties when I'd hardly been born. 'You look like a really pretty boy. Like, Justin Bieber or something.'

Everything he said was a hundred times worse than the last thing he'd said. 'Stop talking, Louis,' said a voice because even Francis thought he was out of order. 'Please stop making words come out of your mouth.'

Louis held up his hands in protest. 'I was saying that you look fit, Franny,' he protested. My heart, which had been somewhere around my ankles, did perk up a little as I waited for him to clarify that statement, but his attention was fixed on something or someone on the other side of the room. 'Right, yeah . . . Were we done 'cause I need to . . .'

He didn't even finish his sentence, but loped off and left me looking like Justin Bieber with a Julius Ceasar haircut. I didn't want to but I turned round to face Francis.

His hair *was* long and messy in front, like mine was supposed to have been, but I could still see his poleaxed expression as he took in the brand new me. 'Wow!' he said. He was so shocked he couldn't even muster a sneer. 'That's quite the reinvention.'

I folded my arms. 'It wasn't meant to be quite so much of a reinvention.'

He walked round me slowly. If it had been anyone but Francis, I would have wondered if they were checking me out. Even so, I went hot and cold at the thought of him, of anyone, seeing the bald spot. 'Oh? What made you change your mind?'

'I didn't. I let Alice loose with a pair of scissors and she did her absolute worst,' I said, even though I didn't want to be one of those girls who badmouthed other girls in front of boys. But I wasn't badmouthing Alice to make myself seem better by comparison. In order to explain my hair, I had to badmouth Alice. I couldn't bear it if Francis thought that I'd *wanted* to look like this.

'It's not so bad,' he said. He was rubbish at sounding like he meant it. 'And you're very silver so that's good.' Now it was his turn to peer intently at me. 'You remind me of someone, can't think who.'

I stood there, arms still folded, and stared at Francis as he stared at me. Sage was right. He wasn't unattractive, not when his face was softened by a slight smile. He'd made no concession to the Halloween-ness of the night and was wearing jeans and a plaid shirt, unbuttoned just enough that I could make out a T-shirt underneath. That whole grunge revival thing was very YSL but he was still ridiculously underdressed, hadn't even made an effort, whereas the more Francis stared, the more I felt that I was ridiculously overdressed.

'Well?' I prompted. 'Who do I remind you of, then?'

Francis screwed up his face like he was in pain. 'John Seeber!' he said triumphantly. 'That's who! John Seeber in Ah Boo the Souffle.'

I didn't know what Ah Boo the Souffle was but it was obviously some dreadful noisenik band, and I knew that John was a boy's name. Francis and, even worse, Louis both thought that I looked like a boy because Alice had destroyed my hair and, unlike Alice, I didn't have any tits that I could shove in people's faces so they'd know I was a girl.

'Thanks! Thanks a lot,' I snarled.

'What? What did I say?' He looked genuinely perturbed, like he'd expected me to be pleased to be compared to some noise-making boy that I'd never heard of. 'It's not a line. You really do look like John See—'

'Oh, just piss off.' I shoved past him so hard he rocked back on his feet.

'I'm going home,' I announced when I got back to our table and immediately dropped to my knees to find my bag, which had my woolly hat stuffed in it. I say announced, but it was closer to actual shouting. 'I'm not staying here to be insulted by *people.*'

'What people?' Mattie looked worried. 'Do I have to fight them for you?'

'They're not worth it,' I assured him, as I found my bag and dug out my hat. 'First Louis compares my hair to Gazza and a Roman emperor *and* says that I look like Justin Bieber and then Francis . . .'

I paused because Paul didn't know who Francis was, then Dora and Sage had another discussion about whether he was fit or not. They still reckoned he'd be a lot fitter if he did something with his clothes and hair.

'What did Francis say then?' Sage finally asked.

'He said that I looked like John Seeper or Seeber or

Seeburgh who's in some band called Ah Boo the Souffle.' The unfairness of it struck me anew. 'Like, if you're going to diss me to my face at least compare me to someone that I know, instead of some bloke in an obscure band. Did he think I was going to find it funny? Did he? Because it's not ... '

'Oh my God, how can you be obsessed with Edie Sedgwick and Andy Warhol and sixties fashion trends and not know who John Seeber is?' Sage's voice dripped with contempt. 'I'm rethinking the whole new best friend thing.'

Sage thought that we were new best friends? That made me feel a bit better. Then it made me feel worse because, despite everything, I kind of maybe missed my old best friend. I hardened my heart and got back to more important matters.

'Please, will someone just tell me who he is?' I said plaintively.

'Not he, *she*. She's French. Jean Seberg.' When Sage said it with an exaggerated French accent, it didn't sound like a bloke's name at all. 'And she was in a film called *A Bout de Souffle*. In English it's called *Breathless*. You know, yeah, Francis is right, you *do* look like her.'

I was already on my BlackBerry, squinting at the screen in the dim light to pull up pictures of Jean Seberg. From what I could see, I could only hope to look a fraction as cool and sophisticated and generally awesome as the girl walking down a Parisian street with a lanky man in suit and hat while she wore cropped black trousers, ballet slippers and a white sleeveless T-shirt that bore the logo of the *New York Herald Tribune*.

I scrolled on until I found a head shot and she did have my hair! My pixie cut, my urchin crop, my butchered sixties do. She even had the tufty bit at the crown, which had been bothering me almost as much as the bald spot, and she was rocking it hard. My heart would be forever Edie's but I could feel a new girl crush brewing.

I'd also been unspeakably rude to Francis when he'd been paying me one hell of a compliment. I looked round for him but he was nowhere to be seen, though Louis waved like it didn't matter that he'd said awful things to me. I wasn't proud of myself but I waved back and then I noticed that Matthew and Dora were kissing and that took priority over everything.

'Hang on! So is Mattie bi then?' I asked Paul, who didn't seem too bothered that his boyfriend was now, cwwww, sucking face with Dora.

'Not that I know of,' he said, staring over my shoulder at my BlackBerry. 'Look! Jean Seberg has a stripy T-shirt just like yours! It's like you were separated at birth or something.'

'But ... what ... you and Matt ...' I looked to Sage for help. She raised her eyebrows like she didn't know what I was talking about. 'I thought you and Mattie were, you know, together.'

Even though Paul was still wearing his Lou Reed dark glasses, he managed to look confused. 'Best mates but nothing else.' He pushed his sunglasses down his nose so he could glare at me. 'Do we have to have the conversation when I explain that just because I'm gay it doesn't mean that I fancy *all* boys? Anyway, Mattie does that whole fop-in-a-suit look, which does nothing for me.'

'I'm not being homophobic.' I was horrified at the accusation. 'I got a very gay vibe off Mattie and you two are always together. My gaydar has never malfunctioned before.' Though, to be fair, my gaydar had never really been tested before either.

I was never going to make it in fashion if my gaydar was wonky, although as Sage pointed out, 'Mattie does act very camp. I did wonder for a couple of days until I saw him holding hands with Dora at the bus stop.'

I'd never seen Mattie and Dora holding hands and she'd never said anything to me. 'But you *are* gay?' I asked Paul.

He sighed. 'I'm the only gay in Merrycliffe. It's my own cross to bear.'

'You're not the only gay in Merrycliffe. The bloke who manages the old people's home next to our house is gay and the lady that runs the Royal Legion Social Club has been with her girlfriend since they were at school together.'

'Yeah, but that's not the kind of gay I choose to associate myself with,' Paul sniffed, and he was just telling me what kinds of gay he did associate with when the music stopped and the lights went up and The Wow Halloween party was over.

Normally on a Saturday night Sean came to pick us up after we'd been to the Market Diner, and now I faced a cold, dark walk home and it was already midnight, my curfew when Dad was home to enforce it.

But I wanted Sage to get the full Merrycliffe Saturday night experience, which meant going to the Market Diner for chips. Even if Dad did ground me, he probably wouldn't stick around long enough to make sure that I was obeying his orders.

We piled out of the club, shrieking as the wind tugged at our clothes, and walked along the seafront. It didn't take long before the paltry tourist attractions – a chippy, a run-down amusement arcade, a boarded-up shop that sold sticks of rock, rude postcards and novelty items in high season and the fifties milk bar – gave way to the bleak industrial estate that housed the companies that used Merrycliffe's port.

Whenever I walked past it, I felt a part of myself shrivelling away. I could also feel another part of me quaking in terror that I might end up working in one of those offices like most other people in Merrycliffe.

It was a relief to see the bright lights of the Market Diner twinkling in the near distance. And it was heavenly to open the door and smell bacon and other pork-based products sizzling on the griddle and be part of the sheer exuberance of the crowd who groaned at the familiar cry of 'Ten minutes for chips!'

We joined the end of the long line and it wasn't until we'd finally got our chips and Sage had admitted that they were better than anything she'd had in Leeds that I saw Francis. He was sitting at Thee Desperadoes' usual table and there was no point in putting this off, even though I didn't want to do it in front of Louis.

'I'll just be a minute,' I told the others and my luck was in. Francis was getting up to visit the condiment station.

He looked at me warily when I walked over. 'Are you still angry at me for some weird reason that I don't understand?'

It was easier when he'd just been a sneering studio tech

instead of having, like, *layers*. 'No! I wanted to apologise for being angry and hopefully you'll think it's a really funny story or else you'll just think that I'm a bit of a twat.'

Francis pushed his hair back so for a second I saw a glint in his hazel eyes that might have been amusement. The glint sort of suited him. 'OK, this had better be good. You've got one minute on the clock, starting now.'

I deserved that, even if I didn't like it, but then I explained how Jean Seberg had got lost in translation 'because you didn't even attempt a French accent', and when I got to the bit about the obscure noise band called Ah Boo the Souffle, Francis laughed so hard that he bent in two, hands resting on his knees so he didn't topple over.

It was a long while, with everyone turning to look at us, before Francis could straighten up. He was a little breathless and pink-faced like maybe he didn't do a lot of laughing and was out of practice.

'So, I'm sorry for getting mad and telling you to piss off,' I concluded. 'But after talking to Louis, then another person coming over to tell me that I looked like a boy ... well, it was just too much.'

Francis nodded. 'I get that and, for the record, I don't think you're a twat. Or that you look like a boy, for that matter.'

When Francis said it, I believed him, in a way that I hadn't when everyone else was telling me that I still looked girl-shaped. There was something quiet and calm about Francis that made me trust him.

I offered him one of my chips and Francis followed me back

to where Sage and the others were hovering at the end of the counter, because there were no tables spare.

Then, half an hour later when there were still no spare tables and I knew that I was in danger of violating my curfew like it had never been violated before, Francis offered to walk me home.

Not like he was waiting to lunge and pull me into a darkened doorway, but everyone else lived in the opposite direction to me and there was this Merrycliffe urban myth that girls could be abducted and within minutes be locked in the hold of a ship en route to somewhere very far away. It had never happened but that's what our parents always told us. That's what Francis told me too, and it was past one in the morning and it would just be my luck to get kidnapped by some vile pervert who wanted to sex-traffic me to the Far East, so I agreed.

18

'Where do you live anyway?' Francis asked, as we waved good-bye to the others. 'You don't live miles away, do you?'

I was tempted to tell him that walking the seven miles to Lytham was nothing, but the friendship we seemed to be forming was too fragile and new to take any more miscommunication. 'Nah. I live on the seafront. About this far from The Wow but in the opposite direction.'

'Didn't think anyone lived on the seafront,' Francis said. 'Apart from the old people in all those retirement homes. What's it like having an ocean view?'

'Very windy,' I replied, just in time to hear Louis shout something that carried on the breeze. Something that sounded a lot like 'Woooh! Yeah! Francis! Don't do anything that I wouldn't do.'

I shuddered and at least it was dark and there wasn't much

in the way of street lights so Francis couldn't see the embarrassed blush that was burning up every millimetre of skin that I possessed.

'Talking of twats,' he said, though we hadn't talked about twats for a good forty minutes. 'Don't take anything Louis says too seriously. He's one of those people who doesn't have a filter. As soon as he's thought it, he says it, but he's not doing it to be evil. The guy doesn't have a malicious bone in his body.'

I didn't say anything while I processed that. Maybe Sage was right when she'd said that Louis wasn't blessed in the brains department. But that was only one part of the Louis whole and the other parts had to be worth all the effort I was going to, otherwise what was the point?

'Well, that's good to know,' I said at last. 'Because there was a moment this evening when I really wanted to smack him.'

'Yeah, I get that feeling a lot too.'

Francis and I shared a smile that was a little awkward and then he asked me if I wanted to borrow his DVD of *Breathless*. I was relieved he'd stopped calling it *A Bout de Souffle*, but I needed to check something. 'It does have sub-titles, right?'

It did and Francis promised me that it wasn't like a lot of French films where people mostly stared out of windows moodily until the camera panned to something random like a bird on a telephone line. 'It's boy meets girl but boy is on the run from the police and the girl is a cool American hipster type who doesn't know that he's a villain.'

It sounded wonderful and I was intrigued by the pictures I'd seen of Jean Seberg and then I told Francis about Edie

Sedgwick and that actually a lot of the Andy Warhol films she was in were really boring and pretentious and I only watched the bits she was in and skipped the rest.

'Probably not as boring and pretentious as some of the films I had to watch when I was at Central St Martin's,' Francis said and my head whipped round in a way that had nothing to do with the force ten gale that was rushing in from the Irish Sea.

'Oh my God! You were at Central St Martin's?' I couldn't make my legs work. 'That's where I want to go. To do a fashion degree. What were you studying?'

'Film.' Francis didn't say anything else. When I glanced sideways at him, I could have sworn he was sneering. I wondered if that was the way his face got when he didn't want to talk.

'So did you decide that you didn't want to study film any more or did you do something awful like destroy a very expensive camera?' I asked.

Francis wasn't sneering quite so hard. 'Nothing like that. I had to defer for a year. My dad isn't well,' he added reluctantly.

I really wanted to reach out and touch him, just on the arm maybe, but I didn't. We were hardly even buddies, let alone touching buddies. Still, I did want Francis to know that I was sorry about his dad but I didn't know where to start.

'I'm sorry' seemed like a good place. 'Um, is it serious?' Well, obviously it was serious if Francis had quit his film course and dragged his heels back to merryless Merrycliffe. 'Like, he is going to get better, isn't he?'

''Fraid not.' Francis swallowed hard and I held my breath a little. 'He's OK at the moment, but back in July his doctor said that at best he has a year and at worst, well . . . he doesn't have a year, so I came back home.'

I could fill in the blanks – Francis had slotted back into the spaces left of his old life while he waited for his dad to get worse. How awful. How horrible. It made my problems seem so small.

'I'm sorry,' I said again, because I didn't know what else to say.

He scuffed his feet. 'Yeah, well, shit happens, doesn't it?'

'It does,' I agreed. It was odd that I'd never really noticed Francis before. He must have been at school with Shuv but she'd never mentioned him. And he'd been in Thee Desperadoes two years ago, but all I ever focused on was Louis. Francis was one of those people who drifted through the shadows of your own life until all of a sudden they were there in front of you. Making you feel things – sad, protective, helpless – that you didn't really want to feel because they made your stomach churn and your head hurt and your skin grow clammy and cold. 'But it must mean a lot to your dad that you came back. And if he's not too, like, poorly at the moment, then you've got the chance to make some more good memories together. Seizing the day and all that stuff, you know?'

'Yeah.' Francis nodded and gave me another of those almost-there smiles. 'Never really thought about it like that.'

I realised that we'd come to a halt outside the fifties milk bar and were just standing there, facing each other. It was hard to have a serious conversation when you were walking into what felt like a tornado. 'Sometimes . . . sometimes when you're in that kind of bad situation, it's hard to see beyond it. To get some perspective.' Jesus. I'd been to one family counselling session with Mum and Dad before Mum decided that it was a waste of time and Dad agreed with her because he had a job booked to deliver some stuff to Dusseldorf and here I was, acting all perceptive like I was Oprah.

'Oh, so did one of your parents—'

'No! No! Nothing like that,' I quickly told Francis before he got the wrong end of that particular stick. 'It's just . . . my mum's sick too.' It was my turn to swallow hard. 'Not sick like your dad but she has depression. Well, she has what the doctors call "a major depressive disorder". It's hardly the same thing but . . .'

'It's not,' Francis said, but he didn't sound angry as we started walking again, the wind getting fiercer so the two of us were almost folded in half as we tried to stay in forward motion. 'But it's still an illness.'

'I know. I've been told that a million times. I've Googled it. I've read about it. I know that she can't help it but there are also times when I want to scream at her to just . . . you know, snap out of it. Pull herself together.'

'Don't think it's as easy as that, Franny.'

'Yeah, but she could still *try*.' I was getting dangerously close to ranting. I took a couple of deep breaths. 'She used to try. She would cry and get really stressed out about stupid stuff like a parking ticket or a letter from the bank or the washing-up being left undone, but after lying on her bed for a little while crying, she was OK. But now she's not.'

I didn't know why I was telling Francis this. Nobody else knew about this, only Alice, and it was probably the last thing he wanted to hear when he had a much heavier burden to carry, but he was listening, he wasn't sneering. 'So, what changed?' he asked so softly the words almost got lost in the night.

I shrugged. 'About two years ago we had a really shitty time. My nan, her mum, died and she got made redundant and part of our roof blew away and my sister, Shuv, she's everyone's favourite, she left home to go to university and Mum just had a nervo.' I preferred to call it that instead of a nervous breakdown, which sounded so clinical. So final. Like once something had broken down, it could be fixed but it was never going to work as well as it used to. Our GP and the registrar at the hospital had called it an 'episode' but it had looked a lot like a nervous breakdown to me. 'She cried for weeks and she was always a bit OCD before but she went totally OCD and she spent all day cleaning and messed up her hands by washing them in bleach, then she went away for a bit.'

She'd agreed to go to a place in Bridlington with a locked ward for really proper menty patients. Mum hadn't been on the locked ward, but she'd had to share a room with this old woman who had dementia, smelt terrible like weeks-old piss and called me Mary the one time I went to visit Mum.

There was no way Mum was ever going to get better in a place like that, she and Dad decided. And because she hadn't been sectioned but had voluntarily admitted herself, it was easy to discharge herself too. So she came home and she was a bit better. And now she wasn't as better as she used to be.

'She could take her pills,' I explained to Francis, who must have been wishing that he hadn't offered to walk me home now. 'She could go to her group counselling sessions. She could stop pretending that everything is OK when my dad and my sisters are around. She never stops to think that she's not the only one who has to deal with her depression; I get a double helping of it too.'

'Maybe it's because she trusts you,' Francis suggested. 'Like, she knows you won't judge her.'

'That's not true,' I muttered, because I judged her all the bloody time. But I think the reason Mum let me see her without the brave face that she showed the rest of the world was because she knew I'd keep her secrets. Other girls went shopping with their mothers or even clubbing with them, but the way Mum and I bonded was that she fell apart and I picked up the pieces. Anyway, it didn't matter – this was the last thing that Francis needed. I couldn't even believe that I'd told him this much. It didn't feel good to vent. Saying the words to another person, instead of going over and over them in my head, made the truth come out instead of lingering in the dirty, dark shadows where it usually hid. The truth was never a friend. 'God, forget I said anything. I'm sorry to dump all this on you. And I'm sorry that I keep on saying sorry when you have enough to deal with.'

We were almost at my house now. I stopped on the corner, hands shoved deep in the pockets of my coat, and grimaced.

Not just because of my oversharing but because the wind felt like it was scouring the skin off my face.

'It's all right, I don't mind,' Francis said, though he should have minded. He probably did but was too polite to say it to my face, now that we were almost mates. 'And you can tell me to piss off again if you hate unsolicited advice, but I find it helps to have stuff that makes you laugh. It gets you through the crap bits. Even if it's convincing Louis that a spaceship was spotted hovering over the Dyke a couple of nights ago and that we should go up there and see if there are any alien rocks.'

'Oh God, please don't tell me stuff like that,' I whimpered because I didn't want to think that Louis would be stupid enough to fall for such a lame joke but I could already hear his excited cries as he spotted alien rocks that were really just normal rocks. Then I thought about what Francis had said and there were lots of good things happening: college, Sage and Dora and the others, figuring out how to do armholes, having a new sixties icon to obsess over and . . .

'Don't forget our trip to London,' Francis reminded me. 'Is that going to be cool with your parents?'

I scoffed. Even waved a casual hand in the air. 'It's going to be fine,' I said, especially as I'd already told them I was going to spend the weekend in Manchester with Shuv. It was going to be harder to convince Mrs Chatterjee to give me the Saturday off than to totally lie to Mum and Dad about where I was going. Though talking of parents, I was in such violation of my curfew that there was still a distinct possibility that Dad would ground me and take away my wifi privileges if I wasn't home soon.

'Anyway, thanks for walking me home and listening to me jaw on . . .'

'You can jaw on to me any time you want,' Francis said and he was *so* nice. He was probably the nicest boy I'd met, now I was past the sneer. There was a lot more to him than simply a way to get closer to Louis. 'And I jawed on too. We both jawed on.'

We were both jawing on now because it's always a bit weird to say goodbye to someone you don't know that well. 'Look, I'll see you Monday at college,' I said. 'And I'll swap you Edie in *Chelsea Girls* for Jean Seberg in *Breathless*. Deal?'

'Deal,' Francis said and then we did this odd little dance like maybe we were going to shake hands or have a quick and awkward hug but we touched each other's elbow instead, and then I felt my phone vibrate with what could only be an irate text message from Dad asking if I'd been abducted and I had to run the last fifty metres.

19

When I finally surfaced the next morning and Dad had finished giving me a stern lecture about how my curfew wasn't just a vague suggestion but to protect me from being abducted by sex traffickers, I checked my phone to find that Francis had added me on Facebook. The boy formerly known as Sneering Studio Tech and I were friends. Or Facebook friends, which meant we were almost real life friends. I'd never expected that! Francis had also invited me to an event he'd created: Thee Desperadoes Go Mad In London. They were playing the Saturday after next in a pub in Camden called the Dublin Castle (I'd have thought that pubs in Camden would have more exotic names) and were driving up in the morning and driving back that night.

I saw that Lexy and Kirsten of Thee Desperadettes had

already joined. I clicked on 'Maybe' because I didn't want to appear too eager and then I saw Alice's name on the invite list.

I hated that when I saw Alice's name my stomach did this horrible swan dive. Though I had to admit that my hair didn't look so bad in the cold light of Sunday. It still had the remains of the silver spray in it (the rest of the silver spray was staining my pillow) and now that I'd seen Jean Seberg, I didn't mind the tufty bit so much. In fact, by the time it was the Saturday after next, my hair would probably have grown enough that the bald spot would no longer be bald and the fringe wouldn't be so nineties footballer any more.

It still felt wrong to have spent another Saturday night without Alice, even wronger not to phone her to debrief about what had happened on Saturday night. And as soon as I thought it, I heard the phone ring.

Not my BlackBerry but our home phone. I was in the kitchen peeling spuds, Dad was making a herb crust for the lamb (Shuv should never have bought him a Nigella Lawson cookery book last Christmas) and Mum was flicking through the Sunday paper. We all looked at each other in horror. Nobody ever rang the landline except ...

'It had better not be anyone trying to sell me something,' Dad said as he picked up the phone. 'Hello?' After a moment, he held the receiver out to me. 'It's for you.'

I took it gingerly. I didn't want anyone trying to sell me something either. 'Hey.'

'It's me,' Alice said. 'I cannot even believe that you blocked my number. That is beyond harsh, Franny. How many more times do I have to apologise about your hair?'

Then I remembered that this wasn't just about my hair. It was about *why* Alice had done what she did. Because getting a boy, a boy that I already had dibs on, was more important than the years we'd been friends.

Also, you didn't fuck about with another girl's hair. It was as bad as punching them. She'd pretty much scalped me – I had a bald spot – so she hadn't apologised enough yet. I wasn't sure she ever could.

'You only apologised in the salon because your parents were there,' I reminded her, painfully aware that my own parents were within earshot and weren't even bothering to hide the fact that they were listening. 'And you let me think that you'd been cutting hair for ages when you're not even allowed to use a blow-dryer unsupervised.'

'Well, yeah, but I'd watched people cut hair for years …'

'Like, that's the same thing …'

'When you don't know how to do some sewing thing, you look up videos of other people doing it on the internet,' Alice pointed out.

'Yeah, but if I bodge a seam, then I'm not going to parade around showing my bodged seam to the world, unlike my hair …'

'It didn't look *that* bad.'

We were going round in circles. Alice was stubborn. She'd never admit that she was wrong: not to other people's irate girl-friends, not when she'd been busted by her mum when she was

195

snogging Raj outside the Spar when she'd sworn she was home revising and not even when she'd tried to sabotage me in her pursuit of Louis.

'You didn't have to do that,' I whispered. I wished we had a cordless phone and not an old-fashioned thing fixed to the wall with a curly wire that was always getting tangled up. 'We both know that when it comes down to looks, you're going to win every time. You didn't have to do what you did and it totally violates the rules we drew up.'

'I didn't do it on purpose. God, you're never going to let this go, are you? I called to apologise, to try and make this right. Jesus, Franny, you do love to play the victim sometimes.'

I gasped at the unfairness of her accusation. 'No, I don't!'

'Yeah, you do. I get that stuff is hard, I really do, but you don't always have to be such a martyr about it,' Alice told me in a tight voice. 'Sometimes I wonder if I should put a sign up in the newsagent's window asking if anyone's seen your sense of humour because it feels like it's been missing for months.'

'Shut up,' I hissed, not as quietly as I thought because Dad's eyebrows shot up and even Mum looked mildly alarmed. 'It's obvious you don't give a toss about our friendship, because if you did you wouldn't be behaving like such a dick.'

'You've been behaving like a dick ever since you started—'

I couldn't bear to listen to what Alice was going to say next and then have to think of something nasty to say in reply. It was much easier to hang up and put the phone back on its little perch with a hand that shook slightly.

I sniffed. The tears were threatening to unleash *yet again*. I took a deep breath and turned round.

Dad became very interested in smearing his herb crust on the lamb, like he was slathering a pasty child with factor 50 sunblock on a hot day at the beach. Mum was transfixed by an ad for nan trousers in the back of the *Sunday Mirror* magazine. They both looked up as soon as I turned round.

'Everything all right, Franular?' Dad asked. He glanced pointedly at Mum for some back-up.

She tore herself away from the nan slacks. 'Is there anything you wanted to talk about? Um, did you want a mother-and-daughter chat?'

I did not. Things weren't *that* bad. Things would never ever be *that* bad.

'Everything is fine. It's better than fine. In fact, it's cool,' I said in a tone of voice that brooked no denial. 'Anyway, I'd love to stay here and chat but I have GCSE revision to do.'

It was my get-out-of-the-kitchen-free card and it had never failed me yet.

I was primed now for my GCSE Maths retake. I'd taken so many timed mock exams and never scored less than 70 per cent that I wasn't even panicking any more. I just wanted it done, marked, then I could get on with the rest of my life.

When I wasn't taking timed mock GCSEs, I worked on my leather dress. I'd done the really scary bit, which was pinning my pattern pieces to my scant metres of leather and cutting them out. Now I was slowly and carefully sewing them together with surgical gloves on my hands so the leather didn't get grubby, though even Barbara said she thought that was going a bit too far.

I was starting to really love college. A place had opened up on one of the beauty courses so Krystal with a K had disappeared and Karen and Sandra were actually hilarious when you got to know them. They entertained us with very rude stories about their ex-husbands and their cut-price package holidays to Turkey where they did unspeakable things with men half their age, so when Barbara wasn't in the workroom I seemed to spend a lot of time listening to their sexcapades and giggling.

Even Barbara wasn't as bad as she had been at the start of term. In fact, she was a mine of information about Martin Sanderson if you caught her in a good mood or she'd had a glass of wine at lunchtime. 'He once tried to make a tartan jacket that I still see in my nightmares' was just one of the gems she'd come out with. 'He worked on it for weeks but he just couldn't get the tartan to match up. It was what you young people would call a hot mess.'

Mostly though it was the five of us: Sage, Dora, Mattie, Paul and me hanging out. I loved that I could talk about fashion for hours on end and no one told me to shut up, like Alice used to; and five should have been an odd number, someone should have been left out, on the sidelines, but it didn't work like that. Anyway, sometimes we became six when Francis hung out with us. Not all the time, but there was always a reason for him to come into our workroom. It was surprising how many times one of the sewing machines stopped working and it was against Health and Safety for us to mend them ourselves.

Once Francis was around he tended to stay so he could join in our heated debates about whether his boss, Ted from Facilities, used to be a woman or if it was true that one of the girls studying Leisure and Tourism was boffing the canteen cook who always scratched his armpit with whatever serving utensil was to hand.

As a new friend, Francis was shaping up quite nicely. We didn't mention that walk home, the secrets we'd shared, but it was like we didn't need to mention them. And because we both knew all this deeply private stuff about each other, it felt like we'd skipped through a lot of the opening chapters in being friends and had settled into a comfortable familiarity that I didn't quite have with the others yet. With Francis, I could just be quiet. Sometimes it was a relief to just be quiet. Also, Francis was an amazing source of cool girls in old films that we'd watch during lunch break or when Barbara wasn't around. 'You need to see Anouk Aimée in *La Dolce Vita*,' he'd say. And 'Brigitte Bardot in *And Man Created Woman* is totally inspiring.' Or 'Let's watch Jean Seberg in *Bonjour Tristesse*.'

Occasionally Sage would join us if she was around, but usually it was just me and Francis, though he jumped every time we heard a noise in the corridor because he was meant to be mending broken sewing machines and logging borrowed equipment, not watching films on a college laptop and sharing my bag of stale pick 'n' mix from the 59p shop.

After so long knowing everything there was to know about Alice, getting to know all these new people was exhilarating. There was so much to discover. Like, I didn't know why Sage's parents had got divorced or how Mattie and Dora got together. Or how Francis felt about watching a kissing scene in a film when I was sitting next to him, because it made *me* feel a bit weird and self-conscious. Or whether he'd mind if I ate all the fizzy cola bottles that were so sour they made my tongue shrink back in my mouth.

The flipside to getting to know so many new people in such a short period of time was that it was also exhausting. It was a relief to be able to talk about hemlines and how there was always a fine dusting of dressmaker's chalk over everything in your bag, but I missed Alice.

I couldn't help it.

Alice and me had our own language; our own personal shorthand. She knew that I took two sugars in my hot drinks, the same way that I knew that she would always have a diet Coke with her chips and that she secretly believed the lack of calories in one totally cancelled out the calories in the other.

My history was tangled up in Alice's history. From all the times we'd cried together and learned to swim together and got scratched by her next-door neighbour's cat when we were six and ever since then we always said we were dog people, to the year when we watched the entire ten seasons of *Friends* again and again. Even now, if either one of us catches two seconds of a repeat on TV we can name the episode and pretty much recite the entire scene from memory. We shared chocolate brownie recipes, fashion disasters, experiments with hair straighteners and liquid eyeliner, long bitching sessions about our parents and teachers, lamented our lack of boobs and got our first period within weeks of each other.

She wasn't family but Alice was imprinted on my DNA and so, just as how I never stopped loving Shuv even though I was mad at her for bailing on the whole Mum thing, I couldn't help loving Alice. Not in a lezza way, but in a way that there was no Franny without Alice. I wouldn't be the person I was today if I'd been best friends with some other girl. But then I'd catch sight of my hair in a mirror or shop window, and Alice was dead to me all over again. Stalemate. Then, when we were hanging out Thursday lunchtime, Francis asked me: 'So, what's the deal with you and that Alice girl? I used to think that you two were like non-identical conjoined twins.'

I noted that even Francis called her 'that Alice girl'. Then I noted that Francis had been aware of Alice and me enough that he'd had a theory about us. I paused with my cheese and pickle sandwich halfway to my mouth. 'There is no deal,' I said. 'You can't have deals with people who are dead to you.'

'Is it because of what she did to your hair?' Francis was sitting next to me and fiddling about with the Quicktime programme on the laptop in front of him, so he couldn't see the dark look I gave my sandwich.

'Well, not just that.' I pulled a face. I could tell Francis about my mum, but talking about Alice seemed so much harder. 'It was *why* she did this to my hair.'

'Yeah? Why?' Francis was deep in the Quicktime settings, double-clicking on stuff I didn't have a clue about. Sage still reckoned that Francis had potential but I wondered if he ever felt like Louis's sidekick, the junior partner, something much less when Louis was around. Did boys have thoughts like that?'

'To do with Louis,' I muttered, though I didn't know why I felt the need to mutter. Francis knew how I felt about Louis. It wasn't exactly a news flash. 'I've fancied him for ages. *Ages*. Then Alice decided that she was going to make a move on him, which is totally against the best friend code . . . '

Francis looked across at me. Now that he didn't sneer so much, it was quite hard to get a read on his facial expressions. 'Oh, I didn't know there was a best friend code.'

'Well, there is,' I said quickly. 'So, then we both agreed that we'd make a move on Louis but she . . . God, it's impossible to try and explain and not sound really immature.'

'You realise that then? Good, 'cause I was worrying about how I was going to break that to you,' Francis said. He straightened up from his hunch over the laptop. 'Please tell me you haven't fallen out over a bloke, over *Louis*? I thought you were better than that, Franny.'

I thought I was too, but apparently I wasn't. Though in my defence . . . 'It's not just that. It's, like, it was always just the two of us, Alice and me, but there was also Alice and all her boy-related dramas, which is why she hasn't got any other friends. It was why I didn't have many other friends either, until I started college and began hanging out with Dora and the others and then Alice felt like I was abandoning her, even though I wasn't.'

There was so much more to it. I hadn't even told him about our pitched battle to win Louis's heart but Francis just said, 'Right, OK, I get it now,' and I knew that he did. 'It's much easier hanging out with lads. You just call them on it when they're acting like tools and it's sorted.'

I shook my head. 'It can't be that easy.'

'Really is. I suppose boys are just more ... what's the word I'm looking for?' Francis paused to consider. 'Oh yeah, we're just more evolved.'

I scoffed and even acted like I was about to throw the rest of my sandwich at Francis, but what had happened between Alice and me wasn't just going to be resolved with some laddish light banter. It was so much more complicated than that. Deeply and darkly complicated, but I guess I was leaning towards at least offering her some kind of olive branch. Maybe unblocking her number would be a start?

'No way, man,' Raj said when I saw him in the shop later that afternoon. 'She's a stone cold killer. If you think she's shed one tear about you, then ...'

'Tears would be a bit much,' I'd protested. 'But maybe she regrets what she did. You can't wipe out sixteen years of being friends like it never happened. We should at least try and put things right, don't you think?'

Raj looked at me pityingly, like I needed help sounding out the big words. 'Franny, she maimed you. You look like one of those women from World War Two who got their hair hacked off for getting freaky wit' the Nazis.'

I glared at him because no matter how awful my hair might

look, it didn't look *that* awful. 'Yeah, you should totally use the phrase "getting freaky wit' the Nazis" in your S levels,' I'd said. Then I teased him for pretending he was gangsta when he was really a history nerd until he threatened to 'bust a cap in my ass', just as Mr Chatterjee brought in a load of clothes that had had to be industrially cleaned off-site and cuffed him round the back of his head.

Which was hilarious, especially when Raj was forced to apologise to me three times for threatening me with physical violence before Mr Chatterjee was satisfied that his son's words came from a place of deep sincerity. But I still didn't know what I was going to do about Alice.

I had all these new people in my life and Alice had only me, except she didn't even have me any more. Over the next couple of days I wondered if I could bear to bow out of our contest and let Alice have Louis as compensation. Here was my opportunity to do something nice, to be the bigger person. But then Louis would tweet a picture of himself about to eat the double burger he'd just constructed or he'd 'Like' the Rolling Stones clip from 1969 that Francis had just posted on my Facebook wall. (Francis was adamant that the 1960s Stones should not be judged by the same standards as the bunch of wrinkly-faced, granddad rocker, twenty-first-century Stones who'd headlined Glastonbury.) Just the slightest sight-ing of Louis on the internet and my stomach did that dippy thing.

Then I'd think about how happy Louis was to see me on the three occasions that we'd talked to each other. It was obvious that there was a spark between us. It was why I'd crushed on Louis for so long – because I knew we could have something really special. Alice should have respected that. But she hadn't. Which meant that she had no respect for me or our friendship.

Call me unevolved, but whichever way I looked at it, Alice and I were over.

20

On Monday, after a parentally approved weekend (no Wow Club, lots of timed mock GCSE Maths exams), I was well rested and sat in a small room on the second floor of the main college building with six other people also taking their Maths GCSE.

Three hours later, I was done. There'd been one question about higher probability that had made me sweaty but generally it had been OK. I was extremely hopeful that I'd passed with a C or higher and would never have to use a protractor again at any given point in my life.

I still had English to retake but that was in June, which was light years away, and right now all I needed to worry about was easing the sleeves into the armholes on my leather dress, which were as puckered and lumpy as Karen's caesarean scar, which she'd shown us on Friday afternoon – she and Sandra had been drinking at lunchtime.

I headed back to the art block. The workroom was deserted but there was a good luck card and a chocolate muffin on my table from the others, which made me feel warm and fuzzy inside. I sat down and stared at the leather on my dress form and waited for inspiration to strike.

Inspiration still hadn't struck when the others trailed in from lunch. Barbara came in five minutes later and made a beeline straight for me. 'How did you get on in your exam?' she demanded, though her eyes glazed over as soon as I mentioned high probability. She then gave me a short armhole tutorial that left me more confused than ever and by the time she bustled out again, saying, 'I'd start that sleeve again if I were you, Franny,' it was gone two. This was normally when Francis liked to turn up and tell me what film we'd be watching that afternoon, but he was nowhere to be seen. Half an hour later Francis was still a no-show – maybe there was a light-bulb emergency in the catering block.

I tacked a sleeve on to my dress and then untacked it, but all my focus had gone for the day so there was no harm in checking Twitter, though usually I didn't indulge when I was doing fashion. I mean, where would Stella McCartney be if she kept stopping every five minutes to tweet about what she was going to have for dinner?

Stella's tweets weren't even that juicy but Martin Sanderson was an excellent tweeter. He was always posting pictures of his two pugs and sneak peeks of his new designs.

He'd just tweeted a picture of a dress made from a gorgeous watered silk with what looked like a digital print of a blown-up snowflake on it, which was fascinating but not as fascinating as the little exchange I found when I scrolled back to yesterday's tweets on my timeline.

@WorstGirlfriendInTheWorld Cant beleve how much skin u were showing last nite!

@LouisDesperado U can talk! But if U got it, flaunt it, amirite? ;)

@WorstGirlfriendInTheWorld Just healing the world with our hotness, babes. ;)

I thought I might start to cry when I realised that Alice was free from the parental chains. Tania, or more likely Sean, had caved and the only punishment she'd got for being totally, completely and utterly out of order was to be grounded for one measly Saturday night. Jesus, there were worse consequences for stealing pick 'n' mix from the 59p shop because they always called the police. Usually you got away with a telling-off but they banned you from the 59p shop for life. They even put your picture up in the window. It had happened to a mate of Raj's.

Alice was meant to be penitent and remorseful. She should also have been barred from any place where she could reasonably expect to have fun until my hair grew back. That was only fair, I thought, as I stuffed the whole of the chocolate muffin in my mouth. Then I could do nothing for a while but chew furiously and come to the slow realisation that I was maybe overreacting. Maybe even being a little immature. I was still annoyed with Alice for flirting up a storm with Louis, but that was the only way that Alice could connect with him.

Whereas I connected with Louis on lots of different levels.

Except, I hadn't quite worked out what those levels were apart from pretending to like cats in sunglasses and the Chicken Hut.

Also I had Francis. Francis was my road less taken to Louis, except actually he really wasn't that any more. He was my friend and he was missing in action.

Francis was still absent the next day. When Sandra broke the overlocking machine with a loud and ominous crunching sound, Amir from Facilities arrived. Not to fix it, like Francis would have done, but to hang an *out of order* notice on it.

'Um, no Francis then?' I asked casually and very quietly because if Sandra and Karen even heard you mention a man's name, they automatically assumed that you were shagging him and wouldn't stop asking questions about his performance and generally taking the piss.

Amir shook his head. 'Nope,' he said.

'So, he's not in college today?'

Amir shook his head again.

'Is he sick?'

Amir shrugged. He was a man of very few words. I gave up.

Francis was still AWOL on Wednesday. I began to wonder if everything was all right. I wanted to call him, but then I remembered that we'd only been friends for not even two weeks and we hadn't swapped phone numbers. I could send him a Facebook message but that seemed inappropriate when we'd only used Facebook so Francis could post that video on my wall of the Rolling Stones performing an eighteen-minute version of 'Sympathy For The Devil' at Hyde Park in 1969 and for me to comment: LOVE, LOVE, LOVE first ten minutes but then it gets a little samey. Francis had replied: Franny! I wish there was an "Unlike" button for your cruel comment. When that was your only Facebook contact with someone, it felt really wrong to send them a very personal message about their father's terminal illness.

All I could do was worry and hope that Francis and his dad were all right and that he'd be back at work soon because I already missed hanging out with him. There was so much I wanted to show and tell. Like, we were both obsessed with the old lady who worked in the Sue Ryder shop who wore nothing but purple and I liked to give him an outfit update each morning when I passed her on the way to college. And I'd amassed a huge quantity of YouTube clips of talking animals, and stale bananas from my 59p shop pick 'n' mix because those were two of Francis's favourite things.

I hadn't known Francis that long, but he'd made major inroads into my daily routine.

'Haven't seen your mate for a while,' Paul commented as he and Mattie left college with me at Wednesday lunchtime. Two books I'd ordered on inter-library loan had come in and they wanted to see what the library had in the way of DVDs. Not much, I'd warned them but they wouldn't be told. 'Has he got the sack for skiving off?'

I lurched into a lamp post. 'Do you think?' Francis did spend a lot of time hanging out with us. 'No! Surely Amir would have said. Though what if there are budget cuts? The news is full of budget cuts. Francis was last in so he'd be first out.'

Now I was properly worried, though Mattie and Paul didn't

understand that Francis losing his job would be kicking a man when he was already down. They were talking about the chances of finding *The Big Bang Theory* boxed set in the library and that left me free to decide that I had to Facebook message Francis tonight even if it was inappropriate.

'Stop frowning, Franny,' Mattie said, as we climbed up the steps to the library. 'Otherwise you'll be caning the Botox before you're twenty.'

I mumbled something in reply, then headed to the Orders desk and they went to the two sparse sets of shelves that were the DVD department. I got my books, a biography of Diana Vreeland, legendary editor of US *Vogue* during the sixties, who pretty much discovered David Bailey and Jean Shrimpton, and yet another book, *Popism*, about Andy Warhol.

I ordered a biography of Alexander McQueen and was just about to join Mattie and Paul to see if the DVD shelves would cough up a copy of something cool when I saw him.

My heart, my fickle heart, did the little salmon leap it always did and then he looked up from the graphic novel he was reading, lips moving in time to the words, smiled and waved.

I couldn't have not gone over. Besides he was now shouting, 'Franny B! Hey, Franny B!' with blatant disregard for keeping quiet in the library.

'Oh, hey, Louis,' I said in a hushed whisper when I reached his table. 'You all right?'

'I think I'm all right but I need to know that you're not still mad at me.' He pulled an exaggerated pouty face. 'You know, for comparing your new haircut to several different dudes. Francis said you were really pissed off.'

'Oh, *that*.' I was over that. Had been ever since Francis had explained that Louis was ... how had he phrased it? That Louis had no filter. 'Yeah, my hair is a bit of a sensitive subject.' I had a cute geometric-patterned Primark scarf tied round my head, but my hand was already creeping up to touch the bald spot, even though everyone said it wasn't a bald spot any more. I still wasn't convinced that twelve days was long enough for a bald spot to stop being bald. 'I'm not pissed off with you. Honestly.'

I couldn't believe Louis had given even a few moments of his time to worrying that he might have upset me, but he gave me a blinding smile as soon as I said that we were cool. 'Great. I hate it when people are mad at me. You'd be surprised at how often it happens.' Actually the more I got to know him, the less surprised I was that not everyone fell under his spell. Apart from girls. All the girls.

Louis looked at me expectantly like he was waiting for me to pull a rabbit out of my tote bag. There were so many things I could have asked him. If he'd noticed that I wasn't at The Wow on Saturday and whether he really thought that Alice was the girl for him. Or I could even screw up every last gram of courage that I possessed and request the pleasure of his company on an actual date, but that could all wait.

'I'm glad I ran into you,' I said and Louis smiled happily again, but I wasn't going to get sidetracked. 'I've been wondering where Francis is. He hasn't been in college for the last three days and I'm not sure if he's been sacked or, well, if there's stuff going on at home.'

Louis scrunched up his features like he was suffering a thousand agonies. 'Home?' he echoed. I could *feel* the effort he was making not to blurt out what he obviously wanted to blurt out. He had one of those faces where you could tell exactly what he was thinking.

'Yeah.' I leaned in closer, not to take great big whiffs of Louis but so I could lower my voice. 'You know, um, with his dad.'

'Oh! So he told you about his dad?' Louis let out a sigh of relief that ruffled my ridiculously short fringe. 'OK! Cool!'

'He mentioned it in passing.' I shrugged like it was no big deal. 'So, is everything all right with his dad? Is that why he's not been in work?'

'Yeah. I mean no! Oh, hang on. Like, um, no, his dad's in hospital and yeah, that's why he's not been around,' Louis clarified. 'Something up with his dad's piss.'

'Ewwwww! *What?*'

There was a loud shushing noise behind me. I didn't dare look round, especially as Louis chose that moment to put his hand on my arm to pull me a little closer.

That should have been my cue to melt into a puddle of gloop that was formerly known as Francesca Barker, but it turned out I was made of stronger stuff. Also, I was so grossed out by what Louis had just said that I wasn't sure I wanted his hands anywhere near me.

'He's got an infection in his pee or his kidneys. Whatever. It was pretty serious. Francis even missed a rehearsal because he was at the hospital.'

'You guys actually rehearse?' Another Merrycliffe mystery solved.

'Every Monday evening,' Louis told me proudly. 'Well, except we don't really do much rehearsing because that goes against the whole spirit of Thee Desperadoes, so mostly we play *Rock Band* in our drummer's basement. But Francis didn't even text to say he wasn't coming.'

'He was probably worried about his dad.' There was a thought I didn't want to think. 'But is his dad getting better? How long is he going to be in hospital for? He will be coming home, won't he?'

Louis was nodding happily again. It was my turn to sigh in relief. How strange to think that time wasn't something that stretched endlessly in front of you but something precious that could run out. How did Francis even get up in the morning and walk and talk and smile and remember to look up clips of films that he knew I'd like?

'Don't worry. It's all cool. Francis' dad and his piss . . . '

'God, please stop saying that . . . '

'Hey, Franny, we all do it,' Louis said earnestly. 'Everyone has to sh—'

I held up my hand in protest. 'I get the picture. Francis's dad is on the mend and Francis will be back at work soon, right?'

'Right. End of the week. I never thought you were this uptight, Franny.'

And I never thought that a) I'd ever go up to Louis and start talking to him like it was the most normal thing in the world and that b) I'd then beg him to shut up because he kept talking about a mutual friend's dad's wee.

'I'm not uptight. I'm actually quite laid-back,' I said, though I was probably more on the uptight part of the life spectrum. I glanced over my shoulder to see Mattie and Paul waiting at the exit for me. 'I have to go but if you see Francis, will you just say hi and that ... Just say hi and that I'm glad everything's all right ... No! Just say I said hi.'

'Sure,' Louis said. His attention was drifting back to the graphic novel he'd been reading. 'Franny B says hi. Got it. OK. Yeah ...'

I'd lost him.

But I found Francis. Or rather I thought I saw him in the distance when I was dropped off at college by my parents the next morning like I was six or something.

They were going to the big wholesale supermarket in Preston. They always went there about a week before Dad headed off on a long European trip. That was usually when I clenched every muscle in my body and kept them clenched until he came back, but this time I was unclenched. The outing to buy catering packs of bacon and Capri-Sun usually coincided with Dad writing the dates he'd be away on the calendar in the kitchen and pinning up his itinerary on the fridge. But this time both calendar and fridge were unmarked so it looked like he was staying in Merrycliffe for a while longer.

I opened the door before Dad had even pulled into the kerb.

'Don't forget to buy me one of those huge glass jars of the pra-lines. Oh and if they've got the nice pizza, not the gross pizza, make sure to get lots and lots.'

Dad muttered something about how he was amazed I hadn't asked for a job lot of cheap vodka and cans of Red Bull and Mum lifted her head up from her shopping list, which she'd been compiling and cross-referencing and amending for three days.

'I'm sure that the cheese on even the nice pizza is full of car-cinogenic chemicals,' she told me. Then she slapped on a cheery smile. 'Have a good day, love!'

It was almost comforting the way we slipped into these roles like we were a normal family, but then Dad would go away again and we would become an abnormal family. Not even a family but just one girl left to cope with her menty mother.

'Bye then,' I said, and hurried after Francis. He was too far away to call out to and I was still swiping my ID at the security gate when he went through the entrance marked *Staff Only*.

But he was back, which meant that his dad was better, and I'd discovered a sixties actress called Julie Christie and wanted to show Francis a scene from a film called *Billy Liar* where she skipped down a street and had adventures. I also needed to give him a tenner for the London petrol kitty and mostly I just wanted to say hi.

This morning as I'd been brushing my teeth, I'd made a vow to myself that I would redo the armholes on my grey leather dress, which were still giving me all kinds of grief. Once they were sussed, I would ease in the sleeves. The sleeves would become my bitches.

'I think a sleeveless dress would be much easier,' Barbara told me when she assessed my work-in-progress later that morning. 'I don't think you're ready for sleeves.'

Of course that just made me want to put sleeves on my dress even more.

'Why do you think so many dresses in the shops are sleeveless?' Barbara asked me.

She had this habit of staring at you without blinking when she was talking and she had her glasses on, which made her eyes look superbig and distorted, and I started blinking a lot more than I normally would. I was beginning to get paranoid that Barbara would think my blinks were taking the piss when the door to the studio opened and my head swivelled in that direction, as it had done all morning whenever anyone even passed by in the corridor outside. This time my head-swivelling wasn't in vain.

It was Francis with his toolkit.

He was walking straight towards me. I smiled. Had the 'Hey!' all ready to go, but then he took a left towards the broken overlocking machine and even though I tried to catch his eye, his eye refused to be caught.

Even after Barbara had moved on to give Paul grief, I didn't have a chance to talk to Francis because Sandra and Karen were busy explaining how it totally wasn't their fault that the overlocker was making a terrible noise, and I had a meeting with my English tutor.

'Hey you,' I said as I walked past but he didn't hear me or look up because he was intent on unscrewing tiny, tiny screws with a tiny, tiny screwdriver.

There was no chance to catch up with Francis at lunch either as I had a lunch date with Lexy of Thee Desperadettes fame who I'd been tweeting with about possible sequinned T-shirt designs. She was going to bring along Kirsten of the allergic-to-false-eyelashes-glue fame.

I was worried that it was going to be awkward and it *was* awk at first. 'So you're the girl that always hangs round with *that* girl,' Kirsten said when we met up outside the posh sandwich shop. Her eyeballs were normal size but she was giving me serious glare action. 'What is her problem?'

Where to begin? 'I don't really see her so much any more,' I mumbled, because it still felt wrong to slag Alice off to other people.

'It looked like Louis was seeing quite a bit of her on Saturday night,' Lexy said drily and I waited for my stomach to drop to the floor. Just as it started to plummet, I thought I saw Francis across the road, but it wasn't him and by then my stomach had righted itself.

I found I could listen to Lexy and Kirsten discussing Alice's Saturday night exploits without flying into a murderous rage even though it sounded like she'd been all up on Louis all evening. I guess now we weren't actually friends any more, none of the rules we'd drawn up applied.

'I would never let Louis that near once he's taken his top off,' Kirsten sniffed. 'His sweat gets everywhere and I love him but sometimes he smells really ripe.'

'Foul,' Lexy agreed. They didn't sound that besotted even though they were members of Louis's entourage of besotted

Desperadettes. 'I also really hate it when he drops to his knees in front of me and beats his chest. I keep telling him that it's not even a little bit funny and then he gets upset and it's impossible to stay angry with him.'

'Why's that?' I asked.

They both looked at me and shook their heads. 'Because it would be like kicking a kitten,' Lexy explained and I wanted to interrogate her further, but then Kirsten asked if it was true that Alice had come at me with a razor blade and that was why my hair was so short, then they both put in orders for sequinned T-shirts.

It turned out to be a pretty good lunch break in the end. After, I hurried back to the studio to wait for Francis but he was nowhere to be seen and he'd taken the overlocker away because apparently Sandra had bodged it up so badly that it needed to be mended off-site.

'Will I have to pay for the repairs?' she asked us. 'Maybe I could wipe off the debt if I agreed to give Amir a blowie round the back of the bins?'

'Oh God, can we all pretend you never said that out loud?' Mattie begged and so of course she spent the rest of the afternoon describing all the ways she was going to work off the money for the overlocker repairs. I spent most of the afternoon bent double with laughter – when she described something particularly wretched involving the student chaplain and an oven glove, I really thought I was going to wet myself.

I was still quite shaky and giggly as I left college and just as I walked past the *Staff Only* door, Francis came through it.

'There you are!' I exclaimed. 'I've wanted to talk to you all day. I was beginning to wonder if you were avoiding me. I'm so glad you're back.'

'Are you?' he said in that old flat way of his.

'Well, of course I am!' I frowned. 'Why wouldn't I be? Come on!'

Francis shook back his hair so for once it wasn't falling into his eyes and I could get the full glory of his furious face. Eyes narrowed, nostrils flared. Lips pinched. Not a sneer. I'd have welcomed a sneer. 'Because now you haven't got an excuse to talk to Louis. Jesus, just how low can you go?'

Wow! And no! And oh my goodness! 'It wasn't like that at all. I was worried when you suddenly weren't around and—'

'Why would you be worried about me?' Francis demanded, like all the time we'd spent together recently meant nothing – that we weren't really friends. Not that I wanted to be friends with Francis now. Not if he actually thought that I was the kind of person who'd use his dad's illness as a great way to get my flirt on with Louis. Which I *so* hadn't done.

'I asked you to put in a good word for me with Louis but that was weeks ago,' I reminded him. 'I didn't know you then and you didn't know me and it's clear you still don't know anything about me, not if you think that's the crappy way I roll.'

I could see him weighing up my words. Testing the heft of them. 'I don't like being used. That's all.'

Francis was going through something terrible but that still didn't give him the right to take it out on me. I was sick of people taking things out on me. 'Yeah? And I don't like people thinking the worst of me when I was just trying to be nice. I thought you were my mate. *I told you about my mum.*' I hissed the last sentence at him and he took a step back because I think there was spittle involved. 'Do you think I did that so you'd trust me enough to get me in good with Louis? Do you?'

'Well, no, but . . . '

His hair was falling in his face again but from the sound of his voice, uncertain and stammery, Francis knew he'd made a big mistake, but he still wasn't rushing to apologise.

'Oh, just get over yourself,' I snapped and I turned sharply enough that I clonked him hard with my bag, though that was a genuine accident, and stomped off as much as anyone can stomp when they're wearing kitten heels and a very tight pencil skirt.

I seethed about it at work as I let out the seams on Mrs Ayers's black party frock because she'd quit Weight Watchers yet again. I was still seething when I got home even though there was a *mahoosive* jar of chocolate pralines on my bedside table and when I tried to give Dad a tenner for them, he smacked my hand away.

Even having the good pizza for dinner couldn't turn my ferocious frown upside down. 'You'll get stuck looking like that, kid,' Dad said to me. 'Come on, cheer up, it might never happen.'

That was the singularly most irritating thing you could say to someone who was already in a bad mood. 'It has already happened,' I said glumly. I had no appetite for even the good pizza and Mum was picking all the cheese off her slice with a look of barely concealed disgust and Dad sighed and said that he wasn't going to waste money on the good pizza again if Mum and I weren't going to eat it.

21

By the next morning, I'd devised a brilliant plan to avoid Francis until I was calm enough not to start shouting at him as soon as I saw him, and he'd seen the extreme error of his ways. It involved making sure I removed myself from any place where Francis was lurking. This meant that I wouldn't be going to The Wow on Saturday night, but that didn't seem like such a tragedy. Not when I also couldn't bear to see Alice, whether or not she was all up on Louis.

My plan worked beautifully. I did see Francis talking to the Desperadettes outside the newsagent at Friday lunchtime but he didn't see me – probably because I crossed over the road and hid behind a postbox until he'd gone. But as I was leaving college later I bumped into Lexy and Kirsten, who was with the other Desperadette.

'This is the famous Franny B. She's not at all stuck-up when you get to know her,' Kirsten said as she introduced me. I'd never thought of myself as stuck-up but that was the problem when you tried to work a cool look; sometimes it backfired. 'This is Bethany.'

Bethany looked doubtful but not unwelcoming. 'So, word is that you're not hanging out with that Alice girl any more?'

I shook my head. 'Nope. I'm pretty much Alice-free these days,' I said lightly. The more times I said it, the less it would feel like a betrayal.

'Well, we have to go now but we'll see you at The Wow tomorrow night,' Lexy said firmly, like saying no wasn't an option.

It was though. Sage was in Leeds with her dad. Dora and Mattie were doing something Steampunk-y, and Paul had already told me that he was never going to The Wow again because they played terrible music and after the Halloween party he'd got disco dirt on his leather jacket that he couldn't shift.

'There's no law that I have to go to The Wow Club on a Saturday night anyway,' I said to Raj the next day when he'd come into the shop to do the afternoon shift. 'Lots of people don't go to The Wow on a Saturday night. You don't. What do you do instead?'

'Oh, I be out with my honeys,' he muttered vaguely.

'No, seriously, what do you do on a Saturday night? You don't have a crew and I can't see your dad letting you borrow the van so you can go out with your alleged honeys.' Raj was the only person I knew whose life was more boring than mine.

'Just drop it, Franny. I will totally bust a cap in your ass for realz this time,' he warned me.

'Yeah, yeah. Like, you're really packing heat.' I looked up from the skirt I was working on. 'You stay in, don't you? No big deal. I'm going to stay in tonight too. Like I said, The Wow is so over.'

'You're only saying The Wow is over because you don't want to turn up on your own and have Alice think that you're lame and friendless without her,' Raj summed up smugly, and he was half right. I also didn't want to turn up on my own and have Francis think the same thing.

'Well, it's not like Alice has a whole bunch of brand new friends,' I muttered. 'She hasn't even got a new boyfriend so she's just as lame and friendless as me.'

I could have sworn Raj's ears pricked up. 'Bitch be single, then?'

'Yes, Alice is currently between partners.' I could hear Shuv's disapproving voice in my head. 'Don't call girls bitches. It's demeaning.'

Raj pretended to choke. 'Yo! You've called her a bitch yourself. Heard it with my own ears.'

I gave him a pitying look. 'That's because she was *being* a bitch. It's completely different.'

'Girl, you be knowing shit about sexual politics.'

I had no comeback and a sneaking suspicion that Raj might be right, so I threw my pincushion at him. He laughed, caught it with one hand and promptly stabbed himself with a pin, which made me laugh.

It was a regular laughfest.

I went back to my hemming and Raj went back to being a human beatbox, which was really irritating until he suddenly stopped.

'So, if you wanted to go to The Wow, I'll come with you. Not on a date,' he added hurriedly, as I put down the skirt to stare at him in surprise. 'As mates. So you don't have to stay at home on your own on Saturday night.'

And so it was that Raj came to my house to pick me up later that evening. It was weird. I've known Raj for ever. We go back as far as me and Alice go back. I know pretty much everything about him. God, he even farts in front of me and I've blown my nose in front of him when I've had a cold and my snot was loud and really green.

Raj was Raj but when I heard him ring the doorbell, my stomach hurled itself from one side of my body to the other and I had to do a complete high-speed circuit of the kitchen until I felt calm enough to open the door.

'You ready then?' he grunted at me, though normally he told me that I was looking fly or super fine or sick.

I think he was trying to establish that we were not going on a date and that to tell me that I looked nice in my sixties-inspired Op Art-print minidress would be really date-like. 'I'm ready,' I said, grabbing the leather jacket I'd borrowed off Mattie for the weekend.

Mum and Dad had gone out on what they did call a date, though I couldn't see anything romantic about sitting in the Dockers' Arms watching middle-aged men with huge bellies play darts, so I didn't have any grief about the shortness of my skirt or what time my curfew was. They also weren't here to see Raj pick me up so they could spend the rest of the week trying to find out if he was my boyfriend.

Up until now they'd been quite relieved I hadn't shown any interest in boys. (Like I would ever admit it to them anyway.) I wanted to keep it that way.

As we set off along the seafront, I was also hugely grateful that Raj was wearing an outfit that wasn't too likely to show me up: sand-coloured drop-crotch skinnies, a large white, long-sleeved T-shirt and an unbuttoned grey short-sleeved shirt over that with Nike high-tops and, thank God, no baseball cap. I'd seen him look a lot worse. 'So, shall we head to the offy first?'

'Not for me.' Raj was such a pussy. 'I have to write a really long essay tomorrow so I can't have any alcohol.'

'But you don't mind if I have some?'

Raj said he didn't and he gallantly turned his back when we came to the seclusion of a wind shelter and I hiked up my dress so I could shove a quarter bottle of off-brand vodka down my tights. He didn't say a word but he looked rather scared.

'I'm not going to get drunk and jump you,' I told him as we joined the back of the very short queue outside The Wow. 'Mates, remember? Mates don't jump their mates. Urgh. It would be like snogging ... actually I don't even want to think about what snogging you would be like.'

'Right back at you,' Raj snapped. 'Anyway, I don't snog drunk girls. I want my honeys to remember every touch they get from the Rajmeister.'

'The Rajmeister!' I snorted happily and we were back in the friendzone, where we spent most of the time insulting each other.

Despite his rubbish gangsta routine, there had been a time when Raj had come to The Wow every week and he knew the routine. He went to the bar to get me a pint of diet Coke so I could pour my vodka into it and I headed for my usual table, safe in the knowledge that I wasn't on my own like a total loser but waiting for my friend to come back from the bar.

But when I got to my table, there was Alice on her own like a total loser. My body gave this quick jerk, like it was pleased to see her. After all it had been over two weeks since I'd last seen Alice and that was the longest we'd ever been apart, unless you counted the summer holidays when the Jenkinses went to Ibiza for three weeks.

'Oh, it's you,' she said. She looked at me nervously like she wasn't sure whether I was going to smack her.

I wasn't but I was having trouble with the sight of Alice in front of me looking as blonde and beautiful as ever, when in my head she'd become a blowsy, brassy tart with an evil glint in her eyes.

I couldn't think of a single thing to say to her so I stood there with my arms folded and put on my most epic bitchface like I wasn't even going to waste any words on her.

'So your hair's looking good,' she said desperately, then shuddered when she remembered that she didn't get to pass judgement on my hair. I was learning to love my hair; I'd resigned myself to having a Jean Seberg cut rather than a messy Edie do, but that didn't make what Alice did all right.

'I get the table,' I said, sitting down. 'You were here last week, even though you were meant to be grounded, and you trashed my hair, so I get the table.'

'Look, Franny, we're too good together to not be mates,' Alice said earnestly, shifting round on the seat to look at me. 'I miss you.'

'You miss me because I was your one friend and without me, you've no one. You don't miss me for *me*,' I pointed out. I thought I was over this. Anyway, I was fine without her, I had new friends, but I could hear the throb in my throat before I even felt it. 'You're just used to having me around. You don't value me otherwise you wouldn't have done what you did . . .'

'I've apologised a hundred times. Well, maybe not a hundred, but I will if you want me to,' Alice said. 'I'm friends with you because you're *you*. You're part of who I am, Franny, even if you can be a really moody bitch.' I stiffened again and she sighed. 'You're still too angry for me to get away with calling you a moody bitch, right?'

'Right,' I agreed, but my heart wasn't in it. It was exhausting being this angry with her when she was sitting there wearing her stretchy tight black Lipsy dress, which she always put on when she needed some extra oomph because she was feeling a bit crap. 'It just feels like I couldn't have been that important to you; that you didn't mind throwing me away if it meant that it got you Louis.'

When Alice took my hand I didn't stiffen. 'Oh, Louis,' she said with an eyeroll. 'Look, it's dumb to let him come between us and I'd rather have you than have hi—'

'Yo, Franny B, why you holding hands with someone who isn't me?' I looked up to see Raj standing there with my pint of diet Coke. 'And why are you holding hands with *her* when we both agreed she is no good?'

I loved Raj but the Rajmeister really was a dick. 'Alice and I are in the middle of maybe, just maybe, becoming friends again, so why don't you sit down and then this would be a great time for you and Alice to become friends again too,' I said. I felt better than I had done in days because finally all the pieces were slotting together.

'No, we're not,' Alice spat, snatching her hand away from mine so suddenly that she scratched me. 'You and I are not becoming friends again, not when you're here with *him*. How could you, Franny?'

'You two broke up ages ago.' Raj was giving Alice evils just as hard as she was giving him evils but when I spoke, they both turned to glare at me. 'Enough time has passed now that you both need to just get over it and then the three of us can hang out like we used to.'

'Why is everything always about you?' Alice cried. 'I was going to let you have Louis, but now you pull this crap on me, you can just forget it.'

'What crap?'

'Bringing him here. Sitting at *our* table with him. Rubbing my nose in it.'

'Just 'cause you don't want me doesn't mean there aren't other ladies begging me to give them some touch,' Raj said and he did some weird thing with his hands, which I guess would have meant something if I spoke fluent 'hood. 'Why you be jealous 'cause Franny wants to get wit' me?'

'What*ever*.' I turned to Alice because she couldn't be buying this or even care because Raj was simply another one of her conquests. She got up and shoved me out of the way to make her escape, so apparently she was buying it and she did care. 'Oh, come on, Alice. Really?'

'No, I won't come on. This is to get me back because of your hair, isn't it? I wish I'd taken the fucking clippers to it now, bitch. If you thought it was on with me and Louis before, then you don't even know what *on* is.'

She was gone, slamming past me with an elbow to my shoulder, then knocking into Raj so hard that he spilt the diet Coke. 'Bitch be tripping out,' he muttered, sitting down. Despite all the drama, he didn't seem that put out. He didn't even seem to mind that he had a brown stain on his white T-shirt.

'She doesn't just act like a bitch, she is a bitch,' I decided. 'Why the hell did you say I wanted to get with you? Like that would ever, ever happen!'

Raj wriggled his shoulders like he was trying to dislodge a cat clinging to his back. 'Yeah, but she doesn't know that. Is time she realised she doesn't own all the hotness. I mean, you're not hot HOT, Franny, but I bet plenty of brothers would want to get breezy with you.'

It was sweet of Raj to say that but I was still mad at him for derailing Alice and me making up. Though she couldn't have been *that* into making up. Probably she wanted to blindside me with fake friendship while she sank her claws even further into Louis.

I was starting to wish that I'd never seen Louis one grey day four years ago and decided that he was a beautiful boy-shaped container to put all my dreams and fantasies in. Really.

'Don't use me to score points,' I told Raj sternly. 'God, you can be a real dickhead sometimes.'

Raj mumbled something under his breath, then reminded me that he he'd just bought me a diet Coke so he wasn't all bad.

I decanted some of the vodka into it and sat there drinking while Raj slagged off every track the DJ played and every single person that walked past. He obviously regretted being my plus one. I should have trusted my instincts and stayed home because tonight had been a complete waste of time.

I didn't even dare move from the table because I didn't want to see Alice and Louis all over each other like a bad case of nits. And I didn't want to see Francis and it wasn't like Raj would dance with me and I wasn't going to dance on my own. There wasn't enough vodka and watered-down diet Coke in the world to make me dance on my own.

I was just about to ask Raj if we should call it a night and head to the Market Diner to get some chips when a crowd of girls suddenly surged around us. Lexy plonked herself down next to me. 'Hey, Franny. Can we sit down? We've always wanted to sit here. Best seat in the house.'

'Er, yeah, sure.'

Someone went to scavenge for spare stools and soon Thee Desperadettes were sitting round the table. Raj had buttoned up his shirt to hide the stain and was sitting up straight. I was surprised he hadn't fashioned his hands into little paws and stuck out his tongue – he was practically panting.

'This is my mate, Raj,' I sighed. 'This is Lexy, Kirsten, Bethany . . .'

I was going to kill Raj if he went all gangsta but he didn't. Instead he was charming and polite and made such a funny joke about Mark the mad dancer that Kirsten and Bethany even snorted.

It was tiny, Merrycliffe, so of course Raj knew three of Thee Desperadettes' younger brothers and he'd seen the others around and soon they were all chatting about the crappy Merrycliffe youth club that everyone went to until they turned fifteen and could sneak into The Wow.

'My mum stopped me going for a while because she'd heard one of the volunteers was a paedo, but it turned out he was training to be a paediatrician,' Bethany was saying and Raj was nodding and making loads of eye contact and she kept biting her bottom lip and nudging Lexy, who was sitting next to her, so that was nice for both of them.

We left them to it and went to dance and maybe I wasn't having such a bad Saturday night when I'd just become an honorary Desperadette.

Inevitably the music stopped, the lights went up, we booed and stomped our feet and that was when I saw them: Alice and Louis against the bar, their heads close together. Not close enough that they were kissing, but too close for comfort, close enough that they could have an intimate, private conversation and Louis could look down the front of Alice's dress.

I turned away because I didn't want to see what might happen next, which *had* to be a kiss, and there was Francis standing in front of me.

22

'Hey,' he said. 'You going to The Market Diner?'

'Well, yeah, but . . .'

'If we go now, we can beat the queue and get a table and chips, before they say that it will be another ten minutes for chips,' he told me, like we were cool and anyway . . .

'It doesn't matter what time you get there, they always say it will be another ten minutes for chips,' I pointed out. 'Anyway, I'm going to the Diner with my friends and I think we've already established that we're not friends because you think I'm a pretty crap excuse for a human being.'

'I don't think that,' Francis said. 'That was my turn to be a twat. I'm trying to say sorry and I'd really like to do it by buying you a polystyrene container full of chips.'

I didn't want to give in that easily, because I never gave in that easily. 'It's styrofoam, not polystyrene,' I said, but I was walking off the dance floor with a sideways glance at Francis so he knew to follow me as I went to get my jacket and my bag.

'Seriously, do you even know the difference? Does anyone?' he asked and because he was talking to my back, he couldn't see me smile.

Raj and Bethany were nose to nose and he just flapped a hand at me when I said I was going to the Market Diner, even though he'd promised to walk me home so I didn't get abducted by sex traffickers.

We were the first people to leave The Wow. Everyone else was slowly congregating in the foyer and huddling in preparation for what would be an icy, windy dash to the diner because we were deep in November now and those Atlantic Ocean winds took no prisoners.

'Shall we save all our breath for walking superfast and keep the rest of my apology for when we're sitting down with hot chips?' Francis shouted. I wasn't even sure if he'd be able to hear my reply over the howl of the nor'-easter.

As it was, my eyes were watering and it was a relief when Francis tucked his arm in mine and we half walked, half ran to the Diner.

It was a miracle but the chips, all golden and sizzling, were ready and as Francis went to get ours I repaired my mascara, which had run down my face in grimy black rivulets. Then I patted down my fringe, and decided against more lipgloss. It would only disappear after the first sip of tea and it was only Francis. He didn't care if my lips were glossy or not.

But he did care enough to bring me a choice of condiments

on the tray with my chips and my tea. I snagged a couple of sachets of brown sauce and spent long moments drizzling them over my chips and when there wasn't anything left to drizzle I had to look up at Francis.

He was staring at me. Not in a creepy way, but a thoughtful way. 'So, sorry,' he said. 'For behaving like a twat and jumping to conclusions.'

Just this once, I realised I had to let something go. 'I think you have a free pass on the twatdom because your dad's not well, but don't push it.'

He smiled ever so faintly. I'd forgotten how much cuter he looked when he smiled. 'Reckon I won't be able to use it for at least another month.'

I really wanted to smile too. 'At least.' I took a sip of tea. 'How is your dad then? Is he over what he had to go to hospital for? I tried to ask Louis what was wrong with him but he wasn't very helpful.'

I took another sip of tea and it turned to ashes in my mouth because I'd mentioned Louis and just as Louis had brought Francis and me together, he also pulled us apart, but Francis shook his head and smiled again.

He'd put on a grey woolly beanie before we'd left The Wow and he hadn't taken it off, so for once, without his hair in the way, I could see his face. The strain of the last week had put hollows underneath his cheekbones and painted dark circles around his eyes. 'My dad had an infection and it gunked up his kidneys. That's the proper medical explanation. It made him go a bit daft in the head, until they pumped him full of drugs and put him on a rapid drip to kickstart his kidneys again. I bet the explanation you got from Louis was a bit more basic than that.'

'Way more basic than that.' I rested my elbows on the table. I was vaguely aware of the door opening and letting in an icy blast of air along with the first wave of Wow-ers, but mostly my attention was focused on Francis. 'I'm glad he's better. Must have been scary.'

'It was. Still is. It's like we know how our bodies work. That they need food and water and sleep and then they pretty much do what we want them to do when we want them to, but my dad's body . . . ' He stopped to eat a chip and almost choked on it. I reached across the table and rested my tea-warmed hand on his.

I didn't know what to say so I said nothing, but curled my fingers round his taut, white knuckles and stared at our hands until I heard Francis take a deep breath and I knew it was all right to look up.

'My dad's body has become a prison,' he said quietly. 'He's trapped inside it. It's stopped doing what it's meant to. Now it does all this weird, unpredictable stuff and he's in pain all the time. I can't even imagine being in pain all the time.'

'Neither can I.' In that moment I felt closer to Francis than I'd ever felt to anybody, even Alice. No one had ever been this honest with me, this brave. 'I'm glad you told me. You can tell me anything and you don't have to worry that I'd tell anyone else. I'm really good at keeping secrets.'

'Oh, don't, Franny. You're making me feel even more of a

twat than I was already,' Francis said and in the time it took him to smile crookedly, he shifted so I wasn't holding his hand any more and for one brief second he was holding mine instead. Then he patted it clumsily and let go so we weren't touching and were simply two people sharing a table. It still felt intimate. 'Anyway, I spoke to Louis again and he said that when you saw him in the library all you wanted to talk about was me.'

'Well, no, not quite,' I said quickly, because even though Francis and I were having a moment – or so many moments all strung together that actually they went beyond anything as temporary and disposable as just a moment – I didn't want him to get the wrong idea. 'I just wanted to make sure your dad was OK. Though we all wondered if you'd been sacked for hanging out with us when you were meant to be working.'

'Yeah? They wouldn't sack me. I'm the only one who knows how to repair the overlocker that you guys keep jamming up.' Francis grinned. He wasn't looking so sad now and there was the tiniest twinkle in his eyes, though that could have been the reflection of the strip lighting. And with all his hair tucked away, I suppose you could call him attractive. Not really hot, he was a bit too sharp for hot, and he could never come close to Louis for sheer male beauty, but he was all right to look at.

'I never jam the overlocker,' I protested, and I had to tell him about Sandra and Karen sexually harassing Amir. Then I had to tell him about Julie Christie in *Billy Liar* and then I had to tell him that the purple lady had a new shopping trolley, which was purple too *and then*, when he could finally get a word in, Francis told me about a video he was making where he edited together lots of clips from old sci-fi movies set to a track from the last Daft Punk album. And then he reminded me that Thee Desperadoes' gig in London was next weekend and I was just giving him a tenner towards the petrol when the last stragglers from The Wow turned up.

'Ten minutes for chips!' went the cry and I barely had time to glance up before a hand was descending towards my plate.

'Budge up, Franny B,' Louis demanded, sliding into the booth next to me. 'And don't hog the chips!'

At the counter a blissed-out Raj was surrounded by Desperadettes, and Louis was eating all my chips and grinning at us. 'So, have you two kissed and made up, then?'

'We've made up,' I muttered as Francis told Louis to 'shut it'.

Shutting it was not something Louis liked doing – I was starting to realise that. 'Like I said, Franny doesn't need an excuse to come and talk to me. You can talk to me any time,' Louis offered kindly. I slumped down in the seat and wondered whether I could make my head completely disappear into my neck. 'Anyway, all we talked about was your dad's piss.'

I didn't care that Louis was the walking embodiment of my teenage dreams made real. I elbowed him so hard that he almost landed on the floor. 'Don't start all that again.'

'See, I told you she goes bright red every time I talk about piss.' Louis actually had the nerve to laugh and maybe it was just as well that he wasn't the most . . . intellectually gifted boy on the planet otherwise he might have guessed that a) I went bright red most times I spoke to him and b) that was because I was pining for him so hard.

Maybe I hadn't been pining quite so hard for Louis lately but I'd had a lot on my plate and as soon as I thought it I was swivelling round in my seat. 'Where's Alice?' I asked. I couldn't even say her name now without my mouth twisting into a horrible shape.

'Her dad came and picked her up. Apparently she has to be in by eleven-thirty. How lame is that?'

I wasn't going to be that girl who ran other girls down but . . . 'So lame,' I said with my best sneer. When I looked over at Francis he was sneering too, but it wasn't about Alice having to be home before midnight.

'Don't,' he said, very quietly, so only I heard because Louis was shouting across the Diner to ask Thee Desperadettes how much longer the chips were going to be. 'Just don't, Franny.'

He was right. I was being all wrong so I nodded and Francis raised his eyebrows at me, before he relented and smiled another one of his crooked smiles and then Raj, Lexy and Bethany came over and insisted that we all scooch even though our table was only meant to have four people sitting round it.

Later, when the last cold chip had been mopped up in the last congealed slick of ketchup and no one had money for any more tea, we left the Market Diner.

Thee Desperadettes and Raj all lived on the wide avenues off the High Street. Raj cast a longing look at Bethany who smiled encouragingly, then he turned to me. 'I'll walk you home, right?' He sighed.

I didn't want to get in the way of someone else's potential snog, but I also didn't fancy getting abducted on my long, lonely walk along the seafront. 'Well, it's just . . .'

'I was heading that way,' Francis cut in casually. I would much rather Francis walked me home so we could talk about films and stuff, instead of Raj moaning that I'd cock-blocked him. 'If that's cool with you, Franny?'

'Supercool,' I said and that just left Louis, who slung an arm round our shoulders and said he'd come with us.

It was everything I'd ever wanted. Well, not everything: there was no kissing, no gazing into each other's eyes, no chance for Louis to tell me that he couldn't stop thinking about me and that the world was a more magical place with me in it.

But even so, it was still Louis walking me home. With Francis.

I was bookended by Desperadoes. Louis tucked his arm into mine, demanded that Francis, who seemed lost in thought, take my other arm, and off we went with Louis trying to persuade us that we should launch into 'Follow The Yellow Brick Road' from *The Wizard of Oz*.

'It will be fun! Franny, you can be Dorothy and we'll do the dance and everything,' he pleaded. When I laughed because he had to be joking, Louis pouted. 'Oh, come on.'

'Please don't make me,' I said, as I tried to fight back the giggles. 'You do not want to hear me sing.'

'But you can't sound any worse than Francis.' Louis tried to skip but Francis and I refused to join in.

'Seriously, you're like a six-year-old girl trapped in the body of a twenty-year-old dude,' Francis said. 'Pipe down, you'll frighten the seagulls.'

There were no seagulls. They usually stuck around during winter, but you never saw them at night. That was Louis's next topic of conversation. 'Do you think they hang out underneath the arches by the old marina, shooting the breeze? What does shooting the breeze actually mean anyway? How could you shoot a breeze? Why would you want to?'

It was as if every single thought that entered Louis's mind came out of his mouth at the same time. It was kind of entertaining and Louis was tucked up in a navy peacoat and I didn't even mind that he'd popped the collar because he looked so cute and snuggly but in a rock 'n' roll way, but I also wished he'd shut up for even thirty seconds. I wanted to ask Francis if he knew any other cool bands from the sixties, and just before we'd left the Diner and Louis had been chatting to Lexy, Francis had quietly asked me how my mum was.

But I'd barely had a chance to tell him before the others had decided that it was time to leave.

It was all right though. Francis and I were friends again and on Monday we'd watch clips from black and white films and I could tell him stuff that I couldn't share with anyone else because he was the kind of person who'd take your secrets to the grave with him.

That didn't mean Francis was boring or dull, but he was a steady presence on my left, matching his pace to mine, while on my right Louis pranced and swung my hand and tried to pull me faster than I wanted to go.

23

My goal for the next week was to finish my leather dress to wear on Saturday when we went to London. My other goal was to get Mum to pay me back for all the money I'd loaned out to her when Dad was away.

On Wednesday evening she finally handed over one hundred and thirty pounds in used notes. She actually owed me closer to one hundred and twenty but she said that the extra was interest.

'You going to buy yourself something nice in Manchester then?' Mum asked. I frowned, until I remembered that she still thought I was spending the weekend with Shuv. 'Maybe some clothes? They've got a big TopShop there, haven't they?'

Mum hovered in the doorway of my sewing room, which was next door to my bedroom. Back in the day, it had probably been home to four Victorian housemaids but now it was home to my proper industrial sewing machine, which the Chatterjees gave

243

me when they bought a new one for the dry-cleaning shop. All my buttons and zippers and findings were neatly stored in an old shop display unit that my dad had bought me from a French flea market, and on the IKEA shelving were all my fabrics arranged according to colour. No one ever bothered me when I was in my sewing room, and while I totally appreciated Mum showing some interest in my life, I'd just successfully sewn the first sleeve into my leather dress and I was keen to start on the second, while my luck was still in and also ... 'Well, I don't buy new clothes,' I explained. 'It's just a waste of money when I could make something or buy vintage or second-hand clothes and repurpose them.'

Mum pulled a face. 'Yeah, but ...'

'And at the same time, it's educational,' I said brightly, as I very carefully positioned the tacked sleeve under the needle. 'Even making that wrap skirt I gave you last Christmas was working towards my future. That's kind of ace, isn't it?'

'I suppose.' Mum didn't sound convinced but she'd loved the denim skirt I'd made her last Christmas. I'd even appliquéd little felt flowers on to it and anyway we were having an actual conversation, and Dad hadn't put any dates on the kitchen calendar and we were deep into November now so there was no way he was going to disappear into the wide blue yonder this close to Christmas.

It was all good. Pretty much all of it. There was still the Alice thing, I thought, as Mum muttered something about an episode of *Don't Tell the Bride* waiting for her on the Sky box, but I was missing her less and less.

I didn't *need* Alice any more. When I thought back to being friends with her, which seemed like a gazillion years ago, my world had been much smaller. There had only been room for Alice in it.

Now my world had expanded to encompass all these new people. Not just Sage and Dora and the others, even Karen and Sandra, but Thee Desperadettes and especially Francis and Louis. Louis was properly in my life now and when I thought about the weekend in London, I'd get a shivery feeling of excitement though it felt a bit like terror too, because I knew something important was going to happen.

'It's my do-or-die weekend,' I said to Sage on Friday afternoon as I put the final touches to my leather dress, though part of me never wanted to see it ever again. The leather had stretched from being worked on so much and the hem had gone seriously wonky.

'You mean it's your do-Louis-or-die weekend.' She smiled slyly when I shuddered because I didn't want to *do* Louis. Not yet anyway. But kissing would be good – if he could stand still and be quiet for long enough. 'So, shall we talk outfit options?'

'Well, I'm wearing this, of course!' I gestured at my grey leather dress. 'With my—'

'No, don't tell us. Let us guess,' Mattie drawled from where he was perched on top of his desk, swinging his legs and flicking through the new *Vogue*. There was a big interview with Martin Sanderson, which we'd all pored over; photographs taken in what he called his atelier (and what I called his workroom) above his first ever shop in Notting Hill. The whole building was painted in his signature shade of pink, a dull, smudgy pink like the dusky Merrycliffe skies in winter. 'You're going to wear thick black tights and . . . '

' . . . either your kitten heels or those block-heel black knee-high boots,' Dora said. She tilted her head and looked at me. 'Maybe with Mattie's black leather jacket. I know you despise double denim but how do you feel about double leather?'

'I think I could make it work,' I decided and Sage made a funny noise at the back of her throat. 'What?'

She shook her head. 'You're going for a fashion look when you should go for a pulling look. Boys don't get fashion looks. They're not that evolved.'

I glanced over at Mattie, who shrugged. 'I am one of the very few who are evolved, but the rest of my kind think girls should do legs *and* cleavage.'

'No!' I was genuinely shocked. Francis had claimed that he was far more evolved than me, but he'd been talking about emotional maturity rather than fashion. Then I thought of Alice's strike rate and the stretchy short black bandage dresses she preferred because they made the most of her three B's. 'Not all boys, surely?'

Mattie looked at me pityingly. 'Most boys don't understand fashion.'

I thought about the smirks and nudges when I wore my cropped trousers, Chanel-ish jacket and brogues to The Wow. Even when I wore one of my Edie-esque slinky T-shirt dresses, boys looked at me in confusion because of the thick black opaques and the lack of six-inch stripper heels.

'But if the boy was, like, in a band or something, he'd be creative and arty and he'd totally go for a girl like me,' I pointed out, but Sage just rolled her eyes and said that most boys in bands would go out with a blonde model given half the chance, even indie boys in indie bands, and that if I was really serious about pulling Louis I'd at least have to wear bootie shorts with my thick black tights.

'The day I wear bootie shorts is the day that I've suffered a mild concussion,' I said grandly but now I was worried that I hadn't thought hard enough about my outfit options. I hoped Sage was wrong.

There were plenty of boys who got fashion. Francis, for instance, had been full of praise for my leather dress and we often discussed sixties designers like Mary Quant and Barbara Hulanicki of Biba. Though even Francis had got a bit glassy-eyed when we watched a film called *Girl on a Motorcycle* because the actress starring in it, Marianne Faithfull, spent all her time in a black leather catsuit.

It was all so confusing.

'Anyway, even if you do wear bootie shorts, you'll have to wear a bum bag or money belt,' Sage reminded me. She'd been to London five times, which was more than any of us. Even Karen and Sandra. She'd even been to Camden and said that the streets of London were not paved with gold but rapists, muggers, pickpockets and gangs of gypsies who'd steal your phone while they distracted you by cursing when you wouldn't buy their lucky heather.

There was so much to worry about, but Francis had told me

that London was also really exciting. It was fast and noisy and there was always something happening, something new to look at, something that you'd never seen before. He'd also said we'd have enough time before Thee Desperadoes soundchecked for him to take me to Berwick Street in Soho where there were loads of fabric shops.

'Take lots of pictures and put them on Instagram,' Paul told me as we left college. 'Live tweet everything so I can pretend I'm in London too.'

He was the only other person who'd never been to London before and he made me promise that I'd have my photo taken next to Camden Town station. Sage stood over me until I'd downloaded a tube map on to my phone and Dora wanted me to go to a particular shop and see if they had a purple leather bustier in her size and they all walked with me to the seafront and waved me off, like I was going to war and they might never see me again.

The giddy, sick feeling of excitement that made my tummy churn and my toes curl up inside my Dunlop Green Flashes (I refused to wear any other kind of trainer) intensified until I thought I might actually throw up.

I was still awake at two the next morning, mentally reviewing my outfit options but always returning to the leather dress. Then it was seven and my alarm was shrieking me awake.

It took a few seconds to penetrate my sleep-fogged brain, then I sat up with a tiny cry because I wasn't going to spend the day doing alterations. I was going to spend a lot of the day in a minibus with Thee Desperadettes and Thee Desperadoes and Louis.

I was going to London.

I should have leapt out of bed and danced my way to the bathroom like I was in a Hollywood musical but I staggered instead, lurching into the wall every now and again when staying upright got too hard.

I had to have a barely lukewarm shower because it was too early for the boiler to come on. It woke me up quite a bit and soon I was squeaky clean and wide-eyed as I assessed my hair in the bathroom mirror.

It was three weeks since my shearing. The bald spot was no more, the tufty bit was a lot less tufty and my fringe was long enough to sweep to one side and smooth down with serum in a very gamine, sixties way. I almost loved it now.

I was also going to have to learn to love my leather dress. The thin leather had stretched so much that it was shapeless rather than A-line and made me look even more stick-like than usual, and one of the three-quarter-length sleeves was tighter than the other one. All I could do was hope that, to the untrained eye, it would look very stylish and directional.

I packed my bag with all the stuff I'd need for the next twenty-four hours. We weren't getting back to Merrycliffe until God knows what time on Sunday morning but Lexy had already said I could stay at hers because Mum and Dad thought I'd be all tucked up on Shuv's sofa in Manchester.

I felt a tiny pang of guilt about lying to Mum and Dad, but it was lying for their own good. And my own good because even if they had agreed to let me go, which was doubtful, there'd have been conditions attached. I was used to Mum's benign neglect but Dad was a bit more hands-on when he was around. He didn't mind what I got up to in Merrycliffe because there wasn't much I could get up to, but whenever I ventured further afield there were hourly texts and phone calls.

Anyway, I was going to be fine in London. It wasn't like I would be chugging down alcohol – no more than I would on a night out in Merrycliffe – and I'd be with older, responsible people. Well, they were older anyway.

It was no use. I still felt guilty. Enough that I decided to make them a cup of tea before I went. Both Mum and Dad had been very suspicious of why I needed to leave for Manchester at eight in the morning but Shuv had told them there was a vintage fair on and we had to get there before all the good stuff went. When it came to lying to the parents, there was still so much Shuv had to teach me.

But she didn't have to teach me anything about sucking up. Not only did I make tea but toast too, and put the jam and butter in little dishes. Then I carried the whole lot upstairs on a tray quietly so as not to ruin the surprise, until I came to their bedroom door. It was always ajar when Dad was home because he said that once you'd had kids you couldn't not sleep with your bedroom door ajar to hear them if they cried out in the middle of the night. Innate primordial instinct he called it, though it had missed Mum out because she managed to sleep with the door tightly shut when he was away.

Anyway, now it was ajar and I paused to listen carefully to make sure I wasn't interrupting anything. Like, sexy times. Oh God, it didn't even bear thinking about. But I couldn't hear anything that was going to require me to have huge amounts of therapy, just Dad saying . . .

'Well, we'll talk to her when she gets back from Manchester, before I head off to the continent.'

My heart sank. Not just to my feet but right down to the floor. He wasn't meant to be going anywhere. And before I could even wonder what they needed to tell me that was so important . . .

'I can't see the harm in Franny staying on to do her fashion BTEC if she passes her retakes,' Mum said. 'Then she'll have a qualification to fall back on.'

'Not a proper qualification though.' I knew I should stop listening, all that chuff about eavesdroppers never hearing any good, but I was rooted to the spot. 'We both thought Franny was as bright as Shuv, but she's not and this ridiculous idea that she's going to do some fancy fashion degree and move to Paris to make frocks for a living? Best nip it in the bud.'

He said it so matter-of-factly that for a long moment I agreed with him. Even getting into Central St Martin's to do a fashion degree would be lottery lucky, but to actually become a successful fashion designer – that would be like winning Euromillions when the jackpot had rolled over week after week. It was a once-in-a-generation kind of deal.

I glanced down at my leather dress. It hadn't turned out as I'd planned, but even Barbara had been grudgingly impressed with what I'd managed to achieve from some off-cuts of cheap, thin leather. That was nothing to do with luck. It was to do with working bloody hard and I needed to be somewhere where I could harness my talent, work even bloody harder.

This was about the time that Mum should have been sticking up for me. It was the least she could do. I waited.

'Well, she could still be a machinist, couldn't she?' she pondered. 'I mean, it's not what she wanted, but it's a career in fashion. Sort of.'

'Yeah, but that's all outsourced to the Far East now,' Dad said and I couldn't believe they thought they had the right to decide how my life was going to be. They wanted to take my dreams and rip them into tiny pieces because their world was too small and narrow to make room for them. 'I looked at the course fees for that fashion degree in London. Thousands and thousands a year, plus rent and whatnot. With her track record, who's to say she'd even stick at it? She's better off going full-time for the Chatterjees. The recession doesn't seem to have affected them.'

Mum grunted in agreement. 'It would be good to have her around for when you're not here,' she decided and I'd heard enough.

I kicked the door open so hard that it crashed back on its hinges. I really wished that I hadn't made them breakfast, because after my dramatic entrance, both of them managing to jump even though they were sitting up in bed, I then had to set the heavy tray down very carefully on top of the chest of drawers.

'I'm staying on at college and getting my BTEC whether you like it or not,' I burst out. 'And then if they'll have me, I'm going to Central St Martin's to do my fashion degree—'

'Now, Franny,' Dad said in that voice of his that he dug out when he thought I was being completely unreasonable. 'I'm sorry you had to hear that but it is what it is. The real world doesn't work the way you think it does.'

I knew all about the real world. It wasn't like I'd spent most of my life at Eurodisney. 'If you don't want to get saddled with my tuition fees, then fine! I'll leave home so I can be means-tested and not have to pay them.' The unfairness of it all made me clench my hands into tight, painful fists. 'You're my parents! You're meant to encourage me to be whoever the hell I want to be! Why can't you be like those parents on *The X-Factor* who support their children even when they can't sing a note? Except I have found something I could be really good at and you're meant to tell me to go after my dreams and—'

'That's all very well, Franny, but you failed half your GCSEs.' It was the worst thing he could have said.

I looked at Mum and she looked back at me with a wary, frightened look. Then her gaze skidded away. I was done with this. 'I didn't fail half my GCSEs.' I'd given up counting how many times I'd said it. 'I didn't even fail my Maths and English GCSEs ...'

'Franny, please, don't ...' It was a frantic little whimper that was easy to ignore.

'But you did fail them,' Dad pointed out, frowning as he

253

glanced from me to Mum because he was still too dumb to work it out.

'I didn't fail them. I would have had to turn up at school to take them in order to fail them. Do you want to know why I missed school on those days? While you were God knows where in the middle of Europe because it's too much to expect that you might phone at least once every day?' I could feel the spittle collecting at the side of my mouth as the words flew out. They were both silent, staring at me in horror, but for very different reasons. 'I didn't dare leave the house because I was terrified that if I did, she'd have done something awful while I was gone. That I'd have come back to find she'd overdosed on the pills that she stops taking the minute you get into your lorry and disappear.'

It didn't even come close to describing those five awful, wretched days in June, Thursday through to Monday, when I'd stayed in the house, curtains drawn so not a chink of blinding sunlight could penetrate, no restorative sea breezes allowed to gently sweep through the house.

Mum had been neither manic nor maudlin. Instead, she'd cried for five days straight and kept saying, 'I can't bear it, I can't bear it,' and when I wanted to phone Linda or the doctor or even Dad and tell him to come home now, she'd cried harder and said she'd be sent away again and she'd never forgive me.

Neither of us had slept. I'd been too scared to close my eyes. How could I when my mother was lying on the bathroom floor telling me that there was no point in going on when she felt like this? And she didn't sleep because all she could do was cry.

I'd spent most of the time on the floor with her, back propped up against the tub. When she'd let me, I'd held her narrow body and it seemed like it was so frail that it might snap in two with the force of her sobs. Every time I ventured downstairs to get a drink or to snatch something out of the fridge, I'd race back up again and it was always a relief to find her still foetal on our tatted blue bathroom rug. I had fallen asleep eventually, head resting on the lip of the bath, and when I'd woken up on the Tuesday morning, she was in her own bed fast asleep. 'God, what do *you* want?' she'd snapped when she woke to find me standing over her, watching the rise and fall of her breath to make sure that she was still alive. 'Leave me alone, Franny. I'm tired.'

I deserved bouquets and a ticker tape parade for making it to school later that afternoon to take my history GCSE (my predicted A grade becoming a shaky C) but my Maths GCSE had been the Thursday before, English on the Monday and it wasn't like I had a sick note or a mother who'd admit that there was anything wrong with her.

I folded my arms, mostly to stop my hands from shaking. No one said anything. The three of us looked everywhere but at each other until the silence began to feel like a person in its own right.

'It's not what you think, Richard,' Mum said at last. I think her hands were shaking too because she shoved them under the duvet. 'You know how Franny exaggerates. The thing is—'

'It's not what you think because you don't think about us at all,' I interrupted. I couldn't believe that I was talking to them like this and that they were sitting up in bed, looking pretty shellshocked but letting me. 'You can't wait to disappear and the minute you do, she stops taking the pills and going to counselling. She just *stops*. But I don't want to stop here with her just because nobody else can bear to.'

Everyone always said it was good to talk. You couldn't bottle things up. You had to get stuff off your chest. But it didn't feel good. It felt awful, like the worst kind of betrayal. That all the stuff we never said was unsaid for a good reason and that I was destroying our home; prising up the floorboards, tearing off the wallpaper, going through each room and smashing everything I could find.

'I don't expect you to, Franny,' Mum said in a tiny, tight voice. She wasn't even crying, though tears were streaming down my face and even Dad was brushing an impatient hand against his cheek. 'I don't need you to take care of me. I don't ask you to.'

'But if I don't, then who will? You don't have to drive across Europe every month,' I shouted and Dad flinched. 'We all know it's why Shuv hardly ever comes home and Anna only turns up when she wants me to do her mending. I'm the only one left. That's the reason you both want me trapped here in Merrycliffe – so I'm around to pick you up every time you fall. Well, it's not fair!'

Dad flung back the covers. 'Franny! Just calm down!'

'I'm sorry, Mum, but I can't do it any more. If you can get your shit together when Dad's back, then why can't you keep it together when he goes away again?'

She shook her head. 'You don't understand, Franny. You don't know what it's like.'

'I've tried to but I'm sick of trying when you won't make any effort.' I'd backed myself up against the wall and I felt like a cornered animal with no place left to hide.

Dad hadn't even made it to his feet but was sitting on the edge of the bed like he wasn't sure that his legs worked. Most other dads that I knew were getting fat – Alice had told me that Sean had a personal trainer because he couldn't do up his fitted shirts over his paunch – but Dad seemed to be getting thinner. 'Is this true, pet?' He looked over his shoulder at Mum, who was staring out of the window, her bottom lip caught between her teeth. 'Are things really this bad? I didn't think you were that depressed any more, love.'

'I'm fine,' Mum insisted. 'Everybody gets down now and again. Everyone has off days. It doesn't mean that I'm depressed. Not like I was before.'

'Stop lying! Nobody ever says what they really mean in this house. It makes me want to scream!' It wasn't enough. I had to get through to them. Shock them into having some kind of reaction otherwise they'd just go back to pretending that everything was mostly all right, nothing to worry about, let's not make a fuss, because it was the easiest way to cope with it. 'You know what? I'm not even going to Manchester! I'm going to London! With a rock band! And you weren't even going to find out because you're not that interested in anything I do that doesn't fit in with your crummy plans to keep me trapped in Merrycliffe for the rest of my life.'

Dad did manage to stand up then and oh, now he was getting red-faced and cross because it was always easy to get cross with me. 'You are not going to London, young lady.'

I was already halfway out of the door. 'I am and I'm going to stay there. There is absolutely nothing worth coming back for.' I meant it. I didn't care if I had to spend ten years doing alterations in the dry-cleaning shops of London until I had enough saved up to go to Central St Martin's, I was done with Merrycliffe. Done with being told that my life was never going to amount to anything.

'You're not going anywhere. You're going to lose the attitude and you're going to apologise to your mother for—'

'I'm not apologising for anything. You should be apologising to me!'

Then I was racing down the stairs, grabbing my Marc by Marc Jacobs tote bag that always sat in the hall and racing out the front door. I ran as fast as I could along the seafront. Ran so hard I thought my lungs might burst and it wasn't until I got to the Wow Club where we'd arranged to meet that I realised there was no one running after me.

24

There was no one waiting for me either. No minibus. All around me was desolation. Well, I was half an hour early.

It was especially cold on the seafront; the wind whipping up the waves, so the iron-grey sea was trimmed with white frills.

I could have walked down to the Market Diner to get coffee and maybe a bacon sandwich, because I'd left my coffee and toast on the tray in my parents' bedroom. I'd fondly imagined that we'd eat breakfast together while I told them some medium-weight lies about how excited I was to be going to Manchester for the weekend.

Now the thought of eating and drinking anything made me gag and I huddled outside the entrance to the club. I tucked my arms around myself and wondered why I was even thinking about breakfast when my world had just come crashing down around me. Funny how it could take ten minutes to destroy your entire life, but I'd still meant every word I'd screamed: I wasn't going to stay in Merrycliffe to stagnate and become bitter and corroded with thwarted ambition and all that other bad shit. I'd end up like Barbara. Or worse, like my mum.

But I was only sixteen and hadn't had any plans to leave Merrycliffe just yet. I'd read about people who'd arrived in a new city or even a new country with nothing but a handful of bank notes and a dream, and ten, twenty years later they were rich and successful. I had ages and ages to go until I got to the rich and successful bit and what was going to happen to me in the meantime? Maybe I really should go to Manchester and then Shuv would have to help me. There was more to being a big sister than forking out for two different kinds of doughballs.

I heard my mobile ring. I pulled it out, only to see Dad's face flashing up on the screen. I cancelled the call and even that was dreadful. Even that felt like the worst thing I'd ever done. Then I did something even more dreadful and I blocked his number and Mum's and the landline. There was nothing left to say.

I'd crossed a line. It couldn't be uncrossed. I had to get away from Merrycliffe. There was no going back now. Stuff could never be sorted out. Mum's head would still be messed up and I'd still be the person who had to deal with it *and* I'd be grounded. Indefinitely. Worse than grounded. Dad would probably march me to college on Monday morning and make me turn in my sewing kit.

My pity party was interrupted by the toot of a horn. I looked up to see Francis leaning out of the window of a minibus borrowed from one of the local retirement homes. You didn't get much more rock 'n' roll than that.

'Hey, Franny,' he called. 'You're early.'

I nodded in agreement. Wasn't quite up to smiling yet. I tried not to shiver as Francis jumped down from the bus along with a guy I vaguely knew from Saturday nights at The Wow. He always wore a trucker hat and a Nirvana T-shirt.

'Olly, our driver slash roadie slash ... what else do you get stuck doing?' Francis asked.

'Babysitting Louis and shoving his head out of the window if it looks like he's going to vom.' Olly dipped his head at me. 'Aren't you cold without a coat?'

'Oh, I'm fine,' I said but as soon as I spoke I realised that talking wasn't a good idea. My voice caught on every word like it didn't know how to behave when it wasn't shouting out awful truths.

Olly turned away to open the back doors of the minibus but Francis peered at my face like he was counting how many open pores I had. 'You all right?'

I shrank back, then realised I could blame my red-rimmed watering eyes on natural causes. 'I told you I'm fine. It's the early start. It's a killer.'

'Whatever.' Generally I liked being friends with Francis, except now that he knew me it made him kind of perceptive about when I might be lying. 'You had breakfast? Shall we drive up to the Diner to grab some coffee and a toastie?'

My stomach clenched at the mention of food but I was saved from having to answer by the arrival of three Desperadettes and two Desperadoes spilling out of a parentally driven people carrier.

'Let's do this thing!' Kirsten exclaimed. She was very excited. I looked at Bethany and Lexy and realised my leather dress was a terrible mistake.

They were all wearing onesies, and though I would never wear a onesie outside the house, not even to go to the Spar for emergency chocolate supplies, I should have planned for this trip better. They all had huge holdalls and it was obvious they were going to change into their Desperadette outfits later on, whereas I was going to be stuck in a thin leather dress all day. Hadn't even brought the bag I'd so carefully packed.

As it was, all three of them were staring at me. 'You all right, Franny? You look a bit weird.'

This time I was saved from having to reply by another toot of a horn and I thought the day couldn't have got any worse, but it just did. Pulling up in a dilapidated Ford Capri was Louis ... and Alice.

Even in the midst of being furious with Alice, I had to admire her sheer, brazen cheek.

She had no truck in wearing a onesie either but was in another short black dress, bare legs and heels. Despite the ungodliness of the time, she was also in full warpaint: red lipstick and flicky eyeliner, which made my nostrils flare like an angry little bull because flicky eyeliner was my thing.

Alice didn't seem to care that she was greeted by cool nods and tight little smiles from Thee Desperadettes. She barely acknowledged their presence and her glance skimmed over me like I wasn't even there but she gave all the boys a flash of her smile, tongue coming out to moisten her bottom lip, that flirty fluttery thing she did with her eyelashes. No shame.

'So, come on,' Olly said and made shooing gestures towards the van. 'Sooner we get going, the sooner we get to London.'

We climbed into the minibus and I didn't even have the heart to roll my eyes along with Thee Desperadettes as Alice made a huge fuss about needing Louis to give her a hand into the bus while simpering, 'But don't you dare look up my skirt while you're doing it, you gigantic perv!'

It didn't take long to reach the motorway. I watched the green blur of endless fields and hedges as we tootled along the M6 in the slow lane because Olly said that the van made a weird grindy noise if he went above sixty miles per hour. I sat next to Bethany in the back of the bus. She was asleep, her head on my shoulder. Anyone who looked over would think I was also asleep but my eyes were open just a sliver so I could see where Alice was sitting by herself. Not that she cared, because Louis was sitting in the seat in front of her with Francis and they'd both turned round so they could chat to her. She was doing that thing where she pressed her tits together with her elbows to make them look ginormous and I couldn't believe that everything Louis and Francis said was so hilarious that Alice had to make an annoying tinkling sound that I guessed she thought was a sexy laugh.

I couldn't blame Louis, creature of impulse that he was, for being captivated by all that Alice was currently offering, but I was disappointed with Francis. I'd hoped he was too smart to be swayed by Alice's boobs. But no, he was like every other boy in Merrycliffe.

We stopped at a service station just before the M6 became the M1. Now instead of feeling like I'd die if I tried to eat something, I felt like I'd die if I didn't. Also, they had Starbucks and Waitrose because even the most humble service station had more thrilling food options than the whole of Merrycliffe. I climbed back into the bus clutching something called a Caramel Macchiato, which was bigger than my face, and a sausage buttie.

Thee Desperadettes, now changed out of onesies into their usual skater dresses, had taken over the front seats so they could chat to Olly and have control of the music. Two Desperadoes were crashed out at the back of the bus. I took the seat that I'd had before.

Louis and Francis were the last to climb into the van. Francis smiled and gestured at the empty space next to me and I really wanted to leech some of his calm, maybe even tell him a little bit about what had happened. He'd give me good advice and he was bound to know someone in London that I could crash with but . . .

'Hey! Franny B! Let's be bus buddies!' Louis had already slipped into the seat next to me, forcing me towards the window because he was all arms and legs and took up a lot of space.

It was just what I needed to take my mind off, well, every-thing. Louis chattered away about how he hoped that there'd be a lot of A&R men at the gig in London and how maybe even some other bands might be there. Really well-known bands.

'Do you think?' I asked, because that would be cool. 'Like who?'

'Well, no one really, really famous,' Louis amended. 'See, the thing is that really famous people don't go out on the weekend. They go out during the week when there's less chance of them being spotted.'

I wasn't sure that was true and I heard Francis snort from where he sat somewhere behind us but it was lovely to have Louis all to myself and to get one up on Alice, who was sitting all by herself across the aisle. Besides, I'd forgotten how pretty Louis was; how blue his eyes were, his cheekbones like geom-etry and his lips ... They were always in motion as Louis talked and talked. I wondered what they'd feel like on mine.

It was lovely to experience all these familiar tingles instead of fear and shame and abject terror. 'I'm so glad you're part of the gang now, Franny,' Louis exclaimed happily.

'Me too. But maybe I want to be more than just part of the gang,' I added bravely because what the hell. I had nothing to lose. 'If you know what I mean.'

Louis nodded. 'Yeah, absolutely!'

Then he took my hand. The fluttery sensation I used to get whenever he was near wasn't as fierce as it used to be, probably because I don't think Louis had had time to shower that morn-ing and he smelled kind of pungent. 'You're not like other girls.'

A genuine thrill ran through me, especially when Alice shifted in her seat then looked right at me. I knew she was listening to every word. 'Well, some girls can be so obvious, can't they?'

Alice narrowed her eyes. I'd never noticed what small, piggy eyes she had before. 'Yeah, but it's also because you're kind of odd,' Louis told me. 'Like all those really weird clothes you wear. I don't get it but Francis says that if I understood anything about fashion I would.'

It wasn't what I wanted to hear but I could work with it. 'They're not *that* weird, but compared to what some Merrycliffe girls wear, they're quite—'

'Like, most girls would wear a leather dress and they'd look really sexy but you don't,' Louis said. Immediately I wanted to rip off my leather dress and never see it again. I'd die rather than make myself look tarty but I wanted Louis to think I had *some* sex appeal. 'You look . . . like you've never got any touch before.'

The urge to cry was overwhelming. I blinked.

'Jesus, Louis, do you ever engage what few brain cells you've actually got before you open your mouth?' I heard Francis say sharply and Louis protested that he'd been paying me a compliment because 'I was saying that Franny never looks like she gives it up that easily.'

'You can say that again.' Alice leaned forward so once more we could all see down her dress. 'You don't give it up at all, do you, Franny?'

'Shut up,' I hissed in that gap between songs so the bus

was silent and everyone could hear. 'I'm not even talking to you.'

'Franny's never even been kissed.' I wanted to rip the smile of smug satisfaction off of Alice's face with my bare hands. 'How is it possible that you can get to sixteen and not have got off with someone?'

'Maybe it's because I'm not a—'

'Hang on, there was the fugly guy with the mullet when we went on the exchange trip to Poland, but oh yeah, he preferred me, didn't he?' Alice glanced over at Louis, who wore a look of utter bemusement like he didn't have a clue what was going on. 'Story of your life, Franny, isn't it? They always prefer me.'

'That's because you've got big tits and you shove them into everyone's face,' I told her furiously. There was a nervous giggle from the front and a sharp intake of breath from behind me. 'You've got off with pretty much every boy we know, so if I'm tight what does that make you?'

Alice reared up in her seat so she could jab one rigid finger at me. 'At least I'm not some frigid cow with no tits who's as moody as her mum. You'll probably end up having a total nervo like her too. And have you ever thought that maybe you chickened out of taking your GCSEs because you knew you were too bloody stupid to pass them?'

Alice couldn't have gone there because no one with a heart would have gone there. We hated each other but there was still an echo, a memory of the friends we used to be, that meant that some secrets we'd shared were sacred. Not any more, apparently.

But I had no comeback. I simply sat there opening and shutting my mouth. Louis patted my hand. 'There, there,' he said. 'No one thinks you're mental.'

I shook his hand away and before I turned to stare out of the window with eyes that stung from the effort of holding back tears, I caught sight of Alice. She'd sunk back on her seat and she didn't look defiant or angry any more, but small and scared, the way she used to when we'd been caught doing something heinous like taking biscuits out of the tin without asking or smearing our faces in her mother's make-up.

I'd have given anything to go back to then.

It took another hour to reach Camden. No one said a word, not even Louis, though he kept shooting everyone these anxious looks as if the terrible atmosphere was like nothing he'd ever experienced before and he was totally out of his depth.

At one point, as we passed a sign that should have thrilled me because it said *Central London 6 miles*, I suddenly felt a hand on my shoulder.

It was Francis sitting behind me. He didn't say anything but kept his hand on my shoulder, his fingers resting in the deep groove of my collarbone, but even that wasn't enough to stop the roaring in my head and the darkness that was welling up in me, trying to suck me under.

Maybe I *was* having a nervo.

Or maybe I just couldn't bear to be trapped in this minibus any longer with my former best friend who was now my arch-nemesis, my deadliest enemy, the one person I'd hate beyond all measure for the rest of my life.

The silence broke as we reached Camden and inched our way along streets thronged with traffic and more people than could possibly be contained in one place. The girls were jabbering excitedly, there was uproar as we passed the covered stalls of the market and panic from Olly because apparently we were stuck in a one-way system that he couldn't get out of.

All I was waiting for was the magic moment when the van pulled into the kerb and Olly turned off the engine.

I didn't wait for anyone else to move – I climbed over Louis, who yelped in surprise when he got my elbow in his face – and shot out of the door that Olly had just opened.

'What's the rush?' he asked in surprise.

I was just about to jump down on to the pavement but I paused so I could turn and stare at Alice. 'You are the nastiest, skeeviest slutbag I've ever met and that's why you have no friends and I never want to see your skanky face again,' I spat at her.

If I was as cool as I thought I was, I'd have said something way better than that but it still had the desired effect. Alice stared at me. Then, as if I'd flicked a switch, her face, which was always going to be beautiful and not skanky, crumpled up like a discarded tissue and she burst into tears.

'Franny . . .' someone called, I think it was Francis but I wasn't staying to find out. As soon as my feet hit the ground, I started to run.

25

I stumbled fast and forward, not quite running any more because there were too many people in the way. It was easy to get pushed one way and pulled another, past a cinema, past a Gap, another Starbucks and come to rest by a bus stop, as a bus pulled up and the doors opened.

'Franny! Wait!'

I got on the bus without thinking. The doors shut behind me. It was that easy. Or it was until the driver told me off for not knowing what an Oyster card was, then charged me an unbelievable two pounds forty pence fare.

I didn't even get a seat but had to stand and the indignation (two pounds and forty pence for a measly bus ticket!) and the fear that Sage had been right and I was going to get mugged as soon as anyone looked at me made the previous events of the day recede. They weren't gone or forgotten but right now my biggest priority was not getting stabbed.

An automated voice announced the unfamiliar names of the streets and I squinted out of the window at tatty discount stores, fancy little dress shops and imposing, minimalist boutiques that only seemed to stock two items of clothing. There were tower blocks and huge houses that looked old and posh. So much traffic. Too much noise. Everything was bright and blaring. Even the people on the bus were not like people on the buses back home.

The little old ladies in front of me jabbered away in a foreign language, a kid in a pushchair was eating half an avocado – I'd only had avocado once and it had tasted gross – there was a gang of young lads all talking gangsta, which made me miss Raj, and they were wearing weird drop-crotch tracksuit bottoms. I stared at two Japanese girls who were so cute I wanted to pack them in my bag and take them with me and a guy who looked like he could be a model and another guy who might have been the ugliest person I'd ever seen.

Maybe all these exotic people were looking at me in my completely not sexy leather dress and thinking I was exotic too. Somehow I doubted it.

Just like that all my other doubts kicked in too, as it suddenly dawned on me that I was on my own in London without a clue where I was going or what my next move should be. I couldn't even go back to Camden because how could I face any of them ever again? Not after what Alice had said. They all knew about Mum now and thought I was an utter headcase just like she was. Maybe I was – I certainly wasn't behaving like the poster girl for rational thought.

'The next stop is Notting Hill Gate station.' There was a flurry of activity. Pushchairs primed, shopping bags gathered up and I was stepping forward too because I knew about Notting Hill. Like, I'd seen the film countless times. It was where celebs lived and it had a market with second-hand clothes stalls. And there was an address in Notting Hill that I'd committed to memory. In fact, it was engraved on my heart and it was reason enough to get off the bus.

I walked without taking any of it in. I passed vintage clothes stores and rail upon rail of faded, pretty dresses without stopping, which proved I wasn't in my right mind. I was simply a stupid girl with stupid ideas and I didn't belong here. I wasn't quite sure where I belonged but it wasn't on these winding, narrow streets packed with people, the houses painted in pretty colours; mint green, cobalt blue, egg-yolk yellow.

And though I had an address engraved on my heart, my crappy BlackBerry wouldn't load Google maps. Despite my very fragile state of mind, I had no choice but to find someone in the sea of scary London people and ask for directions. I stopped a homely-looking old woman but she barked something at me in a harsh-sounding foreign language. Then I tried a middle-aged couple (it seemed like a safe bet that middle-aged people wouldn't give me any grief) but they simply walked past me like I wasn't even there.

I was beginning to feel like I really wasn't there. That maybe Alice had pushed me from the minibus into the oncoming traffic as we travelled down the motorway. I'd ended up under the wheels of one of those big articulated lorries that my dad drove and now I was a ghost. A see-through girl, invisible to all. I sighed heavily as I got to the end of another unfamiliar street. On the corner was a huge house painted a beautiful sludgy pink. Like I was looking out of my bedroom window on to the seafront and marvelling at how the navy-blue sky was streaked through with the same shade of pink.

I didn't even bother to check the street name or number. I knew it was the address I'd been searching for. It was where Martin Sanderson had lived when he first came to London in the late seventies to study at Central St Martin's. He'd squatted in an empty house with his punk friends and held his debut fashion show in the derelict front room. Later, when he'd got his degree and Barneys in New York had ordered his entire collection, he'd bought the Notting Hill house and opened a shop downstairs while he lived and worked upstairs. Even though he now had shops all around the world from Peking to Sydney, Moscow to Mumbai and even on Bond Street, he still had that first shop in Notting Hill in the building he'd painted a sludgy pink so it would remind him of his Merrycliffe roots.

I gave an excited little cry and rushed forward. There was his name on the window in the minimalist font I knew so well and on a dress form was one dress. A simple, elegant black dress, high-necked, long-sleeved, which was cut so severely, so perfectly it made me sigh with longing.

I wanted to wear a dress like that. Mostly, though, I wanted to be able to make a dress like that. And that made everything easier because although I still didn't know what I was doing at this actual moment on this actual day, I knew how I wanted the rest of my life to be. If I wanted it hard enough, then I'd make it happen. I was sure of that, at least.

I couldn't tear my eyes away from the dress. I wondered what it was made from to make it drape like that. It didn't even hang, but curved lovingly around the form. Maybe it was silk jersey. God, I'd never even touched anything made of silk jersey.

I wasn't sure how long I'd been standing there, but suddenly there was a movement to the left of me and my eyes popped so hard that they hurt. A short man wearing a black leather jacket, dark indigo jeans with an audacious turn-up and a red woolly hat was stepping through a side door. He was the definition of dapper; all sleek and tanned, like he lived well and enjoyed living well and no wonder. Jesus. I'd recognise that pencil moustache and those sideburns anywhere.

I had to bite my lip hard to stop myself from crying out. All I could do was stand rooted to the spot as he turned to shut the door and the moment was gone. Almost gone, if I hadn't left it too late and ...

Say something, Franny. Say something cool and amazing so he sees how cool and amazing you are and gives you a job. In Paris! Say something, you twat!

'Martin! Martin Sanderson!' My voice had never sounded like that before. Thin and rusty, like I'd only just learned to speak after years of being mute.

It worked though. I had his attention. Or rather he was frowning at me and not looking terribly impressed. He was looking the absolute opposite of impressed, then he turned away and was almost gone again; the door was swinging shut and . . .

'I'm from Merrycliffe! Market Diner! The fifties milk bar and that gentlemen's outfitters on the High Street that's had that weird yellow mac in the window for as long as I can remember.' Jesus. I was talking gibberish, but he was paused on the doorstep, neither going in nor out, but staring at me with what seemed like a horrified fascination. 'I'm on the fashion course at Merrycliffe College and I'm being taught by this lady called Barbara who says that she knew you back in the day but we're not sure we believe her. She said that the first thing you ever made in class was a pair of trousers with the legs sewn together.'

His nostrils flared. 'They were bondage trousers. The legs were meant to be sewn together,' he said huffily. The door opened wider, I glimpsed a woman standing there and Martin Sanderson stepped past her. I waited for him to turn round, maybe invite me in, but he just said to her, loud enough for me to hear, 'God, these bloody kids,' and then he was gone.

But he was coming back. I was sure of that.

He wasn't coming back. The woman gave me a quizzical look. She was tall and skinny. Taller and skinnier even than me and she was wearing a black dress similar to the one in the window but short-sleeved so I could see that both her arms were covered in seamless, intricate tattoos. 'He gets very annoyed when people try to doorstep him,' she said gently. 'Don't take it personally.'

I couldn't take it any other way. Just like I couldn't help saying, 'But I'm from Merrycliffe!'

She folded her beautiful, multi-coloured arms. 'And what exactly are you doing on our doorstep, Miss Merrycliffe?' she asked.

'Well, the reason I'm in London ... I came down with friends ... they're in a band ... well, actually they're not really my friends. Not now.' Oh God, I knew what was going to happen next and I could stop it if I really tried but somehow nothing I did worked and I was saying it, 'I've run away,' and if that wasn't bad enough, then I burst into loud, snotty tears.

I was still crying ten minutes later as I sat in the kitchen above Martin Sanderson's shop as Jamie, the tattooed woman, placed a mug of tea in front of me. It wasn't some fancy London tea with an unpronounceable name but strong, sweet tea made with the same Yorkshire teabags we used at home.

She also made me toast from a nutty, brown loaf and smeared it with boysenberry jam, though I wasn't entirely sure what a boysenberry was but I didn't really care much right then because I was too busy working my way through the box of tissues she'd placed in front of me.

Eventually, when there were no more tears to be squeezed out from my gritty, swollen eyes and I was gratefully gulping down the tea to ease the ache in my throat, Jamie pulled up the stool next to mine.

'So, why did you run away?' she asked and took a sip of her own tea. She wasn't even looking at me but at the pile of post in front of her.

I didn't want to bore her with the details. Also I was now

deathly afraid that Martin Sanderson might suddenly appear and shout at me but I'd already made a total show of myself and Jamie not looking at me made it easier. Like, she was a disinterested third party and anyway she could have left me weeping on the doorstep if she hadn't cared at all.

So I told Jamie about my five-year plan that ended with me graduating with a BA Hons in Fashion from Central St Martin's and a sell-out final collection. But she was frowning like she didn't understand why the thought of that had had me sobbing and snotting all over the place.

I didn't know who Jamie was. Whether she was Martin Sanderson's right-hand woman or his cleaner or his favourite niece. So, I really was going to keep my mouth shut, be all enigmatic and self-controlled and stuff, but she kept making these encouraging 'hmmm hmmm' noises every time I paused and it all spilled out. About Mum and not taking my GCSEs and how my parents' plans for my future felt as if they were nailing shut the lid on my coffin. And then I found myself telling her about Louis and Alice and about the horrible things she'd said.

'I didn't want to run away but there was nothing else I could do,' I said, when I got to the end of my sad, sorry tale. 'It all got out of control very, very quickly.'

'Well, obviously. You'd have probably put on a coat if you'd planned it,' Jamie said.

She didn't say anything else but carried on flicking through the mail, dividing it into stacks; now that I'd stopped crying and finished ranting, I wanted to pinch myself hard enough to leave bruises. Then I wanted to get my phone out and take photos because if I tried to tell anyone about this, they'd be all 'Pics or it didn't happen.' I mean, I was right here in the flat above Martin Sanderson's first shop. Even I couldn't believe that I was really here.

'Martin uses this flat as a bolthole when he gets tired of Paris,' Jamie said suddenly. 'I know, right? It's hard to understand how anyone would ever be tired of Paris, but when he gets stuck or he's feeling uninspired he says he needs to be in London. It's impossible to be stuck here. Just walking along these streets ...' She tailed off and I wished I knew what she meant. That I'd walked down those streets and sucked it all in instead of stumbling about in a daze.

By now I'd drunk my tea, eaten my toast and overshared like I'd never done before and it was time to apologise profusely and leave the beautiful blindingly white kitchen with its brushed steel worktops.

Jamie still wasn't saying much. She was everything I expected a fashion person to be. Although she wasn't pretty – everything on her face was long and sharp – it was a face you wanted to keep staring at. A bold face made bolder by her jet-black hair, which was even shorter than mine after Alice had done her worst, and a slash of fuchsia-pink lipstick. She was elegant and cool. Probably the coolest person I'd ever met. Everything about her, from the way she didn't say much to the tattoos to her bulbous silver thumb ring, was cool.

I had never felt less cool in my life. And then Jamie looked up in time to catch me staring at her in much the same way that

I used to stare at Louis. The blush, it burned. 'Well, I should be going,' I said, slipping down from the stool. 'Thanks for the tea and the toast and I'm sorry that I went on and . . .'

'When I was sixteen, I was working in a greengrocer's.' She pushed away a little stack of post and looked straight at me. 'I wanted to stay on at school but my dad had buggered off with a woman half his age and there were six of us at home. I was the eldest so it was up to me to pull my weight.'

I frowned. The woman sitting across from me was a million miles away from a greengrocer's in South Shields, although as she'd talked I could hear a little Geordie creep into her voice. 'But how did you . . . I mean, like, what happened? 'Cause you work for him, for Martin Sanderson, now, right?'

Jamie nodded. 'Right. I'm his Creative Director. I oversee MS by Martin Sanderson.' MS by Martin Sanderson was Martin Sanderson's diffusion line. A diffusion line was a fashion designer's younger, edgier label, not quite as eye-wateringly expensive as their main label. Prada had Miu Miu, Marc Jacobs had Marc by Marc Jacobs, Alexander McQueen had McQ and Martin Sanderson had MS by Martin Sanderson, which was run by a woman who'd been selling spuds when she was my age. 'I really wanted it, Franny. Did my BTEC at evening classes. Pored over *Vogue* every spare minute of the day. Do you know how hard it was to get a copy of *Vogue Italia* in South Shields?'

'Yeah, about as hard as it is to get a copy in Merrycliffe.'

'You know what it's like then,' Jamie said, as if I was the same as her. Like we were kindred spirits. 'Then I entered a new fashion talent competition in *Vogue*, made the shortlist, got given a train ticket down to London so I could have lunch with a whole bunch of important fashion people, editors and designers and the like, and I never went home again. Got a job as the lowest of the low at a designer who made dresses for posh old ladies and here I am, twelve years later.'

It was a lot to take in. 'So, I don't even need a degree?'

Jamie didn't reply but gave me a long, hard stare. 'Did you make that dress?'

My leather dress was now as limp as a week-old lettuce, despite the lining I'd sewn in. 'Yeah,' I admitted. 'I saw the leather dresses that Martin did last autumn/winter but I think my leather was a bit too thin.'

'You've buggered up one of the arms too.' She peered critically at my armpit. 'There's a lot of puckering going on.'

'I'm finding armholes and sleeves really difficult. I can't get the hang of easing in the sleeve. Even crotches are easier than armholes and sleeves.'

Jamie climbed down from her stool and started walking out of the kitchen, which was a bit cold. I wasn't expecting her to offer me a job as the lowest of the low but she could at least have said goodbye. 'Come on, then,' she called over her shoulder. 'I'll give you the guided tour.'

The guided tour involved climbing up a metal slatted staircase to a workroom. It was a long, low room flooded with light from the roof windows. One wall was completely taken up with a collection of international *Vogue*s. There were even *Vogue*s from the 1960s. I nearly started hyperventilating when Jamie pulled out a box for me to peek inside.

Another wall was simply a huge moodboard of photos, pictures ripped out of magazines, swatches of fabric, even a packet of Japanese noodles.

There was a table for cutting and a table for sewing, though Jamie said that Martin's assistants mostly did the cutting and sewing but that he liked to keep his hand in. 'I'm the same. I get itchy when I haven't *made* something,' she said.

There were dress forms and rails of clothing all shrouded in garment bags and then Jamie ushered me through a little door. I should have been worried that actually Martin Sanderson might be a successful serial killer as well as an internationally renowned fashion designer and Jamie was his accomplice, and the two of them would chop me into little pieces with a pair of pinking shears, but I wouldn't have cared, because Jamie had just ushered me into heaven.

'Oh my,' I said weakly. 'Oh my days.'

'Only a few bits and bobs,' Jamie said, but it was the first time I'd seen her smile so I think she was pleased with my reaction.

My eyes weren't big enough to take it all in because on floor-to-ceiling shelves were stacked bolts upon bolts of fabric in every colour imaginable. And in colours I could never have imagined. Prints I wouldn't have thought possible. There was wool, silk and taffeta. Chiffon and organza in delicate sherbet shades. Sparkling swathes of gold and silver and bronze.

'Wow.' I did a slow turn, hands on my face. There was a very real possibility I might start crying again. 'I'd quite like to live in this room. Most of the fabric shops back home sell mainly to people making dance costumes so it's all spandex and Lycra and lots of glitter. I was going to go to Berwick Street while I was here.'

'Not so many fabric shops on Berwick Street these days,' Jamie said and I wanted to ask her where the good fabric shops hung out but she was pulling down a bolt of ... 'Watered silk. We were experimenting with a digital print but it took a few practice runs before Martin was happy.'

I looked reverently at the sludgy green and blue broken lines on the white silk. 'It's gorgeous.'

'It is, but those lines are a bitch to match up. Bit out of your league, no offence.'

'Oh, I wasn't on the scrounge.' This was my most painful blush yet. It felt like the top layer of my skin had burned right off. 'I really wasn't.'

Jamie wasn't even paying any attention to me, but staring up at all the gorgeous fabrics. 'See, the thing is no one has the right to call themselves a designer until they've draped with silk jersey. You're probably better off with black, right?'

'Huh?' I'd gone all slack-jawed and gormless but who could blame me? 'Really? No! I couldn't.'

Oh, I'd said that I wasn't on the scrounge but Jamie wouldn't listen to my feeble protests. She selected a black silk jersey, added a few metres of soft black leather because she wanted me to have another try at making a leather dress, and crisp white cotton because she said that making a simple but perfectly executed white dress would be great practice.

She took the bolts to the cutting table to measure them out

while I watched, mesmerised, as the fabric flowed between her hands like it had suddenly become liquid.

'It's too much,' I said, when they were neatly packed away, along with zippers and buttons and other notions in a huge, stiff cardboard bag with sludgy-pink ribbon handles and Martin Sanderson's name embossed on it. 'Won't he ... Martin Sanderson ... be furious?'

'I think he'll probably agree with me that we can spare a few metres of fabric and some notions,' Jamie assured me. I still couldn't believe that this was happening. Part of me was still leaning towards the theory that Alice had killed me, but if she had, then heaven was absolutely lush. 'Can't have you forced to make frocks out of spandex now, can we?'

Clutching the bag to me, I followed Jamie down the stairs and back into what she called with a knowing smile 'the flat above the shop'. This time she led me into a lounge, though it was probably called something like a parlour or a drawing room. Two spotless white couches flanked a huge silver fireplace. There was a painting hanging above the mantelpiece. I thought it might be a Mondrian and I also thought it might have inspired the colour-blocked dresses that Martin had sent down the runway three years before and when I shyly asked Jamie, she beamed.

She had a huge gap between her front teeth, even that was cool. Like eighties Madonna before she had her teeth fixed. 'Clever girl,' she said. 'Glad they've heard of Mondrian back in Merrycliffe.'

'I was planning to do Art A level,' I explained and that

reminder of all those hopes and dreams dashed and left for dead made me shudder. 'But you're right. Nobody cares about anything in Merrycliffe except container shipping. That's why I had to leave.'

Even I knew that was just my bluster talking. There were people in Merrycliffe who cared about more than container shipping. Lexy and Thee Desperadettes were always talking about where they wanted to go to university, and even though they sounded awful Thee Desperadoes at least had had enough drive to start a band. And Francis cared about so many things that it would take hours for me to tell Jamie all about them, and then there was Alice ...

'I know some people say that if you go back, then you're not going forward,' Jamie said as she sat down on one couch and gestured at the space next to her so I sat down too.

'That's so right,' I said feelingly. Although I was down and out in London, I had fabric and findings and now I knew someone in London and I might not have a place to stay or a job but it would be all right. I was sure of it.

'Except, Franny, you're only sixteen and you have to go back to Merrycliffe,' Jamie told me very gently. I sat there on the pristine white couch, terrified I'd leave a stain just from perching uncomfortably on it, and Jamie took my hand and patted it just as gently. 'You need to get your BTEC so when you do come to London to find fame and fortune, it's because you've got a place at Central St Martin's.'

'But I might not get in!' I protested. 'And my dad said that—'

'You can't expect people to believe in you if you won't believe in yourself.' She took her hand away and sounded genuinely cross. 'If you want to get to London on your own terms, it doesn't matter what your dad says. You go to college every day, you pass your retakes and you don't put up with any nonsense from that Barbara because to this day Martin bitches about how she used to cry because she couldn't get her head around seam allowances.'

I'd been on the verge of tears again, but now I giggled. 'It's just the thought of going back there . . .'

'Look, darling, I've been exactly where you are right now. There were lots and lots of times when I thought I'd be bagging up Brussels sprouts for the rest of my life. And when I did get to London, I was alone and depressed and didn't have enough money for food. Cried myself to sleep a few times but I got through it and you'll get through your bad times too. You need to soldier on for the next eighteen months to get to the good stuff. You're going to have lots of good stuff in your life.'

I opened my mouth but Jamie patted my hand again, sharply this time, like she wasn't done speaking. 'You are not your mother's keeper. You can't be responsible for her.'

It was easy enough for Jamie to say, but when I went home Dad would leave soon enough and then it would just be the two of us once more. And she'd go off on one again, though sometimes the fear of her going off on one was worse, and I'd be the one person between her and the darkness that infected her. Eighteen months was a life sentence.

Then I was nudged and I looked down to see Jamie holding

out a business card. 'You take this and every time you design a new piece, you take a picture of it and email it to me,' she commanded. Seriously. She made it sound like a papal decree. 'Now, I'm not promising a thing, you understand, but every now and again Martin doles out a grant so a worthy young soul gets funding for their degree. Sometimes he even gives them a job. But they have to deserve it. And they have to have conquered their fear of armholes.'

That made me giggle again and I took the card and tried to thank Jamie for the fabric and the stirring pep talk and just for existing really. 'You've been so kind and all I've done is moan and cry and take up all your Saturday afternoon.'

Jamie nodded like she was in complete agreement. 'Well, it killed the time while I was waiting for Martin to finish being interviewed by a Japanese film crew.'

She even promised to give me directions to a bus stop so I could find my way back to Camden. 'If your friends are worth a jot, they'll be pleased to see you,' she said as she took me down more stairs and through a door that led to the stockroom of the shop. Even the stockroom was glamorous, with mood lighting and rails upon rails of clothes. 'Also, you should make up with your mate, that Alice. Honestly, I'm sure this Louis is a prince among men but no man is that good that he's worth losing your best friend over.'

'Try telling her that,' I muttered, but Jamie had disappeared through a black curtain. I carefully peeked through the gap so I could see into the shop. It was beautiful. So clean, so white, the light so muted like nothing harsh was allowed.

The film crew was packing up and Jamie was talking to Martin Sanderson. She towered over him as she gestured with her hands, even rolled her eyes at one point. He shrugged. Said something that made Jamie laugh. Then they both looked in my direction as if they could see me peeking through the tiny gap in the curtain and I shrank back.

I waited for Jamie but I was half terrified that Martin Sanderson would come bursting through the curtain and snatch back all the lovely things she'd given me and take my dreams while he was at it. Oh God, he would. He'd called me a bloody kid earlier.

The curtain shifted and my stomach double-back-flipped but it was just Jamie. 'You're an eight, right?' She was riffling through the rack of clothes nearest to her.

'Oh no! Really no this time. I couldn't.' I backed away from the red wool coat she held towards me, the beautiful A-line red coat with a princess collar that would totally rock my twenty-first-century mod girl aesthetic. 'That coat probably costs more than a year's worth of alterations money.'

'Martin says he couldn't live with himself if he let you parade round London without a coat,' she insisted, giving the coat a little shake. 'Come on. Chop, chop! We've ordered you a car. It will be here in a minute.'

I sank into the coat the way women in movies sank into their lover's arms. It felt like a very expensive hug and I wanted to find a quiet spot so I could spend an hour simply stroking the cashmere wool, which was so soft that it made me want to cry, though I could have sworn that I didn't have a drop left in my tear ducts.

There was a discreet shake of the curtain. 'Car's here, Jamie.'

'Back to Camden with you, Franny B,' Jamie said, pulling back the curtain and guiding me through the shop.

Martin Sanderson was talking to a pretty Japanese girl. I stared down at my feet in my Dunlop Green Flashes, held my breath as I drew level and even though there was music playing and Jamie had paused to say something to the man behind the sales desk, I swear on Coco Chanel's grave that Martin Sanderson turned and whispered, 'Ten minutes for chips,' to me as I scurried past him.

And when I snorted with laughter and turned to look at him in surprise, I also swear that he winked at me. For absolute realz.

Then Jamie opened the door and I was out on the street where a big, sleek black car was waiting for me. The driver was standing there holding the door open.

'Thank you. Thank you for everything,' I said and before I lost my nerve, I gave Jamie a very quick, very fierce hug. She smelt expensive and delicious and for a fleeting second she hugged me back. 'I won't let you down.'

'Never mind me. Don't let yourself down.' She watched me climb in the back of the car, then leaned over, her hand on the roof. 'Just between us, Martin has a soft spot for us small-town kids. Says we're hungrier and we want it more than any of the others.'

I couldn't believe that anyone had ever wanted it more than me but all I could say was a hurried goodbye before the driver shut the door.

As I was driven back to Camden, I realised that I wasn't so scared any more at the thought of facing the others. I didn't think anyone would judge me *too* badly for running away and never being kissed. I mean, stuff happens or, like, doesn't happen. And if they believed Alice's evil bullshit about me and my mum, then they didn't deserve my friendship.

I wasn't so scared about my future either. I wasn't an idiot, I knew that Martin Sanderson wouldn't toss me one of those grants of his just because I was from Merrycliffe and I'd bonded with his Creative Director, but maybe he and Jamie had seen something in me, some kind of spark, and as well as giving me a freaking beautiful coat and a treasure chest full of fabric, they'd given me hope.

Hope had not been my friend these last few months. It was about time I made up with hope, even if there were some people that I was never going to call my friend ever again.

The car pulled in outside the Dublin Castle. I took a deep breath, thanked the driver and stepped out of the car just in time to hear someone shout from across the road, 'Franny B! You get your arse over here right this bloody second. I'm going to kill you!'

It was Alice.

26

I stiffened immediately. I even went to turn away, but then she darted across the road, accompanied by an angry cacophony of car horns, and hurled herself at me.

'Where have you been? I've been worried sick about you!' she screamed right in my face. Then Alice was hugging me so hard I almost choked. 'I'm sorry. I'm so sorry. I can't bear this … I just want to be friends again.'

My first reaction was to stiffen again because her words meant nothing to me. So was my second reaction because she was probably creasing my coat, which I loved more than I'd ever loved anything in the world. No contest. And my third reaction was to hug her back because my arms were still used to holding her. 'Well, I'm sorry for calling you a slutbag,' I mumbled, but it didn't *feel* like I was sorry and Alice let go and from the hurt, still wary expression on her face she didn't feel like I was sorry too.

'Franny, please, can't we just put all this behind us? What we had isn't worth throwing away over some guy. Especially not Louis. Yes, he's supercute, but some things are more important than supercute.'

'I told you that!' I said indignantly. Louis had been a beautiful distraction from all the scary parts of my life, but I had to start dealing with them and God, he was dumb as a box of rocks and I really needed to put all my energy into getting my BTEC so I couldn't be doing with any boy-shaped roadblocks. Even when they were as pretty as Louis. 'Though I have to say I never expected Louis to be supernice as well as being supercute.'

'Yeah, I thought he'd be quite up himself but he's not at all,' Alice agreed with a nervous smile like she was going to agree with everything I said until things were right between us. In which case she was going to have to do a lot of nodding and a lot of agreeing because I still wasn't convinced that things could ever be right. Too much stuff had happened. Shit had got too real.

I didn't begin to know how to tell Alice that but then she glanced down at the stiff white bag with the ribbon handles, gave an ear-perforating shriek and started jumping up and down even though she was wearing hoochie heels. 'Oh! My! God! What the what? Where did you get that? Why is it bulging? What's inside it? Franny, where have you been and what have you been doing?'

I realised that I was jumping up and down too because all that best friend DNA was still in my system and Alice was the one person who would understand how huge, how absolutely hugely major it was that 'I totally met Martin Sanderson and I hung out with his Creative Director and she made me tea and toast and gave me fabric and this coat and I think she might help me with my fashion degree.'

I thought Alice's eyes might pop out of their sockets. 'Shut. Up!'

'No, I won't shut up! Jesus.' I covered my face with my hands. 'Oh my God! I can hardly believe it myself.'

And this time when we hugged, it was mutual hugging and then I took Alice's hand and we ran down the crowded street screaming at the top of our vocal registers and bashing into anyone who got in our way.

It was the same obnoxious way we behaved back in Merry-cliffe. I'd really missed it.

We came to a breathless, panting halt outside a Caffè Nero and didn't even have an awkward stilted conversation about whether we were friends any more or if we should go to Starbucks instead. We bolted inside and Alice joined the queue while I positioned myself by a table where one middle-aged man was sitting with an empty cup. If I couldn't get him to shift through the medium of ferocious glaring then I didn't deserve to call myself a teenage girl.

By the time Alice turned up with a laden tray, he'd slunk off and we could spread out though we kept a tight grip on our bags because there were signs everywhere informing us that pickpockets operated in the area.

Then it was a bit awk but I knew it was my turn to meet

Alice somewhere in the middle. 'I thought I hated you and that I never wanted anything to do with you ever again, but actually I don't know how to stop being friends with you.'

Alice smiled that slinky cat-like smile then her shoulders slumped. 'You've got your new fashion friends now and you're well in with Thee Desperadettes.' She started to crumble her triple chocolate muffin. 'I know I denied it at the time but that's why I went after Louis even though I knew it would piss you off. 'Cause I knew I was going to lose you anyway, so on some level I thought I might as well make it sooner rather than later.'

'But you haven't lost me. I wasn't planning on dumping you, Alice. Just because I might have new friends doesn't make what we have together, like, *less* . . .' It was hard to put it into words. 'I don't have a set amount of friendshipness to give out.'

'But it's always been the two of us and *you* might have new friends but all *I* have is you.' Alice pushed away her muffin. 'At school I have no one to hang with apart from lame boys who want to get into my pants, then when I do get to hang with you, you drag along that goth, Cora . . .'

'She's into Steampunk and her name's Dora . . .'

Alice rolled her eyes. 'Whevs. I am so lonely I could die from it.'

'Oh, Alice.' I put my arm round her very carefully so I didn't put any pressure whatsoever on my coat seams. 'You're funny haha and funny weird and you're excellent at doing my nails and inventing dance routines. You'd have loads of friends if you hadn't alienated every single girl in Merrycliffe by making off with their boyfriends.'

'Well, they can't be very boyfriendly if they're up for being made off with,' Alice muttered and we'd been here before but this time we had to dig down deep enough to get to the roots.

'What's the point though? C'mon, you only have to look in the mirror to see that you're hot. It's not like you need to get with boys to prove it.'

'Being hot is the only thing I've got,' Alice said grimly. 'It's all right for you. You're cool, everyone thinks so, and it's so obvious you're going to rule fashion when you're grown up and you can eat what you like and never put on any weight. I always feel like your sidekick. Like the junior partner. So, if being sexy is my USP, then God, I'm going to work it.'

I would have said, even now, despite everything that had happened, that I knew Alice better than anyone. Maybe even better than I knew myself because my ability to act like a twat always took me by surprise, but this was a side of Alice I'd never seen before. 'I didn't know you felt like that,' I said slowly. ''Cause I often thought that people treated me like I was your sidekick. Well, boys do when they trot over to ask if I'll put a good word in. Every time we go out, I end up on my own because you've copped off with someone.'

'But I always leave with you,' Alice protested, but it wasn't with her usual gusto.

'Anyways, we're sixteen, we don't have to have everything figured out. Yeah, I know what I want but I still don't know if I'll get it.' I couldn't help but look down at the cardboard bag with Martin Sanderson's name on it.

'Yeah, you will.' Alice pursed her lips extra tight and didn't even notice the boys queuing up to order coffee, who were staring at her longingly. 'About your hair . . . '

I held up a hand to my head. 'What about my hair?' I was still cross about it and I couldn't see that changing any time soon.

'I didn't do it on purpose. Well, I don't think I did. Maybe it was five per cent on purpose but, like, subconsciously. I'd spoken to my mum the week before about wanting to be a hairdresser. Properly. Going to college and everything and she just laughed and said that I couldn't even master doing a chignon on the practice head in the salon. Even Dad said that it wasn't such a great career and I should concentrate on Business Studies,' Alice recalled bitterly. 'I wanted to prove that I did have what it took. I've watched other people cutting hair all my life and I started out genuinely thinking I'd do this amazing job. I could see exactly the way your hair was going to be but when I started cutting it, it all went wrong. I really am sorry, Franny.'

'Well, it's not so bad now that it's grown out.' I ran a hand through my hair again. 'I quite like it now. Looks OK when I tie it back with a scarf.'

'Yeah, I thought that was a good look for you.' Alice sighed. 'I was going to do the hair, that was the plan. You were going to be the famous fashion designer and I was going to be the famous hair person. And the really sick thing is that the only other thing I'm really good at besides being sexy is Business Studies.' She pulled a disgusted face. 'I have a knack for figures and I totally get supply and demand and why it's important to have brand extensions. It's not exactly cool, is it?'

'But if I do ever get to be a famous fashion designer then I'm totally going to need a Business Manager,' I said very carefully because this really wasn't about me.

Alice smiled just as carefully. 'Yeah? That's true. I suppose that would make being good at Business Studies sort of cool. So, the hair thing – are you going to let it go?'

'Yeah, but only because the bald spot has grown out now, otherwise I wouldn't be so sure.' I guessed we were well on the way to becoming best friends again. Though being best friends with Alice didn't feel like a choice I had, we just were, even now. Er, even though she was suddenly giving me evils.

'What? What have I done?'

'OK, while we're sorting out stuff: you turning up at The Wow with Raj was really harsh, Franny. Really, really harsh.'

I couldn't see why it was *that* harsh. 'You two hating each other is really old news. I mean, you went out with him for a week or something ...'

'I saw him for nearly two months actually,' Alice informed me snottily as she folded her arms. I didn't remember them going out for that long. Nearly two months for Alice was like three years for any other girl. 'I only broke up with him because of *you*. I chose you over him.'

'What did I do?' I asked again, because I'd never shown any interest in Raj as anything other than a mate and my employers' son, who could be a laugh when he wasn't pretending he was gangsta. 'I have never, ever fancied him. Ugh! As if! It would be like perving on my own brother.'

'That's exactly why I broke up with Raj!' Alice pointed an

accusatory finger at my expression of sheer revulsion. 'You kept telling me I could do better than someone who called me his "ho" but he only did that as a joke and I called him a "ho" too. And you moaned on about how awkward it was that I was sucking face with Raj when you worked for his parents and how you never got to see me on my own and you were already sad about Shuv leaving home and all that stuff with your mum and I hated that I'd made you even sadder so I told Raj he was a crap snog and I dumped him.'

'Oh,' I said, because I couldn't think of anything else to say. 'Oh. I never realised. I'm sorry.'

'Well, it's OK. I'm kind of over it now,' Alice said but her cheeks were red and she was wearing a pretty definite scowl.

'You really aren't over it though, are you?' Alice had completely blindsided me. 'I really don't remember you going out for that long.'

'Well, Franny, it's because I might have all the boys but you have all the feelings. There's no room for me to go through difficult stuff because your stuff is always more difficult than mine,' Alice said. She looked guilty but also determined, like she had to say this no matter how painful it was and I had to listen to it. 'I know that the situation with your mum is the pits and I really don't think you're like her, I just said that because I was furious with you, but even before you got all your new college mates I felt like I was halfway to losing you.'

'I didn't know any of this,' I insisted but was that the honest truth? Even as I said it, I was rewinding key scenes from the last two years. Alice was in most of them but I was somewhere else; either worrying about my mum or designing a dress in my head that would distract me from the knotty feeling in my stomach for an hour at least. 'I wish I could say that I'd change. That things will be different and I won't get so absorbed in my own problems, but *she* needs to change for me to be able to do that.'

The Martin Sanderson high was fading now, almost gone, and reality had me firmly back in its icy clutches. A reality where I'd go back to Merrycliffe because I didn't have much choice and it would be like the argument had never happened. Dad would go away for weeks and weeks and Mum would get worse and worse and I couldn't just ignore it if it seemed like she was going to top herself or something. *'I have to go to college now, Mum, please try not to kill yourself for the next few hours.'*

'Maybe things will be better,' Alice suggested weakly. 'Your dad keeps calling me. Have you blocked *his* number too? By the way, you need to stop doing that. It's so passive-aggressive.'

I flushed. 'Well, yeah. What has he said to you?'

'Now that he's established that technically I'm with you, he keeps ringing to speak to you. Says it's urgent and I could hardly tell him that we'd said loads of evil things to each other and that you'd run off on your own, even though it was your first time in London and we manage to get completely lost whenever we go to Blackpool. I had to keep saying you were in the loo.'

'Did he sound angry?' I couldn't help but cringe.

Alice shook her head. 'More like he's worried about you

being violated by the rock group you said you were running away with. Somehow, I can't imagine Thee Desperadoes violating anything except a Ginster's pasty.'

'True that.' I hoped our friendship wasn't like the crumbled muffin debris scattered over our napkins. That our Aliceand-Frannyness could become whole again. Maybe different to how it had been but still there. 'Alice, I'm sorry for not seeing that we were starting to fall apart. I can't promise that everything will get fixed, but I still love you. Do you still love me?'

'Of course I do,' she said right away, like she didn't even have to think about it. Then she did think about it. 'But not in a lezzy way.'

I shook my head. 'Goes without saying.'

It was time to leave Caffè Nero because we were both hungry for something a bit more substantial than a triple chocolate muffin that had been mashed beyond repair.

We gathered up our stuff and left, just in time to bump into Thee Desperadettes.

'Franny B!' they all pretty much said in unison. 'Where have you been?'

I wasn't sure they'd appreciate the amazingness that was my afternoon with Jamie or EVEN believe that I'd hung out in the flat above Martin Sanderson's shop. Besides, it was cool to share a secret with Alice again. 'I went to Notting Hill on the bus. Two pounds forty! Can you believe it?'

They couldn't. They also couldn't believe Alice and I were hanging out together of our own free will. I pushed her forward. Alice was wearing her bitchface, which transformed into a pout when I poked her in the ribs and glared at her. 'OK, I'm swearing off boys who are already going out with someone,' she said sulkily. 'Though any boy who dumps his girlfriend without a second thought isn't worth washing our hair for. Right?'

Alice logic was hard to deny. 'We're friends again,' I said, and I hoped that might seal the deal though Thee Desperadettes, particularly Bethany, didn't seem that convinced. 'Not only does she have mad boy-whispering skillz, but Alice once made me laugh so hard that I wet myself.'

'I did,' Alice said. 'Though one time Franny baked some banana cupcakes that made me vom so we're pretty even when it comes to bodily fluids.'

'She doesn't bite when you get to know her,' I said to Lexy because Lexy was the unofficial leader of Thee Desperadettes. Once you got Lexy on side, the rest usually followed, although Bethany was giving Alice side eye like it would be a long, long time before she rolled out the welcome mat.

Lexy nodded coolly at Alice like she was on probation, then turned to me. 'We wanted to get some tea but we went to a fish and chip shop 'cause everywhere else was quite scary and they wanted eleven fifty for haddock and chips. The haddock was the size of a fish finger.'

'Eleven fifty!' Kirsten and Bethany echoed.

'I did some research this week for places to go in Camden and there's this chain called Wagamama. It does noodles and Japanese stuff but it doesn't seem too fancy. Bit spendy though,' I said, pulling out my BlackBerry. 'It's on Jamestown Street. Where's that?'

When we got to Wagamama, we discovered it was communal dining, but there were six of us sitting on one large table so it wasn't that communal, especially when Lexy got a text from the boys, who wanted to meet up and get some tea as well.

Louis! That was the one thing me and Alice still had to sort out and now I remembered the way I'd angrily removed his comforting hand. Yeah, I was reliving the scene in the minibus in a slo-mo action replay, including the bit when Louis had told me that I wasn't sexy.

It was all right now because I was in a girlspace. Girls knew when there was stuff you didn't want to talk about but I'd learned very quickly over the last few weeks that despite what Francis had said, boys weren't as evolved as us. Or Louis wasn't.

But what Louis might think of me didn't seem as important as what Francis must have thought as he heard me screech horrible things at Alice. Then I'd run away and brought all this drama when he really needed a stress-free weekend in London away from all the horrors of home.

My stomach was doing the knotty thing again and suddenly the plan to have a bowl of teriyaki salmon ramen, which came with something described as a tea-stained egg, wasn't such a great idea. Not when I felt like I might hurl.

'So, what happened after I left?' I hissed at Alice, who was having a slightly stilted conversation with Kirsten. 'What did the boys say?'

'You mean Louis,' she said tartly. Having the Louis conversation with her was going to suck.

'Well, Louis, but mainly Francis. Is he pissed off with me?'

Alice wiggled her head from side to side. 'He's hard to read. Muttering something about going to Soho to look for you in some fabric shops.'

I hoped he hadn't spent hours searching for me when I hadn't been anywhere near Soho. Though I wasn't sure exactly how far Soho was from Notting Hill. I'd ruined any plans he might have had to hang out with London mates or soundcheck and stuff.

'I bet he's pissed off with me now,' I said, my voice all high-pitched and gaspy. Alice looked at me with amusement.

'Oh, Franny, you're having too many feelings again,' she said, which wasn't very helpful so it was a relief when her phone rang.

'Oh hello, Mr Barker,' Alice said as she stared at me. 'No, she's not in the loo, she's sitting right here. I'll pass the phone over.'

I batted away her outstretched hand. 'I can't!' I whispered. 'I'm not ready to talk to him.'

'This is about the tenth time he's called so you're just going to have to be ready,' Alice said, as she shoved her phone right in my face. She was all about the tough love lately.

It was a struggle to swing my legs over the bench seat without flashing my gusset and kicking Kirsten, but I managed it, then scurried to the door. 'Hi,' I muttered as I reached the street. 'I'm all right. I know I said I was going to London with a rock group but it's not quite as bad as I made it seem.'

'Are you in London?' Dad asked. It was hard to get a gauge

on what he was feeling. And by feeling, I meant exactly how angry he was with me.

'Yeah,' I replied.

'With a rock group?'

'Yeah, but that kind of sends out the wrong idea. They're not a very good rock group. Not that they're badly behaved, just that their music sucks.'

'And are you planning on coming home?' It was still that mild voice but that mild voice could quickly turn into a shouting voice or a voice that used to stop my allowance in the days before I started earning my own spending money.

I sighed. 'I am but I don't really want to.'

I heard Dad sigh too, then silence. It was long enough that I wondered if we'd been cut off but then he sighed again. 'I didn't realise that things with your mum had got so bad.'

'Well, I think you kind of did and that's why you're hardly ever around.' I was shocked at my own daring but I only had the guts to say this over the phone. I didn't think I could ever say this to his face. It was the one thing I hadn't been able to yell at him that morning.

'I take the long runs because they pay better and we need the money now that your mother isn't working,' Dad said and we were back to this tired old dance again.

'But we never talk about why isn't she working any more,' I persisted. 'And don't tell me that I don't need to worry about it because you leave me to deal with her for weeks and weeks and all I do is worry. She stops taking her pills and she hasn't gone to her group for months and she's either totally OCD and manic or she's in bed and it's all I can do—'

'Franny . . .'

'I didn't want to screw up my GCSEs. It was the last thing I wanted to do and she promised that if I didn't tell you she'd start getting better. She was scared that she'd have to go away again and it didn't make her better last time. Not really. I don't think she's ever going to get better and be who she was when—'

'Franny,' Dad said more forcefully. 'Just shut up for a second, pet. I'm putting your mum on the phone now.'

'No! Don't!' It was too late. There was a muffled silence as he passed the phone over and then I heard a snuffly sound.

'Franny? Do you hate me very much?'

I sighed. 'No. It's just . . . well, I don't feel like you love me any more. If you did, then you wouldn't treat me the way you do. You'd want to get better for me, not just when Dad's around; not just because you don't want to go away again.'

'I know. For what it's worth I'm sorry.' I wasn't sure that she was going to say any more than that. Then she snuffled again. 'It's hard to explain. When I'm having one of my bad days, it's like I'm outside of myself and I can't get back in. Do you know what I mean?'

I thought back to what Alice had said about how I would shut her out when I was going through stuff and maybe I sort of did know what Mum meant. 'I suppose. But it's just as scary for me as it is for you. There have been times when I was worried that I was going to come home and find you de—'

'Don't even say that, Franny! Don't even think it.' Mum

sniffed like the tears weren't that far away. 'Me and your dad had a long talk this morning. I've already made an appointment to see the doctor next week. Maybe see if I can have some one-on-one therapy and I promise I'm going to start going to the group again. Thing is, it's not like mending a broken arm or getting over chicken pox . . .'

'I get that,' I said, but a part of me did still think it was that easy and I was still angry with her. She was only interested in getting better now that Dad knew what had been going on when he wasn't around. But then, she was still my mum. 'I just miss you, you know.'

I could hear her swallow hard. 'Yeah, I miss me too.' She swallowed again. 'My head gets so messy, Franny, and I just can't seem to get it straightened out, but when I take the tablets they make me feel like I'm underwater.'

'But maybe there are different tablets you can take and I did some googling and this is just an idea, but exercise is meant to be good, you know, for depression and that. You used to do cross-country running when you were my age, didn't you?'

'I was second best in the county,' Mum said proudly. I hadn't known that. 'Look, I'm going to see the doctor with your dad and you know what he's like. He'll stay there all day until we get a proper treatment plan.'

I'd been starting to feel all kinds of hopeful but now doubt settled in again. 'But he's going away soon, isn't he?'

'He phoned the depot and said he'll only do short trips for the time being,' Mum said. 'It'll mean that money's going to be tight. Or tighter.'

'I can pay my own way if I have to,' I said quickly. 'I'll even chip in on the housekeeping but—'

'That's not what I'm saying,' Mum snapped and it was actually kind of nice that she was snapping at me in a Mum-ly kind of way. 'We don't need you to do that. I just want you to know ...'

'Also, I'm still going to do a fashion degree. I'm the only person who gets to decide on what my future's going to be. I'll find the money for my tuition fees or I'll do what everyone else does and run up some student debt.' I didn't want to mention scholarships or grants because I didn't want to jinx my luck. 'I'm not giving up on my dreams.'

'I'm not asking you to. You'll come home and we'll figure stuff out; the three of us,' Mum said, like there was absolutely no wiggle room.

It was like she said; there was no magic button to press that would make everything better and turn us into a happy family, but what she was proposing made the thought of coming home not quite so awful.

'Right, so I'm sorry for storming off like that and ... did I drop any swears?'

Mum actually laughed. 'Nothing above a twelve rating. We were very impressed with that. Obviously, we did something right bringing you up.'

'You did lots of things right.'

'Well, that's good to know, and I'm sorry, Franny, that you've had to go through all this and that I just haven't been there for you. That I've made you feel so scared and unhappy. It cuts me right up. I want us to get back to that place where you feel like you can tell me anything, pet. Where you're free to act like a stroppy teenager and not have to be the grown-up. That's what I want.' Mum made this awful choking sound like she was really going to cry this time, which almost set me off. 'Now I'm handing you back to your Dad because he wants to know what you're getting up to with this rock group.'

She passed the phone over again so I could say fiercely: 'Not getting up to anything.' Chance would be a fine thing. 'They're nice boys. They're pretty rubbish at being rock 'n' roll.'

'Is that so? And what time were you thinking of getting back tomorrow?'

I told him and if he wasn't happy about me spending the night in London with the rock band, he hid it pretty well.

My bowl of ramen must have been cold by now, and even with a cashmere wool coat on I was shivering a little. I glanced down the road and saw the boys walking towards me. 'I've really got to go now, Dad, but I promise I'll be home tomorrow.'

'I'll see you then – and Franny, love?'

'What?'

'Don't think you're not grounded for lying to us that you were going to Manchester when you were really going to London with a bunch of long-haired layabouts. You're *so* grounded, kid.'

I wasn't overjoyed about that, but at the same time it was comforting to be back on familiar ground. 'Whatever,' I said and Dad said, 'I'll whatever you, young lady,' and I hung up just as the boys reached me.

27

It had been such a stressful day that I was amazed that my stomach was still capable of acting like I was on the scary big rollercoaster in Blackpool. I smiled weakly, but didn't have the guts to look directly at either Francis or Louis. I focused on Olly and the other two Desperadoes instead. 'Hey! The girls are inside. They've already ordered.'

'We've eaten,' Olly said, throwing Louis a withering look. 'Some people refuse to eat any food that isn't battered and doesn't come with chips.'

'Eleven pounds fifty for haddock and chips.' Louis sounded like he might cry. 'The haddock was tiny.'

He held up thumb and forefinger a centimetre apart to show how small his fish had been. I tilted my head and tried to look sympathetic.

The others were already trooping inside and I would have

followed them but Francis was staying back. I felt like all I'd done for the past ten hours was apologise to people. But then again, the other thing I'd been doing for the past ten hours was acting all wrong.

'I'm sorry,' I said, as the door closed behind Olly. 'Sorry about me and Alice having a blazing domestic in the minibus, then taking off. Alice said you were going to Soho to look for me.' I winced. 'You didn't, did you?'

Francis was wearing his grey beanie so I had a clear view of the long-suffering look he gave me. The only thing capable of looking more hangdog than Francis was an actual hangdog. 'Well, I did go to Soho but only partly to see if I could find you. I wanted to check out some record shops too.' He rolled his eyes. 'Also, we need to swap phone numbers for next time you flounce off with no idea of where you're going.'

'I'm sorry,' I said again. 'I need to be alone when I'm going through stuff. Usual angsty stuff, not having a total nervo stuff. I'm not like my mum.'

'No one said you were.' He smiled ever so slightly. 'Well, Alice did and she's what my old English teacher would call an unreliable narrator. Have you two made up?'

'Yeah. She's agreed to stop glomming on other girls' boyfriends and I'm going to stop having all the feelings and save some for her,' I told him.

Francis shook his head. 'I understood maybe half of that sentence. Who gets Louis?'

I really didn't want to talk about that with Francis any more. It seemed inappropriate now and I must have used up my quota of feelings for the month, so when I thought about Louis I didn't feel much of anything. 'We never got round to discussing that,' I mumbled, turning to glance through the window so I wouldn't have to see what Francis's face was doing. There was sure to be a lot more eye-rolling involved. 'So, um, did you eat a tiny, expensive portion of fish and chips too?'

'No, I didn't!' I turned back to see Francis looking utterly offended. 'I lived in London for a year. After the first week I stopped letting myself get ripped off by unscrupulous fast food outlets.'

But I'd only been in London for a few turbulent hours. 'Oh, is Wagamama an unscrupulous fast food outlet?'

He shook his head and thank God, he was smiling again. 'No, Franny. Wagamama is perfectly acceptable. Your choice?'

'Yeah.' I peered through the window again. When Alice saw me, she waved frantically, even though Louis was sitting next to her. 'We should go in. I ordered a bowl of ramen ages ago.'

'I always used to get the teriyaki salmon,' Francis said, as he held the door open for me. 'With the tea-stained egg, which isn't as gross as you'd think it would be.'

It was exactly what I'd thought as I ordered it. The only person who got me like that was Alice and she hadn't been getting me at all the last few weeks. It was a long time since I'd thought of Francis as Sneering Studio Tech – now he was a friend, but not in the way I was friends with Sage or Dora or Thee Desperadettes. I knew Francis's hopes and dreams, his fears and the stuff that kept him awake at night. Then I remembered I still hadn't come close to apologising properly because this little weekend in London should have been a break from all the stuff that kept Francis awake at night.

He was already way ahead, striding towards the communal table that we'd now completely taken over. 'Francis!' He turned. 'I didn't want to ruin the weekend for you. I haven't, have I?'

'You've already said sorry.' He made a little 'giddy-up' gesture. 'Come on, I'm starving and you're in luck, the seat next to Louis is free.'

My salmon teriyaki ramen would have been stone cold if Louis hadn't got over his loathing of weird foreign food and kindly eaten it all for me, except 'I left you the egg, Franny. And it's not my fault. I was starving. Eleven pounds fifty for miniature haddock and chips!' he reminded me. It was hard to stay angry at Louis – but not impossible.

I insisted he pay for fresh, piping hot ramen for me, which he did though he moaned about me being tight.

'She's not being tight,' Alice said from Louis's other side. 'Dude, you ate her tea.'

'I liked it better when you two were fighting over me, instead of ganging up on me,' Louis groused and I waited for the horror to overtake me that even Louis had figured that out, which meant that *everyone else* knew too, but the horror never came. I was immune to any more horror for the rest of the year at least. Anyway, Thee Desperadettes all fancied Louis too and none of them had managed to nab him, and they were still my new best mates, so they obviously didn't care. Francis already knew, and Olly and the other two Desperadoes? They were nice but I wasn't going to lose any sleep worrying about what they thought of me.

Still, Alice and I had shared a significant look that said, 'We'll talk about this later and in great length,' because we were back in that place where we could say quite a lot to each other just by raising our eyebrows and wrinkling our noses.

My ramen had only just arrived when the boys left. The headline band wouldn't let them soundcheck because they were 'totally full of themselves for four people who sound like punk never happened', according to Francis, but they were hopeful that they could beg five minutes to check their levels. Whatever the levels were. Who knew?

'Don't know why they're bothering,' Alice muttered to me. 'They're still going to sound terrible.'

'Ssh, they'll hear you,' I whispered, nodding my head at Lexy, Kirsten and Bethany. 'They must really reckon Thee Desperadoes are talented musicians to go to every gig and follow them to London.'

'Well, they must be stupid then,' Alice whispered back. My plan to integrate her into the new life I was creating wasn't working so well.

Especially when Lexy wanted us to pool our booze money so we could go to Sainsbury's and bulk buy. The only problem was that Thee Desperadettes were wine drinkers and 'We always drink vodka and diet Coke,' Alice insisted. 'Or vodka and diet Red Bull. Besides, Franny thinks that white wine tastes like vinegar.'

Shuv said I had a very unsophisticated palate. While 'Alice can't drink red wine on account of the fact that the first time she ever did, she drank so much she hurled like no one has ever hurled before or since,' I explained.

'Still got the stains on my bedroom carpet,' Alice said, but I'd caused enough upset already so I decided I would be part of the solution rather than the wine-hating part of the problem.

'Why don't we compromise and get some Bacardi Breezers? Or some cute little vodka cocktail things? They're bound to be on special offer.'

I felt a lot like Mother Teresa or Princess Di, except less dead, because everyone agreed and when we got to Sainsbury's, which was a huge desolate grey box that made me nostalgic for home, we discovered that they sold *cans* of lime vodka and Coke and even vodka and diet Coke already mixed.

Though it was freezing cold, we all went and sat by the lock to get mildly tipsy, except we were pestered by old drunk men who kept asking us for money and young drunk men who kept asking to see our tits. We decided to head for the Dublin Castle, where the boys were playing, but first we had to hide our spare cans.

Thee Desperadettes were skilled in the art of hiding alcohol. They shoved their cans to the bottom of their bags and made sure a box of tampons was highly visible when the bag was opened and shown to the security guard on the door, who shied away from the sight of sanitary protection products.

Soon we'd fought our way through the crowded pub, had our names ticked off on the three-pound guest list (playing third on the bill didn't qualify the band to put any names on the proper free guest list) and found ourselves in a dark back room. It might have been small by London standards – two girls behind me referred to the place as 'a dump' – but it was about the same size as The Wow Club, although there were very few tables and chairs. Probably people in London were too cool to sit down.

There was also no way to subtly hang about near the back-stage area, but then I didn't really need to do that any more. I could look at Louis any time I wanted. Talk to him. Touch and be touched by him. Not in a sexy-times way but just in the way that he was a boy that I hung out with now. Which was weird because I'd always imagined that I'd either worship Louis from afar or somehow convince him that we were made for each other – there'd been no middle ground in my fantasies.

I wasn't really sure how I felt about the middle ground. It was something that Alice and I needed to talk about but she was more interested in running her eyes over every guy in the room.

'Seen anything you like?' I asked her.

Alice stuck her tongue out at me. 'Not really. London boys look very unwashed. Anyway, I have more important things to do like mocking Thee Desperadoes,' she said, grabbing my hand to tug me forward. I resisted her efforts. 'Franny! It's been ages since we've mocked Thee Desperadoes. Watching them solo was one of the most excruciating half-hours of my life.'

'We can't,' I said. 'Look!' Thee Desperadettes were already

gathered down the front. 'We'll have to mock from a distance.'

'I can't believe you want to be friends with girls who think Thee Desperadoes are any good.' Alice was incapable of keeping her voice to anything other than a muted roar. 'What losers.'

'They're not losers!'

Before we could start bickering, even though we'd only been made up for a couple of hours, the band appeared. In fact, Louis rushed past us so he could take a flying leap on to the stage, grab the microphone and bellow, 'Hello, Camden. Are you ready to rock?'

Camden really wasn't. When Francis straightened up after fiddling with his effect pedals and saw the empty room, he looked beleaguered, like Alice's dog when she was having a wee and caught anyone looking at her.

I let Alice pull me down the front, but now I was with the band rather than gawping at the band I vowed not to laugh. The only smile on my face would be an encouraging smile, I told myself sternly. Then there was an ear-splitting caterwaul of feedback and, with perfectly synchronised movements, Alice and I were digging into our bags for our earplugs.

It was marginally better, though we could still hear Louis screeching away about offering someone a ride on his love rocket, while Francis and the bassist stood stock still, both of them staring fixedly at the floor like they really, really hoped it might suddenly open up and swallow them whole. I was in a thousand agonies as now my hair wasn't long enough to hide behind so I could have a good laugh.

Alice was hugging herself and lurching from foot to foot. 'If

I don't laugh soon I'll burst,' she shouted, but I was painfully aware of Lexy and Kirsten staring up at the stage, eyes rapt, Bethany taking pictures. I gave Alice a warning shove.

Three songs in and Louis suddenly whipped off his T-shirt. He whirled it round his head for a bit, then tossed it into the non-existent crowd where it landed on Kirsten's head. She yanked it off with a revolted expression and it was too much.

A great ugly snort of laughter burst out of me, along with a tiny bit of snot. The dam broke. As soon as I started laughing, Alice laughed too and it wasn't very long, probably only ten seconds, before we were clutching at each other and howling as Louis strutted his stuff on top of one of the speakers and ran a hand down his sweaty chest.

I didn't even care what Lexy and the others might think but as I was having a choked, gaspy breather between guffaws, I heard her shout, 'Oh, put it away, Louis! We've seen it all before.'

'Do you kiss your mum with that mouth?' Bethany added as Louis yowled about 'sexing you up till you can't be sexed no more'. She turned to us and rolled her eyes long and hard. 'Jesus, you'd think after all this time they might have one decent song, but that's obviously asking too much.'

'At this point a cover of "Gangnam Style" would be a relief,' Alice yelled back. 'Can you imagine Louis doing the dance?'

'Oh my God, don't even—' Bethany begged and then all five of us were laughing, though at least I had the dignity not to heckle the band, which was more than I can say of the others. Also we were laughing *with* Thee Desperadoes — Louis kept giving us cheesy grins and even cheesier thumbs-up gestures —

not laughing at them, though I don't think Francis appreciated the difference.

'Fuck my life,' he mouthed very distinctly at one point just before Louis launched into an enthusiastic series of star jumps and landed in the audience, where he tried to persuade us to join him in the chorus of their last song.

'You've got to be kidding,' Lexy shouted, pushing him off her. 'Get away from me, you freak!'

The room had filled up during the band's set and as we joined the crush to get out, the five of us glared at anyone we heard dissing Thee Desperadoes. You only got to diss them when you'd earned your stripes and seen them play The Wow nearly every week for at least a year.

'See, we thought you two were really into the band,' Lexy said, as we fought our way back through the pub. 'Like, massive Desperadoes fangirls. We wondered if you'd been dropped on your heads as children.'

'Yeah, well, we thought exactly the same about you,' Alice said, but she wasn't being belligerent and as we spilled out on to the pavement and retrieved our cans of vodka, we happily discussed all the crappy highlights of Thee Desperadoes' many shows.

' . . . then there was the time that Louis jumped off the stage and he landed badly and twisted his ankle,' Kirsten tried to say though it was hard as we were all giggling hysterically as we remembered how Louis had stopped the song to say, 'No, really, it doesn't hurt at all,' then hobbled back on to the stage.

'Aw, Louis. He is lovely though,' Bethany said.

'So sweet.'

'Not a bad bone in his body.'

'And he is really fit.'

It was hopeless. Every girl in Merrycliffe was in love with him. I looked at Alice and she looked at me. 'We should talk about this,' she said quietly but then she turned and started talking to Bethany, who wanted to dye her fringe bright green. 'You'll need to bleach it first and then you have to . . .'

I made a mental note to pull Bethany to one side and tell her to never take haircare advice from Alice or else live to regret it and once I'd saved it to my memory bank, I blinked. Francis was standing next to me.

'Have you any idea how hard it is to remember what order I need to play the only three chords I know, when you're laughing at me?' he demanded plaintively. 'It's very, very hard.'

'Laughing with you. Not at you,' I said.

'But I wasn't laughing.' He was half laughing now.

'If you'd let yourself look at Louis you'd have been laughing.' I pulled out my purse. 'Do you want a drink? I feel like I owe you a drink. Except you'll have to go to the bar to get it because I'm underage and stuff.'

Francis rested his hand on mine so I couldn't open my purse and pull out a fiver, though I really hoped that a bottle of lager didn't cost *that* much. 'We're cool, Franny,' he said. 'Anyway, we got a rider. Three cans each, though the headline band tried to make out they were theirs.'

'The more I hear about this headline band, the less I like them.'

'Yeah, well, we have to stay and watch their set. It's kind of bad band etiquette if we don't.'

Alice broke off her conversation with Bethany. 'But we want to go to a club.' She fluttered her eyelashes at Francis. I held my breath but he seemed unaffected by the lashes that had melted the hearts of so many other boys. 'Why give time to a band who wouldn't even let you soundcheck?'

'And tried to steal your rider,' I added. Then Francis had the five of us surrounding him for some prolonged nagging.

'Saturday night in Camden, Francis,' Lexy reminded him. 'Why would you try to deprive us of that experience?'

'Don't shoot the messenger,' he said, hands held up in protest, but when the rest of the boys came out they didn't share Francis's noble belief that you had to support your fellow bands.

'Sod that' was the general consensus and besides Louis was far too excited to stand in one spot and watch a band. He kept darting through the other groups congregated on the pavement until a really old punk with a blue Mohican threatened to smack him.

We decided to take to the mean streets of Camden and find somewhere cool to hang out where we could dance, though it was only ten-thirty and Kirsten insisted that 'Most people in London don't get to the clubs until midnight. They stay open till five in the morning. Sometimes even later.'

Olly went back to the minibus because he said he hated clubbing and he wanted to get some sleep before he drove us back to Merrycliffe. I had no choice but to entrust him with my

Martin Sanderson bag of fabric and my new coat because I didn't want to get disco dirt on it.

Yes, it was freezing without a coat and the hem and cuffs of my leather dress were curling up but I tried to think of it as suffering for my art.

'I'll keep you warm,' Louis promised and as we started to walk down the road, with Francis at the head of our little crocodile as he was the only one who knew his way around, he put his arm round me.

It was almost too much to bear. Hanging out in Camden on a Saturday night on our way to a club that might stay open until five in the morning and Louis Allen had his arm around me so that anyone looking at us would think that we were together. That we were a couple. I could feel the heat of him. A prickly hard kind of hot that was strange and *other*, even though Louis himself wasn't that strange any more.

'We rocked it tonight,' he announced as we skirted past a puddle of vomit just outside somewhere called the Jazz Café. 'I love being on stage. Love seeing my girls having a good time at the front.'

I felt a bit guilty at how Louis's girls had really been screaming with laughter but technically we had been having a good time. 'It's always fun when you guys play,' I murmured and Louis beamed at me.

He was so uncomplicated. It was very restful.

'So, anyway, I've been thinking about how, like, you've not snogged anyone and we should do something about it,' Louis continued in a breezy fashion like it was no big deal.

Um, if he was about to propose what I suspected he was about to propose, then it was a big deal. The biggest deal.

'OK, like what did you have in mind?' I asked casually, even though my heart was suddenly beating like it could explode at any moment. It felt terrifying and delicious all at the same time.

'Well, we kiss. Simples, isn't it? If you're freaking out 'cause no one's kissed you, then you need to kiss someone . . . '

'I wouldn't say I was freaking out so much as . . . '

'I've kissed loads of people. I'm really good at it,' Louis told me like I needed the hard sell. Which I didn't. Not really. 'Might as well get it over and done with.'

Louis was right. There was only so long that a girl could remain unkissed before being unkissed turned into such a burden that she'd lock lips with anyone just to rid herself of it. And Louis wasn't just anyone. It was Louis! The boy of my dreams. And I was in London and it was the day I'd met Martin Sanderson. My first kiss wasn't going to get much better than this.

'All right. OK. So . . . I mean, what did you . . . should I?' My mind was made up but it had to be now, otherwise the count-down to my first kiss would lose all its urgency, and knowing me, I'd probably chicken out. One small problem though – we were currently marching down Camden High Street.

'There's no need to be nervous,' Louis said kindly, pulling me through a break in the traffic to the other side of the road where the covered stalls of the closed market beckoned. 'Don't worry. We'll catch up with the others. I've been to Camden at least three times and Francis always takes us to the same place on Chalk Farm Road.'

I squinted up the road. I could just make out Francis's grey beanie in the distance. If he turned round and noticed that we weren't there, then he'd get cross. Maybe even come and look for us and I was going to tell Louis that but he was pulling me further into the deserted market, a maze made out of canvas and metal. It was a bit scary. Not supernatural scary but like some of those tramps that had hassled us earlier probably hung out round here and I was glad Louis still had his arm round my shoulder.

When we were deep in the heart of the market, Louis stopped and turned to me with a slow-burn smile. 'Right, let's get ready to rumble!'

We ended up doing an awkward shuffle to get ourselves in position. I leaned back against a stall and Louis took me in his arms, which should have had me swooning. Instead I was licking my lips then trying to relax them so my mouth would look totally kissable, like Alice had instructed me many, many times when we were discussing the whys and wherefores of kissing.

I didn't want to think about Alice. I stared up at Louis who grinned at me.

'OK, bring it on,' I said enthusiastically and I expected Louis to swoop down and the swooning to start but instead he took a deep breath then clamped his hand over my left boob. I felt nothing. Well, I felt the warmth of his hand and I panicked that there wasn't much boob for him to get hold of, but then Louis bent his head and I decided that my time could be better spent thrilling to the feel of his lips on mine.

His lips went straight for my neck, along with his nose, and he nuzzled against my skin enthusiastically. He was obviously building up to the kiss, wanted to make it special. Meanwhile the tarpaulins fluttered in the wind and we were cocooned away and – ugh!

I felt something moist and warm drag against my neck. Louis made a happy little noise like my skin was bacon-flavoured, then licked a path up towards my chin and actually standing in the freezing cold with my boob clutched in a vice-like hold while Louis slurped over me was not doing it. None of my parts were tingling and I'd much rather have been in a warm pub with Francis and the others as we complained about how expensive everything was in fancy London. What was wrong with me?

'Louis! I think we should stop,' I said. He stopped instantly. Well, he stopped giving my chin a tongue bath but kept his hand on my boob.

'What's up?' he asked, and he was still textbook beautiful, and all right, there was no way in hell he would ever get any of the answers on *Pointless* but he was funny and sweet and not at all up himself and I absolutely did not fancy him. Then I was all like, *woah*! Where did that thought suddenly come from?

I fancied Louis. It was one of the basic facts that made up me. My best friend was Alice. I wanted to be a fashion designer. I was allergic to kiwi fruit. My mum was a bit menty and I had a serious case of unrequited love for Louis Allen from Thee Desperadoes. Except somehow in the last few weeks I'd fallen out of love with Louis and not even realised it.

Once I got to know Louis, he'd become less and less sexy as he talked about chicken's testicles and impersonated the cowardly lion from *The Wizard of Oz*. Also, it was hard to get hot and bothered about a guy when you discovered that he thought antiperspirant was an option rather than something everyone should use once they hit puberty, under pain of death.

There was no mystery to Louis any more. He was no longer a foxy blank canvas to project all my hipster couple dreams on to. He was a real boy and he still had his hand on my tit.

'Franny? I said, what's up?' Louis asked again. He gazed at me with a perplexed expression. 'I was going to get round to the kissing. I have this whole routine I do.'

'Yeah, about that . . . ' There was no easy way to have this conversation and for a microsecond I wondered if I should just kiss Louis rather than explain why I didn't want to. But it wasn't just a kiss. Maybe I was placing way too much importance on it but my first kiss was only going to happen once and it might just as well be special. 'See, I've waited so long that I reckon I could probably wait a bit longer. With the whole kissing thing.'

'Was it something I did? Or I didn't do?' Louis looked heartbroken. 'Do you not fancy me?'

'It's not that. You're really fit,' I said, because he was and Louis was always looking at his reflection in shop windows and ripping his top off on stage so he obviously knew he was all kinds of hot. 'But now we've got to know each other, well, we're more mates than anything else. So, I think we should forget the kissing and carry on being mates, all right?'

I've never been more relieved to get to the end of a speech.

Even more relieved than the time I'd had to confess to killing the class goldfish by overfeeding it.

I knew I was bright red. I think Louis was too. 'If that's what you want but I do really like you . . . Y'know, I get this *all* the time,' he told me in a pouty voice. 'All the girls say that we should just be mates. I don't understand it. I've got the moves.'

'You have. You've got mad moves,' I said, which reminded me of something. I looked down. 'Um, Louis, your hand's still on my . . .'

'Aaaarrggghh! Sorry!' He snatched his hand away from my boob like it had just given him an electric shock.

'We should find the others,' I said and because I did feel guilty and Louis was looking so forlorn, I took his hand and led him out of the market.

I was sad that my crush was dead and that I'd no longer get a contact high from catching a glimpse of Louis on some darker day than usual but friends was good. You couldn't have too many friends, I realised that now.

'Franny? You know I said that Francis always takes us to the same place on the Chalk Farm Road?' Louis piped up as we started walking along Camden High Street again. 'Well, I'm not sure I can remember exactly where it is now.'

Oh, Louis. No, he was never going to make my heart feel like it was about to cave in, not ever again. 'Do you think if we run really fast we might be able to catch them up?'

I looked at Louis and he looked at me and then we grinned at each other and started to run. Scattering passers-by like skittles and shrieking loudly, just like I did with Alice.

28

We caught up with the others just as they were joining the end of a long queue to get into a club, which looked a lot like a pub to me. A pub that cost five quid on the door.

'Five quid!' Lexy and Alice said to me, when Louis and I arrived red-faced and breathless from our sprint. 'Is the bar gold-plated or something?'

'I wanted to go to the Hawley Arms,' Bethany whined. 'Where Amy Winehouse used to hang out.'

'I still don't see why we couldn't have gone to the Underworld,' Kirsten said to Francis, who looked like he wanted to pull down his grey beanie over his eyes so he wouldn't have to see everyone's mardy faces.

'Any more backchat and we're going straight back to the bus so we can go home,' he snapped. He cast a look at me, then Louis. It wasn't a particularly friendly look.

Maybe Francis thought I'd snogged Louis and that we were *on* and now that I'd got what I wanted I didn't need Francis any more, which was crap. Francis and I were friends now. End of. But not in the way that I was mates with Louis. It was way different from …

'So, like, Franny totally wouldn't snog me!' I heard Louis tell the other two Desperadoes. 'I just got the tiniest bit of touch and then we stopped. What's wrong with me?'

There was going to be so much wrong with Louis once I'd finished smacking him, I thought as three separate hands suddenly shot out in front of me.

'Welcome to the gang, Franny,' Bethany said, then she, Lexy and Kirsten all slapped my hand.

'What gang?' I hissed because we were in a queue, all huddled together for warmth and there was no such thing as a private conversation.

'The Let's Not Actually Snog Louis gang,' Lexy said and they all giggled and I giggled too because it explained so much, especially the way they all treated Louis like a much-loved but very annoying little brother, and then I glanced at Alice. She wasn't giggling but staring down at her shoes.

She'd been in her six-inch heels all day. Her feet had to be *killing* her. Five hours was about all her pain threshold could handle. 'Did you bring your Converse with you, Ally?'

'I am queuing to get into a club in London. There is no way I'm putting on my Converse,' she said. 'No bloody way.'

I looked up and down the queue. I couldn't see anything higher than a two-inch Cuban heel. Most of the girls were wearing clumpy boots or sneakers. 'Put on your Converse,' I begged. 'Remember that time when you wore your heels for too long and the next day your foot went into a cramp spasm for twenty-four hours.'

Alice was wavering, I could tell. 'But my heels make me look taller.' She leaned in close so only I could hear. 'And slimmer.'

'Hello! Did you suddenly forget how gorgeous you are?' I asked, because even pain from her shoes couldn't wither her beauty.

Louis had offered me a sympathy snog, but he must want to proper snog Alice. How could he not when she was so pretty? Also, they seemed to get on really well, were always hanging out together, just the two of them. Maybe they were already snogging regularly and when she found out he'd had his hand on my boob and there'd been licking, we'd be bitter enemies once more. I couldn't go through all that again. Alice and I needed to chat the Louis thing out.

'Alice, if you've got your Converse in your bag, then bloody well put them on,' Francis suddenly said in the same tone of voice he used when Krystal with a K had bodged up the over-locker and refused to fess up. 'If you fall over and break an ankle, we're not sticking around in A&E for hours, all right?'

She was already dragging her sneakers out of her huge tote bag. 'Right,' she agreed. 'Keep your hat on.'

I really needed to get me a stern voice too. I glanced over at Francis, sure that his face would match his voice, but when he caught my eye, he winked at me. 'Won't be much longer,' he said about the queue, which suddenly gave a surge forward, so we were almost at the door.

Another five minutes and we were inside. It was hotter than the very bowels of hell. A humid, sweaty kind of heat that made your hair go frizzy and your make-up slide down your face within microseconds.

Upstairs there was a dance floor with a DJ booth at one end and once we'd organised a bar run and found a little spot to dump our stuff, we all clustered together to look at the fancy London folk getting down. I don't know what I expected – something cool and intimidating – but it was just a bunch of beered-up indie kids having a good time. Not unlike a Saturday night at The Wow really.

Louis licked his lips, eyes wide. 'So many sexy ladies,' he cried then he was gone, diving into the dancing masses.

Then it was just me and the boys on the sidelines as Thee Desperadettes and Alice took to the floor. In my experience, boys who weren't Louis didn't dance and I could only dance to tunes that had some kind of beat. These tunes didn't.

I stood there, sipping a lukewarm drink, suddenly shy and conscious of Francis standing behind me where he must have a bird's-eye view of how even the neckline of my leather dress was curling up and my hair, which now reached the back of my neck, was damp and curling up too.

'Franny B! Get your arse over here!' Alice shouted over a loud, thuddy bassline and a hundred voices chattering, then she and Bethany yanked me on to the dance floor.

There's that split-second change when you suddenly and

seamlessly move from shifting your weight from one foot to the other, arms pinned to your sides in a self-conscious, uncoordinated series of movements, to dancing wildly and beautifully to a beat that exactly matches the rhythm of your heart. That's what happened when the DJ began to play an old Beastie Boys track. Alice and I both screamed, then Bethany, Lexy and Kirsten screamed too and the five of us danced like our lives depended on it. Danced like everyone was watching us. Danced like it was a new religion.

For an hour the DJ played old-skool hip hop and sixties soul and that hour was like medicine for me. I didn't have to think or worry, even when Louis kept shouting, 'Merrycliffe represent!' Merrycliffe representing involved Thee Desperadettes taking the piss out of Alice doing her dirty, hoochie dancing by executing a perfectly synchronised triple slut-drop. For one terrifying moment I thought Alice was going to storm off in a monumental huff but then she laughed.

'Really shaky on the dismount, ladies,' she snarked, and showed them how it was done. After that the four of them stopped dancing in favour of trying to outgrind each other.

Alice had said ages ago that she was going to go older and now I could see that having older *girl mates* would work much better for her. And as I watched Alice bumping hips with Kirsten and laughing, I thought that maybe Alice was coming to the same conclusion. Thee Desperadettes weren't as boy-obsessed as she was and they didn't take any nonsense from anyone, whether it was Alice or some random lad who tried to cop a feel of Lexy's arse when she busted out her best Beyoncé moves.

Becoming the fourth and fifth member of Thee Desperadettes was what our friendship needed to stop it going stale and sliding back into bad old habits. Sage and Dora might be a harder sell but they deserved to have Alice in their lives because when she didn't have all her boy phasers set to stun she was ace. Like now, as she danced behind some guy and totally impersonated the weird thing he did with his pelvis.

I was a hot, sweaty mess by the time the music went crap again. I also needed to clear my head a little. So much had happened today and I needed five minutes on my own to process it all.

I fought my way down the stairs and out into the street to stand a little further downwind from the gaggle of smokers congregated outside the entrance. I pulled out my phone.

There was a text message from Mum. Just wanted to let you know that I love you, Franny. Thought it went without saying but I was wrong. Be safe. See you tomorrow, Mum xxx (You're still grounded.)

I decided then that 'I love you' was better than sorry. It didn't make everything OK, but it helped. A lot. As long as there were 'I love you's then you could get through stuff. Love had that effect.

There was so much to think about but it was too cold outside, even without the bitter bite of the sea air that I was used to. But before I could finish my first shiver, someone put a jacket round my shoulders.

'Please don't die of hypothermia before we make it home,' Francis said.

I looked down at his thick plaid flannel jacket. 'Won't you be cold?'

'I'm OK for a bit.'

There was so much I wanted to tell him, but I didn't know where to start. I found myself gazing up at the inky blackness of the sky for inspiration. 'How weird. There are, like, no stars. Is that a London thing?'

'Yeah. I think it's something to do with the pollution.' Francis took my arm. 'Shall we sit there?' he asked, gesturing at a doorstep.

We sat down, so our thighs were pressed together – that made me shiver too. 'You know, I *still* haven't properly apologised for taking off like that this afternoon. You shouldn't have had to waste time trying to find me. You deserved to have a really good day and I screwed that up.'

'It wasn't *that* screwed up and I reckon the day isn't over until we hit the M6, so it's still got time to improve,' Francis said and he looked so serious and I just wanted him to smile. He didn't smile enough.

'I'll totally buy you some overpriced London chips as we're walking back to the bus,' I promised. 'Might even throw in a can of Coke if you're—'

'So, you didn't kiss Louis then?'

I frowned. Where had that come from? And I could tell from the way Francis had gone completely still that he wanted to take the question back. Pretend it had never happened. But it had.

I ducked my head and I knew I was reddening up. I also

thought I might giggle because now I was thinking about Louis with a handful of breast as he rooted about in the crook of my neck.

'No,' I managed to say but I could feel a gurgle of laughter bubbling up and I had to press my lips tightly together so it didn't leak out. 'No kiss.'

'Have you postponed the kissing to a later date?' Francis wasn't looking at me but staring straight ahead at a bollard, like he'd never seen a bollard before in his life.

I swallowed down the giggles again. 'Not postponed. Cancelled.' Now Francis was looking at me like I was even more fascinating than the bollard. 'Turns out that I love Louis like a mate but I don't love *love* him.' All of a sudden it seemed very important to be honest, no matter how embarrassing being honest might be. 'Pity I didn't realise that until after Louis held my boob for a good five minutes and licked my face like it was covered in a secret blend of herbs and spices, but whatevs.'

'Good,' Francis said decisively.

'Good that he held my boob for five minutes?'

'No! I mean, good that you don't fancy him and good that you didn't throw away your first kiss on someone you didn't fancy.' Francis turned to me and I got it now. I didn't need anyone else to explain to me that Francis was really quite cute in his own low-key, lo-fi way, especially when he was smiling at me like I was the only girl in the world. Or the only girl in his world. 'You should save your first kiss for someone special.'

'I plan to,' I said, and when I thought back to all those *years* pining over Louis and being scared of what might happen if I had the nerve to say hello to him, it was a waste. I couldn't spend my life being scared. That wasn't the kind of life I wanted to live.

Somehow at some point when I was falling out of lust with Louis and becoming his friend, I'd stopped thinking of Francis as just a friend. He was something more than that. Something that was undefined. Something that made me feel good when he was near and smiling at me. Something kind of beautiful. How could I have been so blind that I couldn't see what was right in front of me?

It was easy after that. The easiest thing in the world to lean in when we were so close together anyway, and brush my lips against Francis's. I knew one crippling second of fear and rejection, then he was kissing me back, his hand creeping up to tenderly cup the back of my head where the ends of my hair were ragged and damp.

That kiss, that first kiss, felt nothing like it did when I used to practise kissing my pillow or my forearm. I was kissing another living, breathing person. I was kissing Francis and his lips were firm and gentle on mine and then they weren't quite so gentle any more, but I liked that better. I didn't worry about what to do with my tongue or panic when we clashed teeth; that stuff didn't matter. It was just me and Francis and nothing bad could come of anything that was just me and Francis.

When Francis pulled away after quite a while, I could have sworn that maybe there were a few stars in the sky after all. But when I turned to look at him, he wasn't smiling any more.

'See, as soon as you said you didn't fancy Louis, I was working on asking you out on a date,' he said heavily. 'But that might lead to another date and then we're *dating* and that wouldn't be fair on you, Franny.'

'Why not?' That familiar feeling of dread was back. He already had a girlfriend, some hipster in London who'd promised to wait for him, or maybe Francis was like every other guy in Merrycliffe and it was Alice he really wanted.

'Because this year ... it's going to get messy,' he said. 'Really messy.'

Then I remembered about his dad. This was going to be the worst year of Francis's life, which wasn't any reason why we couldn't, like, *date*. 'I know about messy,' I reminded him softly. 'I'm used to dealing with messy. I don't always deal with it well, but I'm getting better at it so I'd be a really good person to have around. Anyways, I want to be there for you.'

Francis stiffened again. 'You don't have to go out with me just because you feel sorry for me.'

'I do feel sorry for you because of the thing with your dad, it's horrible and it's unfair but also I want to go out with you 'cause, well, I like you. Like, I *really* like you.' I did but it had taken me a long time to figure it out because Louis had always got in the way, blocked my view. 'You can mend sewing machines and we've got hundreds of sixties films that we haven't seen yet and the kissing didn't suck.' I had to mumble the last bit and I wasn't sure if Francis had heard until he grinned.

'It can suck next time if you want,' he said and I did.

I don't know how long we sat on the doorstep and kissed.

Long enough for my arse to grow completely numb with cold and for at least five people to walk past and tell us to get a room and after the kissing my lips were sore and I had a crick in my neck. It was worth it though.

Francis stood up first, then pulled me to my feet. He kept a tight hold of my hand but I pulled free once we'd climbed the stairs and could see the others still throwing strange shapes on the dance floor. 'Let me tell Alice first,' I said, because there couldn't be any secrets between her and me any more. 'The two of us, Alice and me, are a package deal. You know that, right?'

'I had my suspicions, yeah.' Francis didn't look too over-joyed at the prospect. 'But she's not coming on dates with us and I don't have to snog her too, do I?'

I decided that we'd reached the stage in our relationship where I could smack Francis, so I did and then he went to the bar and I went to join the others on the dance floor.

29

'Where have you been?' Alice demanded when I shimmied up to her. My heart sank. Then she tossed her hair back and grinned. 'You missed all the fun. Louis took his T-shirt off, then tried to pick Bethany up and twirl her and this girl thought he was a random perv and threw her drink over him.'

'What did Louis do?'

'He said that if she'd given him some warning before she threw her drink, he'd have kept his mouth open.' Alice did her patented slut-drop – the one time I'd tried it, I thought I'd dislocated both knees – then came back up to the surface. 'Actually quite witty for Louis, I thought.'

'Yeah. Like he suddenly turned into Stephen Fry or something.' I touched her arm. 'Listen, shall we go and have a chat?'

Another hair toss. 'Franny! We're in London, in a club ...'

'It's kind of a pub with ideas above its station ...'

'Whevs. London. Club. The indie boys go into a frenzy every time I do a move that I totally stole from Nicki Minaj. We've got the rest of our lives to chat, now dance, Franny! Dance! Dance!'

I danced, because it had been weeks since Alice and I had danced together and now she was pulling out all the routines that made me laugh, from her demented aerobics instructor to her raved-up mime artist.

Francis watched from the sidelines, but he smiled every time I caught his eye and he had assorted Desperadoes to talk to until the music stopped and the lights came on.

Everyone who'd been dancing with such wild abandon looked around a little sheepishly. It was time to reunite with bags and coats and jiggle desperately as we waited in a long, snaking line to go to the Ladies, which was even grimier and stinkier than the Ladies in The Wow.

It felt a lot colder outside than it had been an hour ago when I'd had Francis' arms around me but Lexy had a spare jumper in her bag and Kirsten lent me her scarf and Alice tucked her arm into mine as we started walking back to where the minibus was parked.

Francis walked on the other side of me, brushing his fingers against mine with every step, and though Alice raised her eyebrows and wrinkled her nose she didn't say anything. Well, not about that. Along with the girls who were walking behind us, she kept up a running commentary about our first London clubbing experience.

It was all 'I thought London girls would at least wear makeup when they went out *on a Saturday night*' and 'Yeah, Alice, he was totally into you but who could love a guy whose T-shirts have gone grey in the wash?'

Alice and Bethany seemed to have really bonded and I was pleased but I also felt a sharp jealous pang. I was the only girl that Alice had ever bonded with and what if she thought that Bethany was more fun than me? More best friend-worthy?

'You all right, Franular B?' Alice whispered in my ear and gave my arm an affectionate little squeeze, and I just *knew* I had nothing to worry about on that score. 'Can you lend me two quid to buy some chips? Chips can't cost more than two quid, can they?'

A portion of chips from a kebab shop that couldn't have passed any Environmental Health checks cost a whopping three quid.

'Three quid?' the Merrycliffe posse chorused. 'Three quid for chips!'

'And eleven pounds fifty for haddock and chips!' Louis shouted and then Francis had to leave my side to perform an intervention because Louis wanted to order a doner with all the trimmings and apparently that could never happen because the last two doners with all the trimmings he'd had on the way home from gigs had resulted in vomit and having to drive back to Merrycliffe with the stench of vomit writ large.

'We'll stop at a service station and get you a Ginster's,' Francis promised and all the way back to the van Louis sang a song about pasties.

'*Pasties, pasties, you're so yummy. I can't wait until you're in my tummy.*'

It *was* funny, but I was quite nostalgic for the days when I thought Louis was beautiful and enigmatic and hadn't just done three loud belches in quick succession.

'He'll crash out long before we reach the first service station,' Francis promised me and as soon as we got back to the bus, presented Olly with a three-pound portion of chips and had barely had time to buckle our seatbelts, Louis was curled up on the back seat and snoring loudly.

There was no awkward allocation of seats. Francis sat down next to Olly and promised to supply him with tunes and music trivia during the long journey home so he'd stay awake. That was another thing I liked about Francis; he cared about people in a cool, unfussy way.

I sat next to Alice, because of course I was going to. And because it was Alice, after I'd established that her hands were absolutely free of chip grease, I let her snuggle down under my cashmere coat, which I draped over the two of us.

'Was everything OK with your parents, then?' she asked as the others let out a ragged cheer as we pulled away from the Camden kerb.

'Well, sort of. Mum sent me a really nice text and apparently she's going to get help and Dad's going to be around more, but I'm totally grounded. Like, whatever.'

'Yeah, what*ever*,' Alice snarled in agreement. 'After what you've been through with your mum, I hope you sneer in the face of being grounded.'

'That's what I was planning to do.'

Alice gave me a sideways look. 'I mean, you've had such a

hard time lately that I was thinking that I need to cut you a break too.' She smiled. It was her post-cream cat-like smile. 'You can have Louis. I want you to have Louis.'

My heart fluttered. It was a very unpleasant sensation. 'No, that's OK. You can have him,' I said sweetly. 'It's the least I can do after all the mean things I've done.'

'No, really, he's all yours. You were right. You had first dibs,' Alice reminded me.

'But, see . . .'

'Unless, of course, you don't want him any more because actually you've decided that you fancy someone else. Hmmmm, someone like Sneering Studio Tech, perhaps?'

'How could you know? I only figured it out about two hours ago!'

'Oh, Franny, poor, foolish Franny – how could I not know?' Alice was loving this. 'What about all those flirty chats about the Rolling Stones on Facebook? Today might be the first time I've seen you two together but it couldn't have been any more obvious. You and Sneering Studio Tech – who'd have thought it, eh?'

I nudged her furiously. 'His name's Francis and he is really, really nice and OK, I didn't know how I really felt about him. Not even when I suddenly couldn't bear to have Louis snog me,' I burst out in a heated whisper.

I cringed in expectation of Alice's reaction because she had to have kissed Louis ages before me and they'd danced together loads this evening and maybe they *were* going out. Alice had gone very still and her eyes were narrowed. 'Did you get as far as being licked by him?' she asked, then she giggled. 'And before he licked you, did he take hold of both your tits like he was choosing melons in a supermarket?'

'No.' I giggled too. 'Nothing melon-like about my boobs. So, did you?'

'I snogged him for a bit but it was a lot like having someone go all rinse-cycle in my mouth,' Alice said with a sniggery shudder. 'So, I made him stop and I said we should just be mates.'

'Oh my God, I made him stop way before the rinse cycle and I said we should be mates too. It's so weird 'cause Louis is like textbook hot ...'

Alice nodded vigorously. 'He's so sexy and cool, until you spend a couple of evenings hanging out with him and then you realise that he's just a great big goofy dork. That's not to say that he isn't lovely ...'

'Yeah, he's very lovely but I absolutely don't fancy him.' Something else occurred to me and I giggled again. 'Also, now that I know Louis, I realise our plan had a fundamental flaw in it.'

'What?'

'Even if one of us had ended up getting married to him, he'd never, ever have got round to changing his relationship status on Facebook,' I spluttered and then Alice and I were clutching each other and laughing and wiping away the odd tear until I begged her to stop because I really was going to wet myself.

Once we'd settled back down, she gave me another sideways look. 'So, you and Francis then?'

'Yeah, me and Francis but I'm going to make loads of time for you. I've already told him you and me are a two-for-one deal.' I took her hand. 'I am sorry about you and Raj and coming between you. I could talk to him, unless he and Bethany ...' I frowned. 'But you are done with that, aren't you? You're not going to go for the boys that are already taken?'

'Well, Bethany said that she and Raj went on one date and he spent most of it talking about me,' Alice said with a quiet note of satisfaction. 'So, I don't know. Maybe we could start being civil with each other and see where it goes, but also Lexy and Kirsten have already said that if I did want to go older then we should head for the University of Lancaster student union bar one Saturday night, so I have options.'

'You are unstoppable,' I told her.

'I like to think so and it seems only fair that I let you and SST have a *little* alone time.'

I pinched her arm. 'He hasn't been Sneering Studio Tech for quite some time now.'

Alice peered down the bus. 'He's not so bad-looking,' she decided. 'You could do a lot worse. He'd be even cuter if he did something about his hair. Hey! I could cut it for him, as a nice, friendly gesture.'

Was she on crack? Was I going to have to persuade Francis to let Alice butcher his hair for the sake of my best friend getting on with my boyfriend?

'Oh, for God's sake, Franny! It was a joke!' Alice snorted. 'You know I don't cut boys' hair.'

'And you should know that it's always going to be too soon

for you to make jokes about *that*,' I snorted back and then we slapped each other's hands a bit until Alice yawned and rested her head on my shoulder and I thought she might be asleep, until she suddenly sat up.

'We're cool, aren't we, Franny?' she asked, all laughter gone. 'We're different to how we were, but we're still cool, right?'

'The coolest.' I looked down the bus to see the back of Francis's head and just the sight of his grey beanie hat nodding as he talked to Olly filled me with a sharp thrill of what we had to come. Then Alice shifted against me, huddled in tighter, because we were both cold. Being with Alice was warm and comforting, like coming home. 'Chicks before dicks.'

'Every time,' she stated firmly. 'Boys may come and go, but you're stuck with me, bitch.'

'I wouldn't have it any other way.'